# TEXAS STANDOFF

# Forge Books by Elmer Kelton

*Badger Boy*
*Bitter Trail*
*The Buckskin Line*
*Buffalo Wagons*
*Cloudy in the West*
*Hard Trail to Follow*
*Hot Iron*
*Jericho's Road*
*Many a River*
*Other Men's Horses*
*The Pumpkin Rollers*
*Sons of Texas*
*The Raiders*
*The Rebels*
*Ranger's Trail*
*Six Bits a Day*
*The Smiling Country*
*Sons of Texas*
*The Texas Rifles*
*Texas Standoff*
*Texas Vendetta*
*The Way of the Coyote*

*Lone Star Rising*
(comprising *The Buckskin Line, Badger Boy,* and
*The Way of the Coyote*)

*Brush Country*
(comprising *Barbed Wire* and *Llano River*)

*Texas Showdown*
(comprising *Pecos Crossing* and *Shotgun*)

# Elmer Kelton

# TEXAS

# STANDOFF

## A Novel of the Texas Rangers

A Tom Doherty Associates Book

New York

TEXAS STANDOFF: A NOVEL OF THE TEXAS RANGERS

Copyright © 2010 by The Estate of Elmer Kelton

A Forge Book
Published by Tom Doherty Associates, LLC
175 Fifth Avenue
New York, NY 10010

www.tor-forge.com

Forge® is a registered trademark of Tom Doherty Associates, LLC.

ISBN 978-0-7653-2579-2

First Edition: October 2010

Printed in the United States of America

0  9  8  7  6  5  4  3  2  1

# TEXAS
# STANDOFF

# CHAPTER

## 1

Andy Pickard had often considered leaving the Texas Rangers. His young wife, Bethel, had been urging him to take up the more stable life of a stockman, or even a storekeeper—anything that would keep him close to home. Now he almost wished he had given in to her, for his sergeant had assigned him to hunt down a lowly sneak thief. Not only that, but he was sending a stranger with Andy in the search.

It seemed a waste of two Rangers' time to trail after the likes of Jasper Biggs when murderers and horse thieves roamed the land. But Sergeant Ryker had wearied of hearing complaints about the man's petty larceny. He said, "We need to slam the cell door on this chicken-stealin' tramp. I'm sendin' Logan Daggett with you. Do you know him?"

"Never met him," Andy said without enthusiasm, "but I've heard of him. I reckon everybody has."

Daggett had a long record with the Rangers, not all of it positive. Stories indicated that he had a short fuse and was given to sudden violence. He considered consequences later, if at all.

By contrast, Andy liked to think things through before jumping into deep water, weighing the costs against the gain. After giving most of his youth to Ranger service, he felt he was due a little extra consideration. He said, "It'd suit me better to ride with somebody I know, like Len Tanner."

His comment appeared to annoy the sergeant. He was used to a quick "Yes, sir," when he gave an order. "I've sent Tanner off on another job. Daggett just got into camp last night, so he's available."

Andy said, "They say he's too quick to go on the fight."

Ryker's narrowed eyes hinted at sarcasm. "And *you've* sometimes been a little slow about it. I figure you should be a good team, makin' up for each other's weaknesses."

In Andy's view, Jasper Biggs was a two-bit night-prowling scavenger. He said, "This looks like a job for some deputy sheriff to do in his spare time. It shouldn't take two of us. I could handle it by myself, easy."

"If you could locate him. But he's at home down in those Llano River oak and cedar thickets. Logan is a good tracker, and I've seen that you're not."

Andy admitted, "There's things I do better."

"Most of Logan's service has been up on the plains. Lately he got into an unpleasant incident at Tascosa. Took a bullet in his leg. They transferred him down here so he wouldn't take another in the back."

*An unpleasant incident.* That did not bode well, Andy thought. He wondered what Daggett had done, but he would not ask. "Which of us will be in charge?"

"He's older than you, and been a Ranger longer. But I

hope you'll gee-haw together so that the question of command won't come up."

Andy thought of Bethel. This might be the time to quit, as she had long wanted. She would fret about him the whole time he was gone. Anyway, this seemed too piddling a mission for someone with his record of service. Maybe it was a sign that they were gradually edging him out. The state's money counters were always trying to cut expenses.

Ryker recognized Andy's reluctance. He said, "This'll give your bride a chance to rest. She probably gets more sleep when she has her bed to herself."

Andy's face warmed. What went on between him and Bethel was personal. They had bought a modest parcel of land on the Guadalupe River near Kerrville, and she had been pressing him to build a house on it so they could be together all the time. But he wanted to give her something better than a one-room shack. He wanted a livestock operation large enough to provide her a comfortable living. He was managing to bank some of his Ranger wages and an occasional reward, but the process of accumulation was slower than he liked.

He doubted there would be much, if any, reward for Biggs. The man's crimes were more nuisance than hardship for his victims, though Ryker said he had recently been discovered burglarizing a farmhouse at night. He had struck the owner with a chunk of stove wood before escaping into the dark.

"It's the first time I've heard of him resortin' to

violence," the sergeant said. "It may mean he's gone a little crazy. Hermits like him are usually halfway down that hill anyhow. We've got to bring him in before he hurts somebody real bad."

That put a different complexion on the situation. Andy had assumed Biggs was simply lazy, though he probably worked harder at his minor thievery than if he had a conventional job, and gained less for his efforts. Even other men of the outlaw stripe looked down on him for his limited ambition.

Andy was headquartered in a company tent camp on the San Saba River near Fort McKavett. He spent his off time, limited though it was, with Bethel in a small frame house he rented at the edge of the village. She heard his horse and came out to stand on the front step, a wisp of a woman still in her mid-twenties. The wind tugged gently at her brown hair and ruffled the apron tied around her narrow waist. Looking at her after an absence took his breath away. Leaving her was always difficult.

She had developed an uncanny knack of reading his mind. With a slight tone of impatience she asked, "How long will you be gone this time?"

That was a question he could seldom answer with certainty. Some assignments were short. Others dragged on and on. He said, "No longer than I have to. I'd be obliged for somethin' to eat before I report back to camp." He paused, striving for his most persuasive voice. "No tellin' when I'll get another meal that's half as good as what you fix."

Despite herself, she allowed a tiny smile to escape. She

still reacted warmly to compliments. "Tie up your horse, and I'll see what scraps I can find in the kitchen." She tip-toed, inviting a kiss.

While bustling about the small iron stove, she asked, "Who are they sending you after this time? Is he somebody I should worry about?"

He said, "He's a grubby, low-life thief who lives like a coyote down in the thickets. They claim he's too much of a coward to be dangerous."

"They say it's the cowards you have to watch the most. They come at you when you're not looking."

He said, "I always watch out for myself." He started to add that it was not in his plan for her to become a widow, but he left the thought unspoken. It might cause her to worry more, knowing that such a notion had even crossed his mind.

She baked biscuits, fried a thick slice of ham, and heated beans left over from yesterday. He could hardly take his eyes from her while she worked. Mentally he cursed Biggs for causing him to leave. But if not for Biggs, he would be going out to hunt for someone else. The desk-bound ac-countants in Austin could not abide seeing a Ranger idle.

Finished eating, he carried his plate and utensils to a tin pan on top of the cabinet. There, not entirely by accident, he bumped against Bethel as she put away the leftover bis-cuits. He folded his arms around her tiny waist. "I don't want to go," he said.

She smiled. "Then stay a while. Tell them your horse broke the bridle reins and ran away."

"He's too well trained. He never does that."

"I could run him off."

"He'd come right back."

Mischief sparkled in her eyes. "Then just lie to them a little."

He tightened his hold and kissed her. "I can do that."

Andy rode back into Ranger camp in time for supper. He found Ryker waiting, standing beside a dark-skinned, muscular man whose full mustache was mostly dark but speckled with gray. Logan Daggett stood half a head taller than Andy, and broader across the shoulders.

Ryker asked, "Did you leave her happy?"

Andy said, "I tried to."

Ryker introduced him to Daggett, then said, "Andy's got him a young wife. It's hard to juggle Ranger duty with a new marriage. You're not married, are you?"

Daggett answered solemnly, "Was once." It was clear that he did not intend to expand on that statement, and Ryker did not press the question.

Daggett asked Andy, "This man Biggs, do you know him?"

"Saw him one time, is all."

Biggs had been picked up in a Ranger sweep through the oak and cedar thickets along the Llano River and its tributaries. Like a little fish tossed back into the water, he was accorded scant notice compared to men whose names were written in the Rangers' fugitive books for serious breaches of the law. He was released with a strong suggestion that he henceforth seek honest employment, and in some distant state. He had not, of course.

Andy said, "The last I heard, he was livin' in the brush." The thickets were a haven for men who sought solitude.

Daggett said, "I hate that brushy country. Always makes me feel closed in. I like the open plains, where a man don't feel like he's bein' smothered to death."

As they saddled fresh horses, Andy noticed that Daggett had a pronounced limp. The Ranger swore under his breath as he put his weight on the right leg and lifted his left foot to the stirrup. The wound was still giving him pain.

Andy asked him, "Are you sure you're up to the ride?"

Daggett reacted negatively to the question. He said, "Never show them any weakness, or they'll come and get you."

They set out southeastward on a wagon road that led toward the town of Junction on the Llano River. A Ranger packmule followed as it had been trained to do. Daggett hardly spoke. Andy wondered what was going on behind those hooded eyes, but Daggett gave him no clue. Andy introduced him to the Kimble County sheriff. The lawman was mildly amused by their mission. He said, "Biggs is just a triflin' no-account footpad. I'm surprised they'd waste your time with him."

Andy said, "A chigger bite is triflin', too, but after a while it itches to where you've got to scratch it."

Daggett said grimly, "A little bug needs squashin' same as a big one."

The sheriff said, "There's not a chicken roost or a

smokehouse in three counties that's safe from Biggs. They tell me he's got several places back in the brush where he holes up. He changes dens oftener than he changes clothes."

Daggett declared, "Even a coyote leaves tracks."

"Most people figure Biggs's petty pilferin' is a normal cost of livin' in these hills, like property taxes. I just had a complaint from a goat rancher down close to Pegleg Crossin'. You might start from there."

Andy said, "Biggs is stealin' goats now? Sounds like he's comin' up in the world."

"He takes a kid goat now and then to eat. Mostly he lives off of the land. There's hogs runnin' free in the thickets, and wild turkeys and such. He'll break into a store occasionally. One thing he never steals is soap. Last time I had him in jail, it took two days to air out the place."

Andy glanced at Daggett. "Sounds like we just have to follow our noses."

Daggett gave no hint of a smile.

The sheriff drew a rough map of the roads and trails he knew about but cautioned, "Some people who live down there are careful not to invite company. If they have to cross a road, they'll stop and wipe out their tracks. Was I you, I'd watch my back."

Andy said, "Sounds like the whole bunch deserve to be in jail."

Daggett added, "Or dead."

The sheriff frowned. "Maybe so, but we have to respect people's rights. We can't allow the law to be worse than the outlaw."

Daggett said, "An outlaw ought to not have any rights."

A buildup of clouds suggested rain. Though experience told Andy that was unlikely, he did not want to camp in the open. He asked the sheriff, "Be all right if we sleep in the jail tonight? The Austin money counters hate to pay for a cot in the wagon yard, much less for a room in a hotel."

"Sure, if you don't mind wakin' up with a sore back. Pick whatever cell you want. One bed is about as hard as another."

The jail held two prisoners. Daggett gave each of them a critical study through the bars. "What're they in for?" he asked.

The sheriff shrugged. "Nothin' serious. They took on too much brave-maker last night. They're still too red-eyed to be turned loose. They might get run over by a freight wagon or somethin'."

Daggett said without sympathy, "A man ought to have better control of himself."

The sheriff's admonition about the hard bed proved to be no exaggeration. Andy awakened with an ache in his shoulders. He worked his arms until the tension eased.

If Daggett felt any pain, he accepted it stoically, without conversation. He walked in circles a few minutes until his leg gained stability and his limp became less severe.

A deputy brought breakfast for the two Rangers and the prisoners, who seemed more than ready to put something in their stomachs besides cheap whiskey. The sheriff watched Andy finish his coffee. He asked, "Are you-all sure you wouldn't like for me to send a deputy with you, one who knows the country?"

Andy said, "Thanks, but I've been in those thickets before. I don't think Biggs will be much of a problem, once we find him."

"That's the catch . . . findin' him."

Andy doubted that they would be lucky enough simply to stumble upon a man who had a dozen hiding places. They would have to ask questions of people who had no reason to want to help a peace officer, and try to read more into their words than they intended to let slip.

Daggett finished his breakfast quickly and headed toward the door without saying anything. Andy still had eggs on his plate, but he said reluctantly, "I'm comin'." He held on to a biscuit as they went out to retrieve their horses. It irritated him to be rushed unnecessarily. Five minutes one way or the other was unlikely to make much difference. But he gathered that patience was not one of Daggett's strong points.

Making it into a bit of a contest, he saddled up in a hurry. He was determined to be on horseback before Daggett. The sheriff's deputy tied a pack on their little Mexican mule, which followed dutifully as the Rangers rode out through the open corral gate. It had been trained well.

Daggett said, "Since you've been in the thickets before, I'll let you lead the way."

*Let* me? Andy bristled at the older man's assumption of authority. He tried not to let his resentment show. They had to work together.

Late in the morning they stopped at the small ranch of a man who had never shown up on the fugitive lists and had always been cooperative with law enforcement officers, up to a point. The rancher wore no gun, which in itself said something about his effort to maintain neutrality. He said, "Jasper Biggs? No, ain't seen him lately, but I missed a ham out of my smokehouse a few nights ago. I figure he's been around. Lost a layin' hen, too, right off of the nest."

Andy asked, "Are you sure it wasn't a coyote that got the chicken?"

"Not unless a coyote has learned to wear boots."

"Do you know whichaway he went?"

"I made it a point not to follow his tracks. I figure a chicken or a ham now and again are a cheap price to pay for peace with my neighbors. Even a lunkhead like Jasper has got a few friends."

Daggett's voice was critical. "If enough honest people would speak up on the side of the law, things would change."

The rancher said, "Maybe, but I wouldn't want to stand on a platform wavin' the flag and find that I was out there all by myself. A man could get hurt."

The rancher invited the Rangers to stay for dinner. Seeing that Daggett wanted to move on, Andy perversely said, "We'd be tickled to break bread with you." Unlike Daggett, he took no offense over the rancher's attitude. He understood the man's thinking.

After the meal, the rancher picked his teeth while he watched Andy tighten his cinch. He said, "I can't afford to tell you Rangers anything straight out, but if I was to give you advice, I'd tell you to travel east. You won't have the afternoon sun in your eyes."

"Much obliged," Andy said. The rancher had just told him more than he had expected to hear. "That's just where we'd intended to go."

Andy assumed that any tracks Biggs left would have disappeared by now. He was not tracker enough to have followed them anyway. But Daggett looked around for a minute and announced, "He went off yonderway." He pointed eastward.

"Are you sure?"

"His trail is plain enough. Can't you see it?"

Andy did not want to admit that he had not, and still couldn't. But Sergeant Ryker had mentioned that Daggett was a good tracker. Maybe he would be useful enough to offset his dour manner.

Andy said, "I'll bet his hideout is somewhere around here. I doubt he'd walk far to steal one chicken."

Daggett shook his head. "You can't be sure with people like that. They think different from us normal folks."

The trail faded out, leaving Daggett frustrated and discussing Biggs's antecedents under his breath. The Rangers came after a while to a wagon road and a ramshackle country store, half hidden by live-oak timber. Andy knew the place. The structure was of rough-sawed lumber, never painted. Cedar bark still clung to a hitching post in front. One saddled horse stood switching flies. A couple more horses lazed in a corral out back, shaded by a large oak.

Andy sensed that he and Daggett had been seen before they dismounted and tied their mounts. The little pack-mule had followed without need of a lead rope and drew up close to Andy's horse. Instinctively Andy felt for the badge he customarily wore. It was inside his shirt pocket. He had thought it prudent not to flash it around among strangers in this environment. If Daggett had a badge, Andy had not seen it. Rangers still had to provide their own, so no two were exactly alike.

A bearded man came outside, gave the Rangers a quick nod, and untied his horse. He was gone before Andy had time for a good look at him. His furtive manner suggested that he might be found in the fugitive book. But that would wait for another time. He was not Jasper Biggs.

The proprietor was a lanky, middle-aged man with a scar beneath one eye and two or three days' growth of salt-and-pepper whiskers. He wiped his hands on a faded flour-sack apron and said, "My name's Smith, and I run this place. How can I serve you gentlemen?" He waved his hand toward a plain pine bar at one end of the dark room. Bottles, lined in a row, were reflected in a cracked mirror on the wall.

Andy said, "I would've bet that your name would be Smith." It probably had not always been. "Nothin' to drink, thanks. We might take a small slab of bacon if you've got any for sale."

"Anything I've got here is for sale. Anything at all."

A girl showed herself at a door that led into a room in the back. She asked, "Did you call for me, Mr. Smith?"

The storekeeper said, "Ain't you done with the washin' yet, Annylee? You'd better get it hung out on the line if you want it to dry before dark." He turned back to Andy, "Seems to me I've seen you before. Ranger, ain't you?"

Andy was mildly surprised that the man remembered, but most people on the shady side of the law had a memory for peace officers' faces. Through a dirty window he could see the girl hanging a tablecloth on a thin rope line. He realized that the cloth was a signal to all comers that lawmen were on the premises. He said, "You've got good recall."

"It pays in this part of the country. Every time one of you fellers comes around, business falls off faster than Annylee's drawers. Lookin' for somebody?"

"Jasper Biggs."

"Jasper? What's he done bad enough to interest the Rangers?"

"Just stayed around too long. Is he a customer of yours?"

The storekeeper's brow wrinkled. It was hard to tell whether he was frowning or enjoying a bitter joke of his own. "Customers come in the daylight, and they pay cash. Jasper comes when everybody's asleep. He seldom pays for anything except an occasional tussle with Annylee when he can steal the money someplace."

"Looks to me like you'd be glad to have him gone."

"So would most other people. But givin' him up to the law . . . that's inethical." The merchant turned toward a counter. "Was you really wantin' that bacon, or was you just passin' the time of day while you look around?"

"We don't really need it."

"I didn't figure you did. Lawmen drop in on me every so often to nose about, and most of them don't buy a damned thing."

"Maybe you're not sellin' what we're lookin' for."

"If I did, somebody would burn this store down, with me in it. Have you-all about finished what you came here for?"

Andy could recognize an invitation to leave. He looked to Daggett, who had not said a word. "I reckon." More than likely a customer or two waited out in the brush. "You can take that tablecloth down from the line."

For the first time, Andy noticed a box at the end of the counter. It had a wooden frame and was covered with metal screen. As he moved near, he heard the unmistakable rattle of a snake. He involuntarily took a step backward.

The storekeeper said, "Everybody needs a pet around the place. That's mine. Ain't he fat?"

Hesitantly Andy stepped closer, confident the snake could not escape through the mesh. "What do you feed him?"

"Mice. There's aplenty of them around here. You can reach in and pet him if you're of a mind to."

"He might not take kindly to a stranger."

The proprietor pointed, his finger near the box. The snake lifted itself partway from its coil, its mouth open, its tongue darting. "I put a ten-dollar gold piece in that cage. It belongs to anybody with guts enough to reach in there and get it. I charge people a dollar apiece to try."

"Anybody ever do it?"

"Been a good many paid the dollar, but they always jerk their hand out as soon as the snake moves."

"Anybody ever get bit?"

"One. He eats his dinner left-handed now."

Andy and Daggett walked out to untie their horses. Daggett remarked, "Looks to me like that snake has got relatives around here, walkin' on two legs."

Andy asked, "Meanin' the storekeeper?"

"I thought I heard him rattle."

The girl stood at the back corner of the store, crooking a finger. Andy led his horse to where she waited, anxiously watching the door. She said in a hoarse voice, "You say you're lookin' for Jasper?"

"We'd be pleased to locate him."

She pointed eastward. "He's got a little throwed-together shack out yonderway. It's in the middle of a thicket and hard to see."

"How come you're willin' to give him away?"

"I don't want to be seein' him no more. I can tolerate the other men who come around here, but Jasper smells bad."

"Mr. Smith might not like you tellin' us this."

"He won't do nothin', not as long as I'm bringin' in money." Looking at the back door again, she asked hopefully, "Reckon there's any reward for Jasper?"

"Not that I know of."

"I just thought . . . well, it'll be nice to be rid of him." She quickly disappeared into the back of the store.

Daggett said, "The storekeeper *is* a rattlesnake, usin' a

girl like that. I've got half a mind to go back in there and whittle on him."

"He's not the man they sent us for."

"He'd be no man at all when I got through with him."

Finding Biggs's hiding place sounded simple, but it was not. Andy and Daggett rode a tiring switchback pattern through the brush for two days without finding anything more than sharp thorns and biting insects. He thought Biggs must have hide like leather to maneuver around in this tangle of hostile growth, especially afoot. Nobody remembered that he ever had a horse.

They camped near a small spring where water bubbled from between layers of moss-covered limestone. Daggett built a fire while Andy unpacked the mule. He surprised Andy by saying, "Ain't much like home, is it?"

Andy shrugged. "It's a livin'."

"A man can make a better livin' bein' a sheriff. In some counties, even bein' a deputy."

"It costs money to run for election. Anyway, my home county has already got a good sheriff, name of Rusty Shannon. I couldn't go back and run against him. He's the best friend I've got."

"If I had my life to live over, I'd be somethin' besides a Ranger. Long days on horseback, poor food or none at all. As often as not, when you finally catch your man, a slick-talkin' lawyer gets him turned loose. You wake up one mornin' achin' all over and realize that half of what you've done with your life has gone for nothin'. Makes you wish you'd shot all the sons of bitches when you had the chance."

It was the longest declaration Andy had heard Daggett make. He considered a reply but did not offer one. He had heard some of the same argument from Bethel. Still, he could not concede that much of his life's work had been for naught. He had helped put some bad men behind bars or under the ground, and the country was the better for it.

Daggett rubbed the wounded leg, his face creased with pain.

Andy said, "Maybe you got back on it too soon. They ought to've let you rest longer."

"I can stand just about anything except bein' idle. It gives a man too much time to think. I was ready and rarin' to get back to work." Daggett poured the first cup of coffee for himself and sat back to savor it. He said, "Sergeant Ryker tells me you've got a pretty young wife. You ought to be with her tonight instead of out here in the middle of nothin' with a shaggy old misfit like me."

Andy said, "You're not shaggy." He realized it would have been better to have said nothing at all. Tired, he rolled up in his blanket soon after they finished their meager supper. The soothing sound of spring water tumbling down the rocky creek bank helped him drift off to sleep.

A curse awakened him as first daylight erased the stars. In long underwear and barefoot, Daggett surveyed the scattered contents of the mule's pack. He said grittily, 'We've been robbed. Somebody got off with our bacon, our coffee, and our sugar."

Andy had not heard a thing all night. He blinked, trying to absorb what Daggett was saying. He glanced around

worriedly until he saw that the horses and the mule remained where they had been picketed. He asked, "You
reckon it was Biggs?"

"A bigger thief would've took the horses too. Camp
cookin' is bad enough, but to have to eat it without coffee to
wash it down, or sugar to sweeten it . . ." Daggett cursed
Biggs's father, his mother, and all his brothers and sisters, if
he had any.

Andy offered, "Maybe he left some tracks."

"I already found them. Let's break camp and get on his
trail. Maybe we can catch him before he uses up all the
coffee."

Andy could sometimes see the tracks, but in the main
he relied on Daggett's keen eyes to lead them. The horsemen moved in a ragged pattern through the thickets of
cedar and oak and several types of scrub brush. After a
couple of hours of starting, stopping, backtracking, they
stirred a hawk from its nest. It flew up and began circling
overhead, screeching a warning that they were encroach-
ing on its territory.

Andy said, "She's probably hatchin' some eggs."

Daggett asked, "Ever been hungry enough to eat a hawk
egg?"

Andy shook his head. "Not as I remember."

"I have. I was better off hungry."

Shortly Daggett raised his hand, signaling to stop. He
pointed silently at a small, crude structure constructed of
tree branches, the top covered by a dirty, stained canvas.
Part shack, part tent, a miserable excuse for shelter, it was

well hidden within a thicket. Andy saw a shallow fire pit ringed with rocks, dark with ash and charred remnants of wood. Approaching carefully, he found a skillet lying upon still-warm coals. Two strips of bacon were burned to tiny curls of black.

Andy whispered, "Looks like he left in a hurry."

"That damned hawk."

"Biggs is afoot. He ought not to be hard to catch."

Daggett seemed enlivened by the near encounter. He dismounted and peered inside the shack. "Gone. You circle to the left. I'll go to the right. Don't take any chances. If he shows fight, shoot him."

Andy might shoot a murderer, or even a horse thief, but not a man whose bite was more like a mosquito's than a snake's. "In the leg, maybe."

"Don't give him a better chance than he would give you."

Andy made his circle and met Daggett on the far side. The older Ranger's questioning eyes told Andy that he had not seen anything either. Daggett said, "I found one solitary track."

Andy said, "He must've lit out like a rabbit, or holed up like one. He could be layin' out there watchin' us right now." The thought made him uneasy, though he knew within reason that Biggs was unlikely to fight unless cornered. Andy had not heard of his ever firing on anyone.

Daggett said, "Right now I'd give my right arm for some coffee. Let's ride back to his den."

"Hadn't we ought to go right after him?"

"He's on foot. If we can find a trail, we'll catch up to him. If we can't . . . he'll turn up someplace. He left his grub behind. He'll be hungry again before long."

Andy put up no more argument. "I'm a little hungry myself."

He looked inside the tiny shelter. It was barely large enough to accommodate one man and his meager belongings. Dirty blankets lay ruffled on a pad of dry grass. Andy did not touch them. He suspected that they contained fleas. Coyotes always had them, so it stood to reason that a man who lived like a coyote would have them too. He said, "I've seen dogs that wouldn't live in a place like this."

"If Biggs was normal, he wouldn't either. But none of them outlaws are normal. They all got a twisted brain."

"Any ideas?"

Daggett grunted. "You said you're hungry. I am, too, so we'll fix somethin' to eat. It's our own grub."

They found little food. Biggs had used up most of it. As for coffee, only a few beans remained. Grumbling about the waste, Daggett led out, searching the ground for sign. He picked up the trail easily at first, for Biggs had left in too much of a hurry to cover his tracks. But after a time Daggett drew up in frustration. "How can somebody so dumb be so damned smart?"

Andy said, "Sometimes nature shorts us one way but makes up for it someplace else. At least we've got a notion of his general direction."

They rode slowly, watching for some indication of Biggs's passage. Dusk caught them still empty-handed.

Regretfully, Daggett said, "Let's turn back and make camp on that creek we just crossed."

Andy had nothing better to offer. They would have water, if nothing else. He said, "I'm beginnin' to think we've been sent on a fool's errand."

Daggett said, "Maybe not. Catch a man while he's still a small crook and lock him away for good. He'll never get to be a big one."

"But they *will* let him out. You know how it is with lawyers."

Shadows from the firelight cut deep furrows in Daggett's face. "There's no appeal from the graveyard."

"There couldn't be much satisfaction in shootin' a miserable thief like Biggs."

"You'd be surprised."

Andy was awakened by a shot. He threw his blanket aside and reached for his pistol. Then he saw Daggett limping into camp, carrying a shotgun and holding a wild turkey at arm's length.

"Breakfast," Daggett said.

The bird had been been shot in the head. "Fancy shootin'," Andy said.

Daggett shrugged. "I cheated. I shot it off of the roost."

They slow-cooked the turkey on two spits above the coals. Andy tore into his half as soon as it was done. "Tastes good."

"Needs salt," Daggett replied. "I reckon we'd better go back to Smith's store and get some more supplies. That Biggs damn near cleaned us out."

Evidently they were seen before they got there, for a tablecloth was already flapping on the line as they rode up. Daggett noted it without comment. Andy felt of it. "Dry," he said. "Probably dry when they hung it out here."

Daggett grunted. "If honest folks would work together like the outlaws do, this would be a better country."

It took a moment for Andy's eyes to adjust to the dark interior of the cramped and crowded store. It smelled of whiskey and leather and kerosene. He saw proprietor Smith slouched in a wooden chair, a bandaged leg stretched out straight, the foot resting upon a pillow atop a three-legged milking stool. Annylee stood beside him, her hand on his shoulder. Smith shouted angrily, "About time you damned Rangers got here! You always show up when nobody wants you, but you're never around when somebody needs you."

Andy said, "You didn't exactly roll out a red carpet for us the last time."

He saw that the lid of the snake box was open, the box empty.

The storekeeper cursed. "That damned Biggs. Snuck in here durin' the night and got my gold piece."

Andy asked, "In spite of the snake?"

"He dumped the snake out, grabbed the coin and ran. Now the rattler's loose somewhere in the store and madder than all hell."

Andy could not suppress a smile. "Looks like he might've taken some of that anger out on you."

"It ain't a bit funny. My leg's swole up bigger than a mesquite stump."

Daggett offered no sympathy. He said, "We've got to have some groceries."

Smith growled, "You'll have to get them for yourself. I can't walk, and I ain't lettin' Annylee risk gettin' snakebit reachin' into them cabinets. She's got to take care of me."

Andy suspected that she had been carrying most of the workload around here for a long time. He said, "Maybe now you'll be more inclined to tell us which way Biggs went."

"Annylee can show you. I'll tell you one thing: if you catch up to him, you won't find him settin' down. He won't be settin' down for a long time."

"How come?"

"I let him have a dose of buckshot where it would do the most good. He squalled like a panther."

Andy said, "You could've killed him."

"I doubt anybody would've cried. Except him."

Andy and Daggett gathered what they needed. Annylee added up the bill. Andy had to correct her on the total. He was not a fast reader, but he had an aptitude with figures. She watched while they put the groceries on the mule. She lifted her foot and placed it on a fence rail, causing her skirt to slide back and expose part of her leg. She suggested, "If you fellers ain't in a big hurry, I don't expect that Mr. Smith needs me for a while."

Andy grinned at her boldness. "All we need is for you to show us which way Biggs went when he left here."

She took them to a set of footprints that led eastward into the brush. She said, "If anybody was to ask, me and Mr. Smith didn't tell you nothin'."

Daggett gave her a look that surprised Andy. It seemed to suggest pity. The big Ranger brought a large silver coin from his pocket and handed it to her. He said, "We wouldn't want the day to be a total loss to you."

She smiled. "Thanks. I'm savin' my money. Someday when I have enough, I'm goin' to leave here and go to some big city, like maybe San Antonio. I'll bet the livin' is easy there."

For her, Andy suspected, life would never be easy anywhere.

Riding away, Daggett looked back once. Regretfully he said, "It appears to me that the country's goin' downhill like a runaway train. People have got no morals anymore."

"They were already sayin' that back in Bible times."

"There was avengin' angels in those days, ready to smite the transgressors. What this country needs is some avengin' angels."

"Do you know any?"

"They'll come, when the time is right. Who knows? Maybe we're them." Daggett went quiet, focusing his attention on Biggs's tracks.

They almost missed seeing the makeshift shelter. It was given away only by yellowed leaves where a few tree branches had been broken off in an effort to hide the entrance. Daggett drew his rifle and stepped down behind his horse. Andy followed his example.

Daggett shouted, "Jasper Biggs! Texas Rangers! Come out with your hands up."

The answer was more plaintive wail than discernible words. Daggett repeated his order.

A weak voice replied from within the shelter, "I can't move. I'm dyin'."

Daggett and Andy exchanged glances. Daggett said quietly, "Be ready to shoot if he as much as wiggles."

Daggett bent at the waist and rushed through the narrow opening. Andy was one step behind him, hands tightly gripping his rifle.

Biggs lay facedown on a dirty blanket, a rail-thin man in clothes too large for him. The back of his shirt and the seat of his filthy trousers were spotted with blood and buckshot holes. Andy was instantly aware of a dank odor and knew it came from Biggs himself. The Junction sheriff had mentioned his aversion to soap.

Daggett said, "High price to pay for a ten-dollar gold piece."

Biggs turned his face upward. Ragged whiskers failed to hide his sunken cheeks and his rheumy gray eyes. He whimpered, "I think that old miser killed me. I feel like that buckshot has worked plumb through to my heart."

Andy said, "From the looks of your britches, that's not where most of it went. We'd better get your shirt off and your pants down."

Panic came into Biggs's voice. "What you fixin' to do?"

Andy said, "If it's as bad as it looks from here, we've got to dig all that shot out of you. Else it may go into blood poisonin', or even gangrene."

"You goin' to use a knife?"

"We've got nothin' else."

Biggs began to weep. He cried out in pain as Andy helped remove his shirt and pull down his long underwear and trousers. "Oh, God, I think I'm about to die."

The corners of the tall Ranger's mustache lifted in pleasure. He said, "The wages of sin."

Andy said, "He must've got some distance away before the shot hit him. They don't look to've gone very deep."

"Deep enough to kill him if they don't come out." Daggett winked. "But we'll do our best to save you, Jasper."

Andy fetched water and washed Biggs's back and rump of dried blood so he and Daggett could see more clearly what they were doing. Daggett said, "You hold him down while I pick a while. He's apt to flounce around a right smart." He took out his pocketknife.

Andy suggested, "Might be a good idea to sterilize that blade in a fire first."

"Good idea. You start one. Now, Jasper, you just lay real still and get yourself ready. This is goin' to hurt like hell. I hope you're man enough to take it."

Biggs moaned and prayed that God would let him die quickly.

Each tiny probe of the blade point prompted a whimper. Most of the shot popped out easily. Daggett wiped sweat onto his sleeve and said, "Here, Andy, you finish it. All this blood is makin' me sick at my stomach." Actually, little fresh blood appeared. The damage was near the surface, and minor.

Daggett said, "Jasper, if you live, and if you ever get

out of jail, I hope you'll remember this and repent your heathen ways. Get yourself an honest job and enjoy the untroubled sleep of a righteous man."

Checking to be certain he had missed no buckshot, Andy said, "He's not goin' to ride a horse for a while."

Daggett said, "Hear that, Jasper? You may never ride again, or maybe even walk. You may have to spend the rest of your days standin' up or layin' on your stomach. Mighty poor way for a man to finish out his time, but you brought it on yourself."

Biggs's thin shoulders heaved with silent weeping.

Outside, Daggett asked Andy, "Know a ranch around here where we can borrow a wagon?"

"I think so." Andy frowned. "You spread it on pretty thick."

"Meant to. A jury is liable to take pity on such a sorry-lookin' specimen and let him get away light. The more scared he was and the more he hurt, the better he'll remember this day when he thinks about liftin' his hand to mischief again."

"I used to know an old preacher named Webb. He'd say you've got a devious mind."

"I believe in due punishment, even if I have to deal it out myself."


Andy sat on the rumbling wagon, holding the reins, his horse tied behind. Daggett was on horseback. They were nearing the outskirts of Junction when a horseman shouted and galloped up from behind. He was a large man, about

the match of Daggett. Eyes ablaze with hostility, he demanded, "What've you done to my brother?"

Andy saw little physical resemblance between this big
man and Jasper Biggs except that both had squinty eyes.
He had always distrusted squinty-eyed people. Irritated, he
said, "We've done nothin' but pick a pound of buckshot
out of him. Now we're haulin' him to jail."

"Who shot him? You?"

"Not us." Andy did not elaborate, though he doubted it
would be hard for the man to find out. Likely as not, the
storekeeper was bragging about it to everybody who would
listen.

The brother said, "He don't belong in jail. He was always kind of simple. He don't know right from wrong."

"He needs to learn. Maybe some jail time will teach
him."

"No jail. You're fixin' to turn that wagon around. I'm
takin' him home where I can watch over him."

Andy saw danger in the brother's eyes. He said, "You
haven't watched over him very good up to now."

"Just the same, I'm takin' him."

The man's hand dropped to the butt of the weapon on
his hip, but Daggett was faster. The Ranger swung the
barrel of his pistol at the man's head. The stranger's hat
sailed away as he slumped in the saddle, then slid off. He
lay in a quivering heap on the ground.

Daggett said, "The conversation was gettin' tedious."

Biggs whined, "You son of a bitch, you could've killed
my brother."

"That I could. Might yet if he don't lay still."

Andy's heart raced. He said to Daggett, "You really would, wouldn't you?"

Daggett's face was grim. "I never draw a gun without I'm prepared to use it." He looked down into the bed of the wagon. "Do you hear me, Jasper?"

Biggs only grunted.

Andy said, "*I* heard you. I don't know what to think about it."

"No thinkin' needed. Just know that I'm serious. Now you'd better catch and tie his horse. He'll be lookin' for it when he wakes up."

# CHAPTER
## 2

They carried the prisoner to the Junction sheriff, who seemed none too thrilled at the present delivered by wagon to the door of his jail. He said, "Couldn't you find some excuse to shoot him? The last time I had him in here, I had to burn sulphur to fumigate the place."

Andy said, "He's clean. We dumped him in the Llano River before we brought him in. Now, if you'll write us a receipt for him . . ."

Riding back toward Fort McKavett, Andy said, "I don't think Jasper's brother would really have shot one of us."

Daggett said, "Then again, he might. A man draws a gun on you, you'd better figure he means it." His voice became accusatory. "I do believe you felt sorry for that two-bit night crawler."

"I did, a little."

"A soft heart can be a liability when you're wearin' a badge. Someday you'll find your head tellin' you to do one thing but your conscience tellin' you to do another. While you're arguin' with yourself, you can get killed."

"Is that what happened to your leg?"

Daggett's face creased as he remembered. "I gave them

every chance to surrender. Instead, they shot me. There's nothin' like the sight of your own blood to clear your mind."

"So you shot them?"

"It was the sensible thing to do."

Fort McKavett was no longer a military outpost. Many of its original buildings had been converted to civilian purposes. Others stood in ruins, their roofs and windows cannibalized for reuse elsewhere. Riding into the village at the edge of the San Saba River, Andy asked Daggett, "Mind if we stop off at the house before we go on into camp? I want to let Bethel know I'm back."

Daggett gave him a questioning look. "This face of mine scares dogs and little kids. She'll say I'm an example of what happens to a man who stays in the Rangers too long."

Andy would admit that Daggett looked the worse for wear, but he did not intend to remain a Ranger as long as Daggett had. He said, "On the other hand, she can see that you're still alive in spite of it all."

"Only because of some people's poor marksmanship."

A little brown dog met them. Chickens fluttered and clucked in protest as the two riders disturbed their hunt for seeds and insects. Bethel stepped out onto the little porch to see what had stirred them up.

"Andy!" she shouted, trying to look displeased but unable to control a joyful smile. "I thought you'd left me for another woman."

"I've thought about it," Andy said, "but I haven't found another one as good-lookin'."

She cocked her head to one side. "Are you bringing home any new wounds that I'll have to take care of?"

"Nary a one. There wasn't a shot fired."

Instead of coming to him as she sometimes did, she waited for him to go to her. She stared at Daggett, a question in her eyes. Andy supposed she felt shy in the presence of the stranger. He said, "This is Logan Daggett. He's been transferred to our company."

He tried in vain to read her reaction. Bethel was accomplished at concealing her opinions when she wanted to.

Daggett lifted his hat. "Ma'am." His hard features seemed to soften as he gave her a long study. He appeared to want to say something more, but nothing came.

She said, "It's nice to meet you, Mr. Daggett. Won't you come into the house? I'll fix some coffee."

Still staring at her, Daggett seemed to drift away into a moment of solemn reverie. Bestirring himself, he said, "That'd please me, ma'am, but it's gettin' late in the day. I'd best go in and report to the sergeant. Pickard, why don't you stay the night here and report in time for mornin' roll call?"

Andy was surprised by Daggett's show of generosity. "You sure you don't mind?"

Daggett turned back to Bethel. "A young lady like this needs a lot of lookin' after. I doubt you're livin' up to the job."

"She doesn't complain."

She said, "Oh yes I do, a lot."

Daggett turned away. The packmule seemed confused but followed Daggett's horse.

Andy dismounted and took Bethel into his arms.

She said, "I guess you caught your man?"

"There wasn't much to it, once we found him."

She turned and looked in the direction Daggett had taken. "How was Mr. Daggett to work with?"

"He didn't load me down with a lot of idle talk, like Len Tanner would've. He can ride for miles and not say a word."

"His eyes bother me, like something dark is hidden behind them."

"He's been through some hard times. He didn't tell me much, and I didn't ask him."

"Is that the way you'll look after being a Ranger a few more years?"

"I'll quit before it comes to that."

She frowned. "I wonder if you'll ever quit." She turned toward the door. "I'll get supper started. Or are you anxious to get back to camp?"

"Like Daggett said, camp can wait till mornin'."


Sergeant Ryker looked up from the table that served as a desk in the headquarters tent. He nodded as Andy walked in to report. He asked, "Had breakfast?"

"Yes, sir, before I left the house."

"A better one than mine, I'd wager. Daggett told me how you-all got your man. It took you longer than I expected."

"Jasper didn't leave a lot of tracks. Even Daggett had trouble followin' them."

Ryker unfolded himself from behind the table and walked outside, looking around as if to assure himself that no one else was within earshot. "I want the truth, with no holdin' back. What is your opinion of Logan Daggett?"

Andy disliked being pinned down to a judgment of a fellow officer. He said, "He's a good tracker."

"I already knew that. What about his attitude? Is he a complainer?"

Daggett had made a couple of negative remarks about the Ranger service, specifically the holders of the purse strings, but nothing stronger than Andy himself had said on occasion. "No, sir, he was determined to finish what we set out to do. As far as I could tell, that was the only thing on his mind."

"How did he treat the prisoner?"

"He took pleasure in pickin' buckshot out of Jasper's butt, and listenin' to Jasper howl. Fact is, I enjoyed it myself after the chase he put us through."

Ryker mulled over what Andy had told him. "Takin' everything into consideration, do you like him?"

Andy wished he had not been asked that question. He said, "I'm still tryin' to make up my mind."

"How would you feel if I was to send you off on another assignment with him?"

"I'd rather go with Len Tanner."

"Tanner's off runnin' down a horse thief."

"Whatever you say, then. You're the sergeant." Andy wondered how long he might be away this time.

Ryker said, "Daggett's good at enforcin' the law, but he's got a reputation for goin' off like a shotgun from time to time. You could be a stable influence."

"I'm supposed to keep the lid on him?"

Ryker nodded. "But don't look at this as a command. Consider it a challenge."

Andy could not see much difference.

Ryker said, "You know Central Texas, don't you?"

"I've spent time there."

"A sheriff friend of mine is sittin' on a keg of gunpowder. There's been vigilance committee activity and some shootin's. I'm volunteerin' you and Daggett to go help him put an end to the troubles."

"Any idea what's behind it all?"

"It started with folks accusin' one another of stealin' cattle and horses. I'm more inclined to think it's really about who's goin' to run that part of the country. There's nothin' like local politics to cause a fight. If I had my way, I'd put all the politicians on a boat at Galveston, sail it out into the Gulf, and sink it."

"Feelin' that way, how have you managed to keep bein' a sergeant?"

"By knowin' when to talk and when to bite my tongue."

Andy kissed Bethel in the house. He felt awkward about doing it outside with Daggett watching. Daggett waited with the packmule, outfitted with enough grub to last more than a week. After that, they would have to buy more, but with a stern admonition to keep the cost down to the lowest possible figure. The headquarters office in Austin was suffering through one of its frequent spasms of acute frugality.

Bethel clung to his hand. "They didn't give us much time," she said.

"Ryker has promised me a few days off when we finish this job," Andy told her. "I promise, we'll camp together in the hills. We'll even stake out the ground where we'll build the house and the barn and corrals someday."

"Someday never seems to get any closer."

"While I'm gone, you could go back home and visit your brother Farley and his wife and the little one. It's been a long time."

"But I want to be here when you get back."

"Think about it anyway."

"Write to me as soon as you get things sized up and have some idea how long you may be gone."

"You know I don't write very good."

"I've found that out. But try."

He kissed her once more, then walked briskly through the door. The early morning sun hit him squarely in the eyes. It made tears start. "Ready?" he asked Daggett.

"Always ready." Daggett tipped his hat to Bethel as she came out onto the porch. "I'll bring him home soon as I can, ma'am."

"But in one piece, please. Seems like half the time when he comes home he has a new bullet hole in him."

"It's the low class of criminals we have to deal with. Maybe someday we'll have a better sort." Daggett set off into a long trot, taking the lead. Andy followed, turning in the saddle to wave at Bethel. She watched, but she did not wave back. Her hands were clasped in front of her.

When they were well away from the house, Daggett slowed and let Andy catch up. Frowning, he said in a critical voice, "Maybe you don't know what a good thing you've got. A pretty little miss like that don't deserve to be left cryin' while you ride away to the devil knows where."

Defensively Andy said, "She wasn't cryin'."

"She was cryin' inside. Every time you leave, she wonders if the next time she sees you will be at your buryin'."

"Before we married, I warned her what it'd be like."

"It's one thing for her to hear it. It's another to live with it."

Andy was irritated by Daggett's lecturing. "How do you know so much about a woman's feelin's?"

"I had a woman once, a lot like yours. God, what I'd give to go back and do right by her this time."

"Can't you?"

"Too late." Daggett's eyes were bleak. He spurred his horse. "Come on, we've got a far piece ahead of us."

The trail at one point climbed up a layered limestone hill, strewn with loose rocks that could slip and cripple a horse. It followed along the top of a long hogback ridge. Andy could see for miles off either side across broad expanses of live oak trees and cedars, hackberries and other mixed timber, which in the far distance melded into a thin blue haze.

Daggett said, "It's a lot different from the plains. Are you sure we haven't strayed out of Texas?"

Andy said, "I think I'd know if we had. The air would feel different."

"The Central Texas hills won't be this big or this rocky, will they?"

Andy said, "Not quite. The Comanches stole me when I was a boy and kept me for a long time. They used to come down into this country to hunt, all the way from the Canadian River breaks."

Daggett said, "The sergeant told me about your time with the Indians. As far as I'm concerned, the Indians can have this part of the country."

Though settlers in recent years had thinned out the game, Andy and Daggett had frequently seen deer bound away into the sanctuary of heavy thickets. To Andy, they were a pleasant sight.

He said, "Bethel and me have bought us a piece of land in the Kerrville country. It's got good grass and water, and game."

"You ought to be there now instead of wanderin' the country like a gypsy. You're workin' on other people's problems when you ought to be takin' care of your own."

"You've been at this longer than I have. Why haven't you quit?"

"Been at it so long that it's easier to stay than to leave and start somethin' new. But you're young enough for just anything you set your mind to. Your wife talked like she's patched up some bullet holes in you."

"Several, but not all at one time."

"You're liable to get one she can't patch. Widow's black wouldn't look good on her."

"Bethel's little, but she's a strong woman."

Daggett gave Andy a silent look that called him a fool.

They took their time, making about thirty miles a day, sparing their horses and the little Mexican packmule. Andy remembered the various counties: Mason, Kimble, San Saba, Lampasas . . .

Working his way down from a hill into a broad valley, he saw a man on horseback herding sheep toward a corral of cedar stakes tied so closely together that a rabbit might not wiggle through. A dog trotted alongside him, wagging its tail and acting pleased with itself as if it were doing the whole job alone.

Andy said, "We'd just as well start introducin' ourselves to the folks."

Daggett frowned. "If we have to shoot any of them, knowin' them might make it harder on your conscience."

"I'm hopin' we won't have to do that."

"Sometimes you've got to shoot a few people before you can make things peaceful."

The dog barked at the two riders and the packmule until its owner bade it to hush. It took a cautious stance behind the stockman's horse, poised to run away at its first perception of threat.

Andy tried to present a pleasant smile. "Howdy. Are we on the right road to town?"

The sheepman was middle-aged, his stomach flat as a slab of bacon. A black pipe extended beyond several days'

growth of bristly gray whiskers. He considered a moment before he answered, carefully sizing up the visitors. He said,
"There are better ones, but this'll get you there."

Andy said, "I'm Andy Pickard. This here is Logan
Daggett. We'll be glad to help you take the sheep the rest
of the way in."

"The dog and me, we've been doing it a long time. But
you're welcome to ride along with us to the house. Stay
the night if you're of a mind to."

Andy said, "That'd be kind of you."

"My pleasure. We don't get much company out here.
Most people regard me as a crazy old sheepherder and stay
away. My name's August Hawkins."

Andy had encountered many sheepmen in his travels. As
a rule he had found them to be smarter than those who criti-
cized them, and better off financially. Sheep tended to be
more profitable than cattle. Hawkins's manner of speaking
indicated that he had education.

He said, "I let them spread out to graze in the daytime, but
I pen them at night. There are lots of four-legged varmints
around here."

"What about two-legged ones?"

"They'd rather steal cattle and horses. Sheep move too
slowly. They can get a thief caught." He stared at Andy,
then at Daggett. "I'm trying to decide whether you two
are laws or outlaws. Sometimes the difference is hard to
see."

"We're Rangers," Andy said. "We've been told there's
trouble in this part of the country."

"I stay out here with my sheep. I try to keep far away from trouble that doesn't concern me."

It was the same eyes-averted attitude that Andy had observed in the Llano River thickets. He said, "Anything you might tell us wouldn't go any farther than me and Daggett."

"It won't even go that far. I have nothing to tell you." A ewe strayed away from the others, nibbling at low weeds. The dog paid no attention until the sheepman pointed a finger and shouted, "Dog, wake up and go bring her back!"

The dog sprinted out and nipped at the ewe. She ran to the others, not stopping until she had plunged in to the middle of the flock.

Andy said, "Hasn't the dog got a name?"

"If I called him what he deserves, he would probably bite me." Hawkins whistled the dog back to its place at his side. "I hope you don't mind goat meat for supper."

"Goat?"

"I don't eat my sheep. I keep them for the wool. Goat tastes quite good when it's prepared properly. My little old wife knows a dozen ways to cook it."

Andy said, "Sounds fine."

The sheepman turned to Daggett. "So far you haven't said a word."

The comment caught Daggett off guard. "All I know I learned by listenin' while others talked."

The corral gate was open. The sheep knew the routine, filing through in good order. Several lambs spooked at the shadow of the gate's crossbar and leaped over it. Andy dismounted to close the gate, built solid so no predator could work its way through. Hawkins pointed to another pen. "You can turn your horses and the mule loose in there with mine. I'll fork out some hay."

A milk cow stood outside another pen, her calf eagerly awaiting her on the inside. Hawkins said, "I'll milk first, then we'll have supper."

He led them to a log cabin. Smoke was rising from its chimney, and Andy caught the pleasant aroma of freshly baked bread.

Hawkins asked, "Does either of you speak Spanish? My wife Serafina doesn't know much English."

Andy had a smattering of it, though not enough for a deep discussion about philosophy. Daggett said he knew only *manos arriba* and *adiós,* hands up and good-bye.

Mrs. Hawkins was a busy, dark-faced little woman who might not weigh a hundred pounds. She smiled and chattered so rapidly that Andy could pick out only a word here and there. But he understood the food she placed on the table.

Hawkins said, "I hired her after my first wife died. She was a widow woman, washing clothes and cleaning other people's houses. It didn't look right, her living out here with me, so I married her. After all, I'm a churchgoing man. I go every month or two."

Andy asked, "Any children?"

"Grown and gone in four different directions. I have grandchildren I've never seen and likely never will. So it's just Serafina and me, the dog and the sheep. And this little piece of land."

After the meal, the three men sat on the porch, enjoying the cool of early evening. Hawkins puffed on the old black pipe. He said, "I suppose Sheriff Seymour sent for you. I'm surprised he'd ask for Ranger help."

Andy said, "He didn't. We got a letter from somebody who didn't sign his name."

"Didn't sign? That's not surprising. Pete Seymour has a bull by the tail. That job has made him touchy as an old bear. You'll need to handle him gently."

Andy glanced at Daggett before saying, "We try to handle everybody gently."

Hawkins said, "It got quiet around here for a while, but things have commenced happening again. A man was murdered last week."

Andy straightened. "We didn't know about that."

"A rancher by the name of Callender. Somebody ambushed him in the door of his barn."

"Any idea why?" Andy asked.

"Just a suspicion. He must've known something that somebody was afraid he'd tell."

Daggett said grimly, "Sounds to me like the work of a mob."

"Around here they are known as the regulators." The sheepman paused to take a couple of draws on his pipe. "To begin with, we have old family enmities that should have been resolved long ago. On top of that we are up against changing times. New people come into the country, crowding the ones already here. I stay out of it. I bought my place free and clear, but much of the land still belongs to the state. Anyone can use it if he has the nerve to take and hold it."

Andy said, "Things'll be a lot more peaceful when the land is all bought up. Then there'll be legal property lines."

Daggett broke his silence. "But folks'll start puttin' up wire fences, and there won't be open land anymore." That thought appeared to depress him.

Hawkins said, "I plan to put a fence around mine. Already have the wire and posts ordered. It'll keep other people's cattle out and leave more grass for my sheep."

Daggett said, "You may have a fight over it. I've seen it happen up in the Panhandle."

Hawkins argued, "If the land belongs to me, free and clear, no one else has any say-so."

Daggett shook his head. "If one owner fences his land, others'll follow. Then the free range will be gone. You'd best test the temper of your neighbors before you dig that first posthole."

Hawkins argued, "I've always gone out of my way to avoid a fight, ever since back in the sixties when I was dragged into a war that was none of my doing."

Daggett leaned forward, his voice earnest. "If I was you I'd wait and let the big operators put up their fences first. If there's to be fightin', let them do it. In the long run they always win, and you'll get a free ride."

Hawkins mused, "I never asked for a free ride during the war. Were you in that fight, Daggett?"

"I was. I learned when to stick my head up and when to

keep it down. I took other people's mistakes to heart and tried not to make the same ones myself."

Hawkins's pipe had gone out. He tapped it against a post to knock the ashes from it, then refilled it with tobacco. He said, "I understand what you're saying, but I won't be letting others tell me what I can do on my own land. That's part of what the war was all about."

Andy pointed out, "The Confederacy lost."

Hawkins smiled, a ring of tobacco smoke encircling his face. "What makes you think I was a Confederate?"

Two horsemen appeared from a row of brush to the east. One wore a long beard, gray except for a few dark strands. The other was like a younger version without the whiskers. Andy guessed they were father and son.

Hawkins stood up when the two were within hailing distance. "Welcome, Mr. McIntosh. Howdy, Jake. Traveling late, aren't you?"

The old man reined up and slowly, stiffly dismounted. "Me and my boy, we've been out talkin' to neighbors." He stretched, flinching from arthritis pain. "These horses trot rougher than they used to. Must be some slippage in their breedin'."

The younger man left the saddle with an easy grace and no sign of pain. The father gave him a look of envy.

Hawkins introduced Andy and Daggett but did not mention that they were Rangers. McIntosh acknowledged them without much interest, then asked Hawkins, "Had any trouble with Old Man Teal or his boys?"

Hawkins looked surprised. "Trouble? No. They came

by here with a small herd one day and asked if they could water them in my creek. I told them to go ahead. The creek bed belongs to me, but the Lord puts the water in it."

"They could've watered anywhere up or down the creek. Why do you suppose they picked your place?"

Hawkins shook his head. "It was handy, I guess. Never gave it much thought."

"They were testin' you. They were tryin' to see how far you'd let them go. Next time they won't stop with water. They'll be turnin' cattle loose on you. I heard talk in town that they've got a herd comin' up from the brush country. They'll need to put them someplace."

"I've never had any trouble with the Teals. I've left them alone, and they haven't bothered me."

McIntosh scowled. "I've known Harper Teal for years. He's an evil, greedy old man. Always was, and he's raised them boys in his own likeness. They'd steal the shroud off of a dead man."

Hawkins repeated, "They've never bothered me."

"Not yet, maybe, but mind what I've told you. All us neighbors have got to stick together. First sign of trouble, you come to us. Me and my boys'll throw in with you."

Hawkins said, "If any trouble comes, I'll go to the sheriff."

"Pete Seymour?" McIntosh scoffed. "He couldn't even protect a prisoner in his own jail."

McIntosh remounted even more slowly than he had gotten down, groaning as he settled into the saddle. "I rode too many mean broncs when I was Jake's age, and wrestled too many snuffy cattle. Now they've come back to haunt me. Be glad you're a sheepman, Hawkins. They don't fight you."

Hawkins smiled. "I have scars all over my back from rams that knocked me down and ran over me."

Andy watched the two ride away. He said, "It sounds like that letter writer knew what he was talkin' about."

Hawkins shook his head. "Old Man McIntosh has a wrong notion about the Teals. They're redheaded and bound together with barbed wire and rawhide, but they've never given me reason to be afraid of them."

"Maybe they're fixin' to."

"It's all in Old Man McIntosh's mind. He and Harper Teal have hated each other so long they probably don't even remember what started it."

Daggett said, "Once we get the lay of the land, we may have to knock some heads together."

Andy asked, "What did he mean, that the sheriff couldn't protect a prisoner?"

Hawkins said, "A year or so ago, Pete caught the leader of a ring of horse and cattle thieves. Some masked men forced their way into the jail and shot him in his cell. Caused a considerable ruckus, but it slowed down the thievery for a while. It's started up again lately."

Daggett nodded approval. "There's times when some vigilantes can help move the law along."

Hawkins said, "The prisoner was Old Harper Teal's son-in-law."

Andy said, "The Teals were part of the ring?"

"I never wanted to believe that. I like them in spite of

their rough edges. And that Teal girl . . . it was hard to understand her marrying somebody like Vincent Skeen in the first place. But she was a country girl and hadn't seen much of the world. I guess his good looks and smooth talk got the best of her."

"Do you figure the McIntoshes shot him?"

"It stands to reason, they or some of their friends and kin. Skeen was a snake, and nobody blamed them much. Pete didn't break his back trying to arrest anybody." Hawkins arose. "Would you like a little drink to settle your supper?"

Andy and Daggett rolled out their blankets on the barn floor. Lying on his back, Andy said, "Hawkins seems like a good old man."

Daggett snorted. "He ain't that much older than I am. Anyway, the best old man I ever knew took a shot at me once. I haven't trusted a good old man since."

Next morning, on the way to town, Andy heard something crashing through the brush. He reined up to listen. A large brindle bull burst out of the scrub timber and onto the wagon trail in a hard run. Before Andy could shout "Look out!" it smashed into Daggett's mount and sent it tumbling. Daggett shouted in surprise, then in pain. His wounded right leg was pinned beneath the struggling horse. The bull shook itself and went running off down the trail, hooves clattering on the rocks.

A horseman broke from the brush, a rope in his hand. He pulled hard on the reins as he saw Daggett on the ground. He took a quick look at the fleeing bull, then swung from the saddle. Daggett's horse was thrashing about, trying to regain its feet. The stranger grabbed it about the neck and took a firm hold on its head. "Whoa now," he said in a quiet voice. "Be still." To Daggett he said, "Can you wiggle out from under him before I let him up?"

Daggett grimaced, straining hard. He wheezed, "See if you can raise him just a little more." Grunting, the stranger managed, and Daggett crawled backward until his leg was free. He tried to push to his feet but fell. Andy, on the ground now, caught him under the arms and dragged him far enough that the horse would not step on him in its struggle to get up.

Andy said, "I hope that leg's not broke."

Daggett's voice was laced with pain. "*You* hope? It's not yours. It's mine." He bent forward and carefully felt of the leg, starting above the knee and working down. "I think it's still in one piece." Blood seeped from a long tear in the pant's leg. "Busted that bullet wound open again just when I thought I was about to be shed of it."

With his pocketknife Andy ripped the pant's leg open to get a better look. Daggett sucked in a sharp breath and said, "That was a good pair of pants."

"You can buy another pair and bill it as groceries." Even the most honest of Rangers might use such a subterfuge to get around the state's penny-pinchers.

The stranger knelt beside Daggett and examined the reopened hole in his leg. He asked, "Got any whiskey with you?"

Daggett said, "The state don't pay for whiskey."

The stranger said, "Then we'd better bind the leg up tight anyway, to stop the bleedin'." He took out a pocketknife and cut off part of Daggett's pant's leg. He used it for wrapping.

The first thing Andy noticed about the stranger was his size. Probably thirty-something, he was as large as Daggett, all muscle and bone. His hair was a rusty red, his jaw square, the mouth broad. A scar on his left cheek showed through several days' growth of reddish whiskers. Andy would have to rate him as one of the least handsome men he had seen in a while. Not quite ugly, perhaps, but close enough to it.

The man said, "I didn't mean to run that bull over you. I didn't even know you was there. I've been tryin' for a month to get a loop over that old rascal's horns."

Andy wondered if the stranger's horse was stout enough to handle the bull's weight on the opposite end of a rope, especially if the animal was on the fight.

The stranger said, "I was goin' to throw him down and turn him into a steer. We're ashamed to put the family brand on the sorry calves he sires."

Andy asked, "What family is that?"

"The Teals. I'm Bud Teal."

Andy remembered the name. Ethan McIntosh had had much to say about the Teals, none of it good. Andy said, "I'm Andy Pickard. This here is Logan Daggett."

Teal said, "Seems like I've heard the name Daggett. Ranger, ain't you?"

Daggett's voice was strained. "Almost ever since I was weaned."

Teal examined Andy's horse, feeling of its legs, running his hand along the chest, then the flanks. "He don't seem to be hurt none, just a little spooked. Let's get you on your feet and make sure you're able to stand."

Grittily Daggett said, "I can stand. I can walk. I can even ride if you and Pickard will give me a lift up."

Teal said, "I'll take you to our house. We'll get that wound cleaned and wrapped proper. Wouldn't want you to have blood poisonin' on account of me and that sorry bull."

Andy had mixed feelings about accepting Teal's offer. It was generous, and Daggett's injury needed attention. On the other hand, if the Teals turned out to be antagonists here as McIntosh charged, any favors accepted now might compromise the Rangers later.

Teal did not give Andy long to consider the dilemma. He helped Daggett into the saddle. Andy asked, "How far to the house?"

Teal said, "Just a hop, skip, and a jump. It's closer than town."

Andy decided there might be some advantage in gaining knowledge about the Teals on their home ground. He would give the McIntoshes a look-see later.

The frightened packmule had run fifty yards before stopping. Andy brought it back. He gave Daggett a quick study and asked, "Are you sure you're up to ridin'?"

"I don't see any choice. I can't stay here like this."

"You're turnin' as white as milk."

Daggett held his right leg straight, the foot out of

the stirrup. He was suffering from shock, Andy realized. Shock could knock the legs out from under the strongest of men.

Teal gave Daggett a look of concern and said, "Sooner we start, the sooner we get there." He set out in the lead. Daggett rode in one wheel rut. Andy stayed even with him in the other, ready to lend a hand if he started to fall from the saddle. But Daggett seemed determined not to show weakness. He stubbornly sat straight and kept a firm hold on the reins, his jaw rigid. He avoided touching the horn, which might be taken as a sign of vulnerability.

Teal looked back with concern from time to time. He asked, "You Rangers just passin' through the country?"

Andy said, "We haven't decided."

"Did Ethan McIntosh ask for you?"

"What makes you say that?"

Teal said, "We've been expectin' him to do some such of a thing."

Andy evaded the question. He said, "We were on our way to consult with the sheriff."

"Pete Seymour?" Teal sighed. "He ought to be runnin' a ranch instead of wearin' a badge. His boots ain't big enough anymore for the job he's got."

"How so?"

Teal said, "He's gettin' old, and he can't see very good. He ain't made a move against the McIntoshes. Been a killin' lately that nobody's answered for. Been a few fistfights over one thing and another, and a drunken shootin' scrape where nobody got hurt. You can bet that if worse trouble comes, you won't need to look any farther than the McIntosh bunch."

Andy noted that Teal was saying essentially the same thing about the McIntoshes that Ethan McIntosh had said about the Teals.

Andy said, "We heard that a mob murdered your brother-in-law while he was in jail."

Teal frowned. "In our family we don't talk about him anymore. He wasn't no Teal." He moved ahead, making it clear that the subject was closed.

Andy had not seen many signs of real prosperity in these hills, and he found few at the Teals' ranch headquarters. The main house was of rough lumber, not painted. A log bunkhouse stood off to one side. The barns were built in much the same way. The corrals were of tied-together posts set upright, their bases sunk in the ground. Most of the structures were of natural materials taken close at hand. Only the main house appeared to represent a cash investment, and even it was short of ornamentation. Andy saw no gingerbread trim.

This was pretty much what his own place would look like someday when he left the Rangers and set out upon the life of a stockman, he thought. It would be spare, at least in the beginning, but it would be his—his and Bethel's.

Teal led them directly to the frame house. Dismounting, he tied his horse to a post and turned to help Andy lift Daggett down from the saddle. He said, "My sister wasn't much at pickin' a husband, but she's pretty good at fixin' up folks hurt handlin' wild cattle and rough horses. Not to say that our horses are really bad. You'd just best not go to sleep in the saddle. They'll wake you up."

The house had a generous porch that helped offset its overall plainness. Teal said, "Let's set him in the rockin' chair out here. In case there's any leakage, I expect Carrie would rather it wasn't in the house."

Andy asked, "Who's Carrie?"

"My sister. She was named Carolina, after the state where our mother came from, but everybody just calls her Carrie. None of us has ever been to Carolina."

Andy wondered if Teal's sister would look anything like him. Whatever Bud Teal had inherited from his fore-bears, good looks were not among them.

Blood had soaked through the rough binding, but it appeared dry. The bleeding had stopped. Andy remained on the porch with Daggett while Bud went inside. He heard voices from within the house. Shortly he saw the dark outline of a woman coming down a hallway that divided the house into two segments. Her stride was firm and determined. She came out onto the porch, a tallish woman of thirty or so, slender to the point of being skinny. She held a bottle in one hand, a bundle of white cloth in the other. She stared a moment at Andy before Bud directed her attention to Daggett.

He said, "The big feller is the one that's hurt."

Her appearance took Andy by surprise. He had expected her to be plain, even homely, like her brother. Instead, her features were pleasant, her large eyes the dark brown of coffee beans. Her hair bore a hint of red. In a country where men outnumbered women by a considerable margin, Andy wondered why somebody had not put an end to her widowhood.

Shaking her head in reproach, she untied the cut-off pant's leg that Bud had wrapped around the wound. She asked him, "Was this the best thing you could find?"

Bud said, "In a pinch, you use what you've got."

She said, "This looks like an old gunshot wound."

Daggett did not reply, so Andy said, "It is. It just got busted open again."

She poured a cloudy-looking liquid from the bottle directly into the wound. Daggett stiffened as if she had set him afire, but through strong will he made no sound except a faint whistling as he sucked air between his teeth.

The woman said, "I'll give you one thing: most men would holler to high heaven." She glanced at her brother. "Bud did, the last time I used this stuff on him."

Bud protested, "I didn't, either."

Tears came into Daggett's eyes. He turned his head and quickly blinked them away. The woman cleaned the wound with a piece of cloth, then bound his leg. She said, "This is going to be awful sore. You won't be chasing any bulls for a few days."

"I wasn't chasin' this one," Daggett wheezed. "I was tryin' to get out of his way."

Teal told his sister, "These two men are Rangers."

Her eyebrows raised a little. She said to Daggett, "Only two of you? I thought you traveled in bunches."

Daggett was still struggling with the burn. Andy said, "Only when the trouble is big enough. We don't know yet how big it is here."

Bud said, "I'll bet Old Man McIntosh sent for you."

Andy said, "Somebody wrote us a letter but forgot to sign his name. We were on our way to see the sheriff."

Carrie's voice snapped, "The sheriff. Pete Seymour can't find his butt with both hands."

Bud took up for the lawman. "Pete's all right. It's just that people are pullin' at him from all sides. And he's gettin' a little old."

She said, "He wasn't much help when we needed him."

"He never claimed to be no Pinkerton detective."

"No," she replied sharply, "and he's sure as hell not." She picked up the bottle of disinfectant and started for the door. She stopped to tell the Rangers, "You-all are staying for supper." It was not a question; it was a command.

Andy said, "We wouldn't want to put you to any trouble."

She nodded toward Daggett. "You already have. A little more won't make any difference." She was halfway through the door when she stopped again. "In case you wonder about it, any beef you eat at our table is our own."

Andy was taken aback by her forceful attitude. He stared after her until she disappeared into the back of the house. He asked Teal, "Did we say anything to make her believe we thought otherwise?"

Teal said, "No, but lots of people have. She gets touchy as hell about it. Feels like everybody is against us."

"Are they?"

"Some, like the McIntoshes and them that follow Old Man Ethan and his boys. But we've got friends, too. Sometimes our side wins the elections, sometimes the McIntosh side does. It makes a difference who sets the taxes."

"Tax rates are supposed to be the same for everybody."

"Depends on who counts the cattle. Some count ours twice but can't find half of the McIntoshes'."

So, Andy thought, it comes down to money, as most quarrels do.

He saw movement at the barn, five horsemen riding into a corral and dismounting. Bud said, "It's Pa and the boys. They've been ridin' the line, keepin' our cattle pushed back onto our own ground."

Andy asked, "If it's state land, what difference does it make?"

"We're taxpayers. What belongs to the state belongs to us. Ain't that right?"

That was one way to look at it, Andy thought, but anyone who wanted to squat on state land could make the same argument. It left much room for disagreement and, ultimately, violence.

He found it easy to pick out the Teals. The father and the other two sons bore a close resemblance to Bud. They were sturdy, muscular men whose confident stride bespoke a certainty that they could whip the world. And like Bud, they were some of the homeliest men Andy had ever seen. The sons' hair was a darkish red, the father's a mix of red and gray. The older man spat a stream of tobacco juice, then wiped his mouth on his sleeve. His beard was streaked with dark stains. He gave his full attention to Andy and Daggett. Andy saw no welcome in his eyes.

Stopping just short of the porch, Harper Teal looked at the fresh bandage on Daggett's leg. "Who shot you?" he asked.

Bud said, "That old brindle bull ran over him."

"That bull's a stray. He don't belong to us. We've got no obligation."

"I feel like we do. It happened on our place."

The older man's eyes were sharp with criticism. "Bud, I told you to get rid of that beast."

"I was right on his tail when he ran into this Ranger. I had to stop and help, so the bull got away."

"Ranger or not, you ought to never leave a job half done." Teal's gaze cut back to Daggett. "If you're nosin' around for a payoff, like most of the badge toters I ever knew, you ain't findin' it here."

Teal's rough manner stirred Andy to defensive anger. "We don't take bribes. We'll even pay for your daughter wrappin' his leg, if you figure we owe you."

"Keep your money in your pocket. Us Teals don't take payment for small favors, and any favors we do for a Ranger are goin' to be small ones."

Daggett angrily jerked his head at Andy. "Let's be goin'. We've been here too long already."

Andy was dubious. "You're not in shape to ride."

"If I can't ride, I'll walk. If I can't walk, I'll crawl."

Bud moved between his father and Daggett. He said,

"No use in you-all leavin' here mad. Pa talks rough, but he don't mean half of it. You-all stay for supper, at least. Maybe you'll feel better after you've eaten."

Andy said, "He's talkin' sense. We'll stay for supper."

Daggett flinched in response to a surge of pain. Reconsidering, he said to Bud, "As long as you-all don't expect any special favors. If we find you breakin' the law, we'll treat you the same as everybody else."

Bud assured him, "The only laws we've ever broke were those we disagreed with."

Daggett said, "I don't agree with all of them myself."

The older man's bushy eyebrows were still mostly red. They nearly joined in a frown as he said, "Bud, you invited them, so you look after them. I don't remember a time that the law ever brought me good news." He started into the house, then stopped. Muttering something about womenfolks' rules, he wiped his feet on a sack lying by the door.

Bud introduced his brothers, Cecil and Lanny. Their attitude was much like their father's. They nodded but did not offer to shake hands.

Bud said, "Daggett, you can't go around wearin' pants with one leg cut off. I'll find an extra pair for you."

Daggett said stiffly, "I'll pay you for them."

Bud turned to Andy in frustration. "I'm tryin' to act civil. What's the matter with him?"

Andy started to say but didn't, *He's thinking he might have to shoot you someday.*

# CHAPTER

## 3

Carrie Teal watched with silent criticism as Daggett limped to the supper table. She said, "We've got a set of crutches. Lord knows that with bad horses and salty cattle, we've needed them."

Daggett's reply was firm. "I'm not crippled. I'd feel like a fool, tryin' to manipulate a set of crutches."

"We can lend you a cane if it won't hurt your pride too much."

"I'll get by."

Her eyes flashed. "Nobody's going to beg you even if it is for your own good."

The elder Teal pulled out a chair at the head of the long table and unceremoniously seated himself. Reaching with a fork to spear a biscuit, he said, "He's been off of the tit long enough to make up his own mind. Don't you get enough, girl, bossin' this family around? Have you got to boss strangers too?"

She said, "I worked hard to fix his leg. I don't want him to waste all that effort like some stubborn schoolboy."

Daggett was no schoolboy. He was forty if he was a day. Stubborn, though . . . Andy had seen that from the first.

Harper Teal declared, "There's a time for talkin' and a

time for eatin'. Right now I want to eat." His plate was heaped with beef and beans. He dug into it as if he had a hollow leg to fill. His sons and the two cowboys followed his lead. Carrie took a seat at the foot of the table, getting up once to bring the coffeepot and refill the men's cups. Only one cowboy murmured, "Thanks." Andy said, "Much obliged, ma'am."

"You're welcome," she said, a little surprised by his manners. She probably was not used to seeing any.

Daggett picked over his food, taking a few bites without enthusiasm. His glazed eyes indicated that he was running a fever.

Carrie said, "You need to eat something and build up your strength."

"Maybe I could, if this beef came from the bull that ran over me."

Bud said, "I'll bring that old brindle down with a rifle if I have to. We've got no grass to spare for the likes of him."

The old man grunted. "You'd ought to've gone ahead and done it today. Wouldn't've hurt this Ranger to've laid there a while till you finished your job. On account of that bull, we've got these two sittin' here at our table like invited company."

Daggett flared. "We'll be gone in the mornin'. In fact . . ." He pushed himself to his feet, leaning heavily on the table. "We'll be goin' right now. Come on, Pickard."

Andy did not arise. He said, "You'd better sit back down before you fall."

Daggett limped heavily toward the door, each step

painful. Andy argued, "That leg'll hurt like hell if you try to ride."

"It already hurts like hell. Come on."

Carrie and Bud caught up to Daggett on the porch. She said, "Hold up a minute. If you abuse that leg, you could lose it."

Bud said, "Pa's like an old dog with a loud growl but no teeth. I feel responsible for what happened to you."

Daggett wavered. The leg was giving him a lot of pain.

Andy said, "These folks are talkin' sense."

Daggett faced toward the barn where his and Andy's horses were enjoying some grain. It looked a mile away. Turning back to Carrie and Bud, he said, "Since you ask so nicely, we'll stay."

Bud said, "You'll like the bunkhouse. We've got plenty of room, and you won't have to listen to Pa rave. He sleeps here."

Carrie's voice softened. "I'll fetch you that cane. Maybe it'll keep you from spoiling my work."

Daggett seemed embarrassed. "I didn't intend to fly off the handle like that. I reckon it's because this thing hurts so damned bad."

Carrie brought a cane and watched as Daggett took a couple of awkward steps, trying to get a feel for it. He and Andy fell behind Bud on the way to the bunkhouse.

Carrie shouted, "Bud, if he needs anything, you come and get it! He ought not to walk any more than he has to."

Daggett muttered to Andy, "Last thing I wanted was to get us beholden to one side or the other."

Andy said, "I saw that bull in time to dodge him. Why didn't you?"

"Are you sayin' I need glasses, Pickard?"

"When are you goin' to start callin' me *Andy*?"

"When you stop bein' a pain in the ass."

Bud pointed to two empty steel cots. "Sorry we've got no corn-shuck mattresses, but it's better than layin' on the ground."

Andy said, "I'll bring in our beddin'."

Daggett sat, sighing as he straightened his hurt leg. To Bud he said, "I appreciate what you folks have done for me, but we can't play favorites. When it comes to duty, a Ranger has got no friends."

Bud said, "We ask for no favors." He frowned. "And we damned seldom get any."

The other two Teal brothers and the two cowboys drifted down to the bunkhouse after a while. Away from the old man, they spoke civilly enough to Andy and Daggett. Bud asked, "Leg feelin' any better?"

Daggett said, "If so, I can't tell it."

"I'll bring you that bull's ears, and get Carrie to fix you some mountain oysters."

Lanny was the youngest of the brothers. He resembled the others in the roughness of his features, though the freshness of youth had not yet deserted him. His brother Cecil said, "If I read the calendar right, tomorrow's Saturday. There'll be a dance in town. You figurin' on goin' in to spark the storekeeper's daughter?"

Uncomfortably Lanny said, "Maybe. Ain't thought about it."

Cecil laughed. "You ain't thought of nothin' else for days. You know Jake McIntosh is after her too. You'd better watch that he don't beat your time."

Lanny's face reddened. Bud, the oldest, said, "Cecil, don't badger your little brother. He's of age to go courtin' if he's of a mind to."

Cecil said, "I'm just tryin' to help him see after his interests. This country ain't overrun with good-lookin' gals like Lucy."

Bud said, "Good looks don't guarantee what's inside."

Lanny stiffened. "Are you sayin' Lucy's not a good girl?"

"I don't hardly know her. I'm just sayin' you need to look farther than her blue eyes. You remember that pretty bay colt of mine? He had the roughest trot of any horse I ever rode. Kept my innards achin' all the time. Passin' him off to that horse trader was one of the smartest things I ever did."

Lanny argued, "Lucy's the nicest girl I know."

Cecil asked, "How many girls have you known?"

"I'm no green kid. I've been to town."

Bud nodded. "You came home all bruised up the last time. Some of them town boys don't like to see Teals courtin' their girls."

"I whipped two of them. I'd've been all right if a third one hadn't piled on."

Bud said, "There'll always be a third one, little brother.

We're outnumbered every time. They're liable to waylay you on your way to town."

Andy thought all the Teal brothers looked as if they could handle themselves well in a fight. They had the tight muscles and calloused, big-knuckled hands that came from hard work. Daggett said, "Maybe I'll be able to ride by tomorrow. He can go along with me and Pickard."

Andy lay on his cot, listening. He said, "It'll be just me. I'll be goin' in to talk to the sheriff. You'll stay here and try to heal up."

Daggett said, "You're forgettin' that I outrank you, so you can't tell me what to do. I'll be ready by tomorrow." He held his leg straight, resting it over the edge of the cot. The pain in his face indicated that he wouldn't be on horseback for at least two or three days.

Andy said, "That leg'll tell you. I won't have to."

Lanny said, "What would folks think, seein' a Ranger bodyguardin' me?"

Bud said, "They'd think you're the smartest man in town."

Daggett arose next morning in a bad temper. His stomach was angry because the aching wound had not allowed him much sleep. Andy had not slept much either, listening to him tossing much of the night. Daggett swung his legs off the side of the cot, then gingerly pushed to his feet. He reached for the cane and hobbled about the bunkhouse, testing the sore leg. He winced with every step but said, "It's damn near healed."

Andy said, "You can't hardly walk, much less ride. I'll have to work alone if you fiddle around and cripple yourself."

Daggett glanced about, making sure no one but Andy could hear. "How'll it look, me stayin' here with the people who may be the cause of the trouble?"

"How better to keep a watch on them?"

Daggett thought about that. "You might have a point."

Carrie stepped out onto the porch and beat an iron rod against a steel ring, signaling breakfast.

Andy offered, "I'll bring you some breakfast so you won't have to walk on that leg."

Sternly Daggett declared, "Nobody's ever had to fetch and carry for me. I'll go for myself."

Andy knew it was useless to argue. He walked slowly to keep from outpacing Daggett. The older Ranger hobbled toward the main house, stopping three times to catch his breath and let the throbbing subside. A less determined man would have given up, Andy thought.

Bud Teal walked beside them. He told Daggett, "You're the stubbornest man I ever saw except maybe for Pa. If you and him ever seriously butted heads, it'd be like two bulls tryin' to knock each other's brains out."

Andy wanted to help Daggett up the steps, but he knew he would be rebuffed in the sternest terms. Watching the Ranger struggle, he imagined he shared the pain.

Carrie greeted them at the door. She asked Daggett, "Is the leg any better?"

"Hardly feel it at all," Daggett lied.

Her expression told Andy that she knew the truth. She said, "We'll take a look at it after breakfast and wrap it fresh."

Daggett said, "You've got no call to be concerned about me. You never saw me till yesterday."

Bud said, "She's a nurse at heart. Dogie calves, stray cats, she takes care of them all."

"I sure ain't no dogie calf."

The kitchen offered the pleasant aroma of coffee, freshly baked biscuits, and fried bacon. Steam arose from a large platter of scrambled eggs on the table. Old Harper Teal was already seated in his accustomed place, eating. He said, "Hurry up, boys. We're wastin' daylight. We got work to do." He gave Daggett a swift appraisal. "I see you're on your feet. I expect you'll be wantin' to go."

Andy said, "He can't ride. I'm leavin' him here for a couple of days."

The old man did not appear pleased. Bud said, "We all agreed that it would be the best thing."

Harper said, "I didn't agree, but I reckon we can put up with him. Just don't let him get in the way of the work." He cut his gaze to Andy. "You're leavin', are you?"

Bud said, "He'll be ridin' in with Lanny. Maybe that'll keep the town boys from jumpin' all over baby brother."

The old man arched his red eyebrows and glared at his youngest son. "What're you goin' to town for? You need to stay here and tend to business."

Uneasily, Lanny said, "It's Saturday, Pa."

"Saturday, Sunday . . . one's like another. They're all workin' days around here."

Lanny's face reddened. "I promised Lucy I'd take her to the dance tonight."

Harper asked, "Who the hell is Lucy?"

Carrie broke in. "She's a nice girl in town. The store-keeper's daughter. You've seen her."

"Never did pay attention to town girls. They're spoiled and addle-brained, flighty as a bunch of heifer yearlin's. Country girls are the best. They know how to work."

Carrie said, "Besides, I need some groceries. Lanny's going to bring them home."

The surprise in Lanny's face indicated that this was news to him, but he nodded agreement. "I'll be takin' the wagon."

The old man gave in grudgingly. "All right, but don't come home all hungover. You'll have work to do tomorrow."

Lanny said, "Tomorrow's Sunday."

Harper said harshly, "Kids! There don't none of them want to work anymore. The whole world has gone plumb to hell." He pushed up from the table. "The rest of you boys, get up from there and get your horses saddled. Mornin's half gone already." He stomped out the door, loudly clearing his throat.

Carrie watched him with a thin smile, then said, "Finish your breakfast, all of you. He'll holler whether you hurry or not."

\*    \*    \*

Daggett left half of his breakfast uneaten. Leaning heavily on the cane, he went out onto the porch and sat on a bench, gingerly rubbing his leg. Carrie watched him through the kitchen window, then turned to Andy, still seated at the table. "Strange man," she said. "Doesn't talk much, does he?"

Andy shook his head. "I don't know much more about him now than I did when I met him."

"I get a feeling that a lot goes on behind his eyes, but they're like a window blind. You can't see through them."

"It might be better not to."

"I couldn't see past my husband's eyes either. I wished I had, when it was too late." She turned away and busied herself with the dishpan on the cabinet.

Andy tried what was left of his coffee, but it was cold. "I heard what happened. I'm sorry."

Her voice thinned. "He had his faults, but that was a miserable way for a man to die."

"Yes'm."

"Odd. Your Mr. Daggett took me by surprise the first time I saw him. He looks a little like Vincent. Same size and build. The eyes are different, though. There's a wildness in them, but there's sadness, too. Vincent's were just wild."

"He told me he had a wife once. He doesn't anymore."

"That might account for the sadness. Do you know what happened to her?"

"He hasn't said. And I'd rather get run over by that bull than to ask him."

"It's none of our business anyway."

Andy guessed that she would give a lot to know. He said, "He may not tell you so, but he appreciates what you did for him."

She frowned. "He could say that himself. He doesn't need you to do his talking for him."

"That's his way."

"Hardheaded. He would fit right in with the Teal family."

Lanny Teal was eating a second helping of breakfast. Andy told him, "Better hurry it up if you plan to ride to town with me."

Bud Teal grinned. "Lanny'll be ready. He's been dreamin' about that girl all night."

Lanny argued, "I still don't see where I need a Ranger to protect me."

Bud said, "You need a guardian angel, but angels are scarce in this part of the country."

Carrie took cloth and scissors and antiseptic out onto the porch where Daggett sat. She said, "Let's take a look at that leg."

"I told you it's all right." He moved the leg and grimaced. His voice softened. "But if you really want to . . ."

The wound was swollen and angry around the edges. She washed it clean, then applied antiseptic. Daggett tensed until the burning subsided. "What is that stuff?" he asked. "It feels like a white-hot brandin' iron."

She said, "If it didn't burn, it wouldn't do you any good." She bound the leg with fresh white cloth. "That's the best I can do."

Daggett said, "I don't reckon a town doctor could do any better." His face furrowed as if he dreaded what he had to say. "I'm sorry I've acted like a sore-footed badger. I'm not used to people makin' a fuss over me."

"We didn't exactly throw roses in your path, either. We Teals have been put upon by so many people, for so long, that we sometimes bristle up for no good reason. Whenever something bad happens, they decide right off that the Teals are responsible."

Andy felt emboldened to ask, "Are they?"

She almost smiled. "Now and then."

Andy saddled his horse. Lanny, wearing a clean shirt and a bow tie, drove the wagon to the front of the house. Carrie stood on the porch, watching. As Lanny started to pull away she said, "Don't lose my list. We're almost out of coffee and flour."

Andy touched fingers to the brim of his hat. "Thanks for both of us, ma'am, me and Daggett."

Riding toward town, Andy kept thinking about Carrie. He pulled in close to Lanny and said, "It's kind of your sister to look after Daggett like she has."

Lanny shrugged his broad shoulders. "She feels obliged, I guess."

"Just the same, it's kind." Andy rode in silence a while, then ventured, "She never said much about her husband."

Lanny's eyes hardened. "He's dead and buried. There's nothin' to say."

"It must've been tough on her."

"She's strong. She got over it." Lanny looked back over his shoulder as if he feared someone would overhear. "Son of a bitch was a thief and a wife beater."

Andy took a chance. "Then you ought to be grateful to the McIntoshes for takin' care of him."

Lanny grunted. "I reckon." The somber look in his face said he did not want to talk about it.

Nearing town, they passed two young horsemen who gave Lanny a hostile study but made no move against him. Once they were out of hearing, Andy said, "They looked like they didn't mean you any good. They might've jumped you if you'd been by yourself."

"I can whip two of them at a time, and they know it. I've done it before without any help."

"So I heard."

Lanny said, "When we get to town I want you to go your way, and I'll go mine. I don't want them ginks thinkin' I need Ranger protection."

Andy said, "If you decide different, I'll try to be easy to find."

In Andy's estimation, the town didn't amount to much. Biggest thing was the courthouse, with an outsized clock tower that seemed too pretentious for its setting. He counted three modest church steeples and half a dozen saloons or dramshops.

Lanny said dryly, "That's two to one in favor of whiskey over religion."

Andy said, "At least the Lord's got a toenail hold."

Lanny hauled up on the reins, stopping the wagon in front of a general store. "Here's where I get Carrie's groceries," he said.

Andy asked, "Are you sure you'll be all right by yourself?"

"Sure. I'd have come by myself if Bud had kept his mouth shut. Him and Carrie both."

Andy said, "They're just worried about you. You're their little brother."

"I'm as big as any of them."

*And about as stubborn,* Andy thought.

Pete Seymour, the sheriff, was middle-aged and trail-worn, his hair graying, his waist broadening. He wore black-rimmed glasses with thick lenses that made his eyes look larger than they were. He appeared annoyed when Andy walked into his office and introduced himself. He turned to a tall, lanky young man and grumbled, "Salty, I didn't send for any Rangers. Did you?"

Salty Willis was slight of build and wore clothes a size too large for him, giving him a rumpled look. Andy would have taken him for a cowboy if he had not seen the deputy's badge. "Never would've thought about it."

The sheriff said, "If I had, I'd've asked for a whole company. I don't see where one will help much."

Andy said, "There's one other." He explained about Daggett's absence. "Even two's enough to make the bookkeepers holler. They'd like to disband the whole Ranger service and save the money."

The sheriff continued to frown. "Salty, you'd better go see Mason Gaines about that missin' horse. I never knew a man with so damned much to complain about." He waited until the deputy had left, then told Andy, "I wish you hadn't ridden in with that Teal boy."

"Lanny was comin' to town anyway. I thought it might prevent a fight if I rode along with him."

"It could be bad business, lookin' like you've lined up with one side against the other."

That had been Daggett's concern too. "I made it clear that we won't play favorites."

The sheriff took off his glasses and squinted at them, then put them back on. They needed cleaning. "I hate these damned things, but it's gettin' to where I can't see nothin' without them. It's hell to get old." '

His eyes narrowed. "As long as you're here, I'd just as well try to get some use out of you. What did you think about the Teals?"

"None of them shot at us. I can't say the old daddy was any too friendly, though."

"Old Harper has got a grudge against Rangers. It goes back to trouble with the carpetbag police after the war."

Andy said, "But those weren't real Rangers. We've come a long way since the days of the state police."

"Harper Teal hasn't."

"What about the McIntoshes?"

"They're Yankees, come here right after the war. Old Man McIntosh once called out the state police against Harper. Even after all these years, neither family can put the war behind them. It's like an old friend they can't say good-bye to."

"And the other folks around here?"

"Some take sides because of family ties or politics. The rest try to keep out of the way. That ain't always easy." He looked as if he had bitten into a bad-tasting pill. "Did you say Lanny Teal is stayin' in town for the dance tonight?"

Andy said, "That was his intention."

"The kid's askin' for trouble. Somebody's always itchin' to try the Teal boys on for size."

Andy suggested, "It might be a good idea if I showed up at the dance myself."

The sheriff said, "I'll be there, too. Maybe if I'm lucky I won't have to throw anybody into a cell tonight. Then I won't have to feed anybody breakfast in the mornin'."

Andy said, "We heard you lost a prisoner in that jail, a Teal brother-in-law."

Seymour frowned, the memory painful. "I got a false report of a shootin' down in the south end of the county. Come dark, several masked men rushed in and got the drop on my deputy. They didn't even bother to take the prisoner out of his cell. They poured enough lead into him to sink a boat."

"You figure it was the McIntoshes?"

"Skeen was stealin' from just about everybody. You could say that whoever killed him did the community a service. There wasn't but a few people at his funeral, and I didn't see anybody cry except his widow."

Andy said, "Too bad about her."

"I guess she still blames me, but what's done is done." Seymour took off his glasses again, wet the tip of a finger on his tongue, then rubbed the lenses. He wiped them dry with a handkerchief. "As long as you're here, you'd just as well show yourself. Visit the saloons. Set a spell on the spit-and-whittle benches. Let folks know there's a Ranger in town."

Andy stood up. "I'll start now."

The sheriff said, "One thing: you've got too friendly a face. Try to look a little mean."

Andy said, "I'll leave that to Daggett. It comes natural with him."

As Andy started toward the door, he was blocked by a middle-aged man wearing a wrinkled white suit. Seymour said, "Ranger Pickard, I want you to meet Judge Zachary."

The visitor removed a long black cigar from between a neatly brushed gray mustache and a spade beard. It was evident that he paid more attention to his beard than to his clothing. Dark eyes almost black focused on Andy, making him feel like a horse being examined by a potential buyer. "Ranger, eh? I didn't know you'd become desperate enough to send for a Ranger, Pete."

Seymour said, "I didn't send for him. He just showed up. There's another one out at the Teals'."

"The Teals? What have they done this time?"

Andy said, "Nothin' that we know of." He explained about Daggett and the brindle bull.

The judge said, "Daggett? I have heard stories about him. Not all happy stories, I am sad to say."

Andy shook his head. "They're probably way yonder exaggerated. You know how stories grow, once enough people have told them."

Seymour said, "Like the stories you hear about the Teals and the McIntoshes."

The judge said, "But there is usually an element of truth behind them. They are all contentious people. How much more peaceful the county would be if one of the families left. Even better, both of them."

Seymour said, "They're not so bad, Judge. The boys, anyway. It's those two old soreheaded daddies that need a good butt-kickin'."

"And I've given it to them the times they appeared in my court." Zachary gave Andy an intense study. "You seem an agreeable young man. How long have you been in the Ranger service?"

Andy said, "Off and on, ever since my first shave. But it's my intention to retire before long. My wife wants me to stay home."

"A commendable goal. As a lifelong bachelor, I can appreciate how difficult it must be to try to maintain a decent family life when one is always on the move."

The sheriff said, "The judge has got him a nice little ranch outside of town."

The judge said, "It is my refuge, my retreat from the daily humdrum of official duty. You must come out and visit me there sometime."

Andy said, "I'd be pleased."

"Feel free to come to my office any time you need

anything from me. Warrants, that sort of thing. I have great respect for the Rangers." He glanced at Seymour. "And for county sheriffs, who too often go unappreciated and under-paid."

Andy and Seymour watched the judge leave, trailed by cigar smoke. Seymour said, "He's a man to ride the river with. He's sharp-tongued and uses his court like a club against those who would disturb the peace, but he's held this county together for many a year."

"I'll make it a point to get better acquainted. I don't think I'd want him against me."

Seated on a wooden bench across the dirt street from the general store, Andy watched a long-legged man in a white shirt and a loose string tie approaching him. He noticed ink stains on the man's hands. Most of all he noticed the man's heavy mustache, which flared upward at the ends. Andy thought he might be able to hang a bucket from either tip.

The stranger halted and gave Andy a critical study be-fore he said, "I understand you're a Ranger."

Andy made a small nod. "I am."

"I'm Jefferson T. Tolliver, editor of the local newspaper, *The Clarion*. Do you mind if I ask you a few questions?

Andy was hesitant but decided this was one way to let everyone know of his presence. "I'll tell you what I know, which isn't much."

"What brings you to this neglected corner of the Texas paradise?"

"Somebody sent us a letter, askin' us to come. They didn't sign it."

Tolliver looked around to be sure no one could overhear. He said, "For good reason. They could get seriously hurt if it were known that they invited the Rangers."

"By talkin' to me now in plain daylight, aren't you afraid you might raise suspicions about yourself?"

"People are used to seeing me interview visitors to town. Have you seen enough to appraise the local situation?"

"I can see the problems. I don't know yet what to do about them."

"You are the only Ranger they sent?"

"There's one more, Logan Daggett. He got hurt along the way, so he's laid up out at the Teals' ranch."

"Daggett!" Tolliver's eyes lighted up. "I know that name. I would give my eyeteeth to write a book about him. Do you think he would consent to an interview?"

"I doubt it. I haven't seen him consent to much of anything since I've known him."

"So he is at the Teals', in the lion's den. One of the dens, at least. Do you know that Lanny Teal is across the street, loading a wagon?"

"I rode into town with him."

"I suspect that the Teals are of Appalachian fighting stock. You may have noticed that they are all redheaded. It has been only a few generations since they left the cave and gave up stone in favor of iron. The McIntosh forebears came from the Scottish highlands, and fighting is in their blood, too. It will be interesting to see which you have to shoot first, a Teal or a McIntosh."

Andy said dryly, "Either way would make a story for your paper, wouldn't it?"

"I hope I may be able to write an eyewitness account."

"And I hope to disappoint you."

A middle-aged man wearing a stained apron came out of the general store, carrying a heavy bag and dropping it into the wagon bed. A slip of a girl stood on the porch. From the distance, Andy could not tell much about her except that her hair was a light brown, and she flashed a broad smile in Lanny's direction.

Tolliver said, "That is Lucy Babcock. Lanny's been sparking her, and so has Jake McIntosh. A perfect recipe for a knockdown, drag-out fight."

Andy heard Lanny tell the storekeeper, "By loadin' up now, I can make an early start for home in the mornin'."

The girl said, "Don't forget. Come for me about seven thirty."

Lanny said, "I'll be there with bells on."

"And no drinking."

"You know I don't drink. Hardly ever. Much."

Two young men stopped near Andy and watched the scene across the street. He thought they might be the two he had seen on the trail, but he was not certain.

One said, "Look at that, would you? Lanny Teal, shinin' up to Lucy."

The other said, "What can we do about it? The last time we jumped him, he like to've broke my jaw."

"We'll tell Jake McIntosh. He's been tryin' to get under Lucy's dress for a good while."

"Yeah. We could sell tickets to that fight."

Andy had pinned his badge to his shirt so it would be conspicuous. He cleared his throat to be sure they noticed him. He made a show of taking the fugitive book out of his pocket and flipping it open.

"What are your boys' names?" he asked.

The two fell into startled silence. One finally said, "Smith. We're both named Smith." They walked briskly on down the street.

Tolliver said, "They lied to you about their names."

"I figured that."

"One is Harold Pearcy. The other is Sonny Vernon. They'd like to be bad men, but I doubt they've done anything serious enough to be in your Ranger book."

"Any kin to the McIntosh family?"

"No, but they do some work now and then for the McIntoshes. They tag along after Jake like coon dog pups."

Two men emerged from a nearby saloon door, one of them the deputy, Salty Willis. He mounted his horse and rode away. The other man cupped his hands around a lighted match and touched the flame to a carelessly rolled cigarette. He walked up to Andy and said, "I am given to understand, sir, that you are a Ranger. It would serve the community greatly if you were to knock those boys' heads together." His tone indicated that he thought Andy should already have done it.

Andy tensed a little. "I'd need a reason. You got one?"

"Nothing I can prove, but keep an eye on them. Sooner or later they'll give you reason." The cigarette appeared to bite the man's tongue. He spat out a bit of tobacco. "I suspect you are here to forestall trouble between the Teals and the McIntoshes."

Andy could not think of an appropriate reply, so he offered none.

The tall man said, "Perhaps you should back off and let the parties fight. A few funerals might clear the air."

"That's a hard way to look at it."

"It could break the stranglehold a few big people have on state land around here. Then the little people would have a better chance."

Andy argued, "They could buy it. That'd settle the matter for once and for all."

"It takes money to buy land. The poor man can't afford it."

"It won't be free forever. Texas is sellin' off pieces of it every day."

The man flicked ashes with the tip of a finger. He said, "We'll burn that bridge when we get to it." He turned and walked briskly toward Scanlon's wagon yard.

Andy looked at Tolliver, his eyes asking.

Tolliver shrugged. "Mason Gaines. The biggest blowhard and bellyacher in the county. Like so many, he wants something for nothing. But nothing comes free. One way or another, everything must be paid for."

# CHAPTER

## 4

Sitting beside the sheriff at the dance, Andy tapped his foot to the rhythm of a banjo and fiddle. He had heard better fiddlers, but he had heard worse too. The wooden floor creaked under the weight of dancers, some gliding with grace, some sliding awkwardly across the boards.

Seymour's feet were still. He did not seem to enjoy the music. He was here out of duty, not by choice. Andy had learned that the sheriff had been widowed for many years.

Editor Tolliver came up and stood beside Andy. He said, "There are several nice-looking ladies whose husbands are too busy drinking to pay attention to them. They'd be glad to dance with you."

"They'd change their minds when we got out on the floor."

"Do you have a wife?"

"Yes, and I wish she was here." If Andy had Bethel in his arms, it would make no difference that he danced with the grace of a wounded buffalo.

"I am a bachelor myself. Sometimes that offers advantages." Tolliver soon was whirling a young matron across the floor.

Deputy Willis was checking weapons at the door, though

only a few men appeared to have brought any. So far as Andy could tell, these people were interested only in having a good time. Judge Zachary appeared in his crumpled white suit. Willis greeted him a little too warmly, as if trying to curry favor. The judge responded in a dignified but noncommittal manner.

Some men absented themselves for a while, then returned with a glow in their eyes and less sureness in their step. As they passed, Andy caught the strong aroma of whiskey.

Lanny Teal danced by him often, always with the same girl. She was a little thing, thin enough to be picked up by the wind and blown away. Her shiny brown hair, done up in curls, sparkled with tiny glass ornaments meant to imitate diamonds. Her eyes seemed to see no one except Lanny, and he appeared to be aware of no one but her.

Seymour nudged Andy and muttered, "There's a storm brewin' up."

Standing against a far wall were the two young men Andy had seen earlier on the sidewalk. They conversed with a youth he recognized as Jake McIntosh. Jake glared at Lanny and the girl, though they seemed unaware of him. They were too absorbed in each other.

The three young men walked outside together. Andy said, "Maybe they're leavin'."

Seymour said, "They've just gone for a drink. They'll come back braver than when they left."

In a while the three returned, Jake in the lead. His unsteady gait told Andy he was bent on trouble. He walked out onto the floor and gave Lanny an unfriendly slap on the shoulder.

"I'm cuttin' in," he declared. "You've danced with Lucy long enough."

Lanny bristled. "I'm the one brung her, and I'll dance with her all night if I want to."

The crowd drew away in alarm as Jake drove a fist against Lanny's jaw. Lanny's head snapped back, but he was stunned for only a moment. His right fist came up from the floor and slammed into Jake's face. Jake staggered. His two friends rushed in and began to pummel Lanny. While trying to shake them off, Lanny kept hitting Jake.

Seymour jumped to his feet. He said, "We'd better stop this before it turns into a free-for-all."

The judge stepped out onto the floor, waving his arms. "Gentlemen! Gentlemen, let's have order."

Andy saw that the crowd had mixed allegiances, some cheering for Jake, others for Lanny. He stepped between the fighters, grabbing the collars of the two who had joined the fray uninvited. He yanked them backward so hard that one stumbled and went down. The other struggled to keep his feet.

On his knees, Harold Pearcy complained, "This ain't Ranger business."

Andy jerked him to his feet. "You'll get your chance, but one at a time."

Seymour said, "Harold, Sonny, this is a private fight. Back off and wait your turn."

It was Lanny's fight, all the way. In no time Jake was

curled up on the floor, his arms folded over his face to ward off Lanny's fists. He cried, "Enough. Enough." Lanny stepped back, red face glistening with sweat, one shirt-sleeve split past the elbow.

To the two young men Andy said, "Which one of you wants to be next?"

Neither appeared ready to face Lanny's fists alone. Both stood with heads down, humiliated in front of the crowd.

The judge said sternly, "You young gentlemen should be ashamed. If charges are filed against you, I promise that you will not enjoy your day in court."

Mason Gaines stepped forward, carelessly flipping a half-smoked cigarette across the dance floor. He said, "You are arresting them, aren't you, Ranger?"

Andy gripped Pearcy's collar and shook him soundly. "I was studyin' on it. But it looks like they've lost interest in fightin'."

"You said all you needed was to see them break the law."

"The boys got excited when they saw their friend gettin' his plow cleaned. I'll bet they'll know better next time."

Gaines made no secret of his disappointment. He muttered, "Maybe you'll do something when these ruffians kill somebody."

Andy wondered why Gaines displayed such an interest in these young men. He suspected they had done something in the past that irritated him. Gaines appeared to be a man easily irritated.

Andy looked to the sheriff. Seymour said, "There wasn't

any real harm done except to Jake, and he asked for it. As long as they'll all leave town right now, I'll forget this happened." He shifted his attention to Lanny. "That goes for you too."

Lanny remained defiant. "I need to take Lucy home first."

"I'll see that she gets home. I want you to leave, right now. Get your wagon and travel."

He turned his attention to Jake, whose face was beginning to darken with bruises and abrasions. Resentfully Jake said, "All right, I'm goin'. The evenin's lost its flavor anyhow."

Silently Andy and Seymour followed Lanny to the wagon yard where he had left the grocery-laden wagon and his team. Scanlon, owner of the yard, said, "Leavin' already? I can still hear the music."

The sheriff said, "It took on a sour note."

The three men helped Lanny hitch up the horses and climb shakily into the wagon. Seymour's voice sounded like the messenger of doom. He said, "Go straight home, Lanny. I'll say good-bye to the girl for you."

"The dance ain't even over."

"It is for you."

Lanny said curtly, "All I done was defend myself."

Andy suppressed a grin. He thought, *A good job it was, too.*

Lanny said, "Jake didn't get half of what he's got comin' to him."

Andy asked, "How did you learn to fight like that?"

"It comes natural, bein' a Teal. With everybody pickin'

on us, we get lots of practice." Lanny spoke sharply to the team and started the wagon rolling. Andy and Seymour followed afoot until satisfied that Lanny had chosen the road that would take him home.

Andy said, "The boy's got spirit."

Seymour said sharply, "I'd be better satisfied if he had less of it. It could get him killed one of these days. Him or somebody else."

Returning to the dance, they found that the crowd had diminished by half. The fight had put a chill over the festivities. Lucy was gone.

Andy said, "Looks like the trouble is over for tonight."

Seymour was not convinced. "Lanny's got two brothers and several friends. Have you ever got yourself tangled up with a feud?"

Andy's face furrowed as he remembered. "A bad one once, down on the border. The graveyards got some bigger before it broke up."

"Ever since my wife died, I've hated funerals. I do what I can to see that they don't get too numerous."

Andy accepted the sheriff's offer to sleep in an empty jail cell and save a little money. Up from his hard cot at daybreak, he ordered breakfast in a chili joint so small that a dozen customers would have been three too many. The steak was thick, however, drowned in grease-and-flour gravy and sided by a generous helping of scrambled eggs. The coffee was strong enough to walk by itself. That was the way Andy liked it.

The cook-proprietor was a stoop-shouldered man named Kennison. He was somewhere on the sunny side of sixty, his thick gray hair needing a comb, his flour-sack apron in need of soap and water. A talkative sort, he did not require much prompting before he launched into a full history of the town and much of the country around it. Andy suspected that his account might be taking a few liberties with the facts.

The cook asked, "What did you think about the fight last night?"

Andy said, "It could've led to worse."

The cook said, "Those boys are slow learners, jumpin' on Lanny Teal the way they do. He winds their clock every time they try."

"They seem to have it in for him."

"For him and all his kin. The Teals are tight with their money and have more of it than most around here. It's human nature not to like somebody who's got more money than you have."

"Wouldn't the same feelin' apply against the McIntoshes too?"

"Sure. There's lots of people who would like to get hold of their land. The Teals and the McIntoshes don't have legal title, except for a little that's on live water. They've just got six-shooter possession of the rest."

"The state will sell it out from under them sooner or later."

"They're like politicians who can't see past the next

election. One day they'll turn their calendar and find there ain't another sheet."

Deputy Willis burst into the little restaurant. "Pete Seymour sent me to look for you, Ranger. Says you need to go over to the doctor's house."

Andy said, "Do you know what for?"

"Somebody brought in Lanny Teal. Looked like a herd of cattle ran over him."

Andy recognized Lanny's wagon in front of the doctor's home. The groceries bought yesterday still lay in it, badly scattered. The sheriff met Andy at the door. He said, "Take a look at what somebody brought in."

Lanny was slumped in a chair, his clothing torn, his face streaked with blood. He appeared to be in a daze, his cheekbones bruised blue and eyes swollen almost shut.

A man in farmer overalls said, "I seen the wagon and team first, standin' there in the trail. Then I found this boy layin' on the ground. Thought at first he was dead. Somebody worked him over like they meant to kill him."

The sheriff put in, "Must've been several of them. One or two couldn't have done this to him. Not him or any of the other Teals."

Lanny struggled to get up. The doctor pressed him back into the chair and said, "Be still, son. You're badly hurt." He had stripped Lanny to the waist. He washed the lacerated face and bruised body with alcohol. Lanny drew himself into a tight knot until the burning eased. The doctor applied a thick ointment to the deep scratches and open wounds.

Seymour said, "Lanny, tell us who did this."

Lanny shook his head, wincing from the burn. "Who said somebody did anything? I just fell out of the wagon."

"We know better than that. Tell us who did it."

"I pay off my own debts. I don't need no squinchy-eyed sheriff."

Annoyed, Seymour persisted, "I can lock them up and throw the key in the river."

Lanny snorted. "In jail they'd get free room and board, with nothin' to do but sleep. Damn poor punishment, the way I see it."

Andy said, "It's as much as the law allows."

"The law! Nobody by the name of Teal ever gets a fair shake from the law."

Seymour argued, "If you try to handle this yourself, you'll wind up in bad trouble."

"I've been in trouble most of my life. It don't scare me none." Lanny looked at the doctor, or tried to. "Hurry up and finish with me, Doc. I want to go home."

The doctor said, "Your eyes are swollen. I doubt that you could even see the road."

"The horses know the way."

Andy said, "I'll go with you. Otherwise that bunch might catch you travelin' alone and do this all over again."

"I'll borrow a gun. It'll be them that needs help."

"With those eyes swollen, you couldn't see well enough to shoot anybody."

"They're cowards. Maybe I can scare them to death."

"That'll be my job."

* * *

Andy drove the wagon, his horse tied on behind. Lanny sat rigidly. Each jolt of the wagon drew his mouth into a tight, thin line, but he did not complain. Old Man Teal had brought his sons up to be tough as a hickory knot.

Andy said, "We'd better stop and rest the horses a while."

Lanny offered no argument. He climbed down slowly and painfully, waving off Andy's move to help him. He said, "As long as I've got two feet under me, I'll do for myself. You can carry me when I'm in my coffin."

"That may be sooner than you think if you keep fightin' all the time."

"Us Teals never set out to aggravate anybody. All we ask for is to be left the hell alone."

About noon Andy became aware of several riders coming up behind. Spotting the wagon, they moved their horses into an easy lope. Andy drew his pistol and conspicuously held it across his lap. It did not go unnoticed.

The riders were young men. They included Pearcy and Vernon, who had jumped on Lanny at the dance. Andy did not see Jake McIntosh. He had probably gone home to nurse his bumps and bruises.

Pearcy gave Andy a hostile look. "Have you taken sides, Ranger?"

"Who would I side with? I haven't seen a halo hangin' over anybody since I've been here."

"We heard Lanny fell out of his wagon and hurt himself. We came out to see that he gets home all right."

Andy raised the pistol to be certain no one had forgotten about it. "You-all can go back to town. I've got the situation well in hand."

"We'll go along and help you."

Andy was sure they would jump him the first time they saw a chance. He said, "Now, boys, I want to be sure we understand one another. See that cow skull lyin' out yonder?" He leveled the pistol and put a bullet between the eyes. The skull shattered in a puff of dust.

Andy gave the surprised young men a moment to consider, then said, "I told you I've got the situation handled."

Pearcy growled, "An old cow skull is one thing. Shootin' a man is different."

"It is," Andy agreed. "A man is bigger, and easier to hit."

Some of the men lost interest after the shot. They were starting to turn away. Pearcy's resentful gaze followed them. Slumped in the saddle, he warned Andy, "We could get you fired. We've got friends in Austin."

Andy said, "So have I."

By this time most of the riders had pulled back. They knew that to hurt a Ranger was dangerous business. To kill one was suicide.

Pearcy muttered about getting a Mexican *curandero* to put a curse on Lanny Teal, and on the Rangers for good measure. Andy watched him turn and follow the others toward town. He said, "I think the horses have rested enough."

The shot had taken Lanny by surprise. He said, "I'd hate to have you aim that six-shooter at me."

Andy said solemnly, "I'd hate to have to."

* * *

They reached the Teals' ranch a little before sundown. Bud, the oldest brother, came down from the porch as Andy stopped the wagon in front of the house. He frowned at Lanny. "Damn it, boy, you look like you took on the Union army and lost."

Lanny's answer was curt. "I won the first fight. If this Ranger hadn't broken it up, I'd've whipped Jake McIntosh to where he'd be in bed for a week."

"What do you mean, the *first* fight?"

"Some of his friends followed me when I started home. They came at me in a bunch."

Andy asked, "Which of Jake's friends?"

Lanny realized he had said more than he intended. He spoke quickly, "I was talkin' to Bud."

Daggett limped out onto the porch, followed by Carrie. For a moment her eyes betrayed anxiety over her battered brother. Taking a grip on her emotions, she said, "Did you bring everything I asked you to?"

Lanny said, "It's all there. Look for yourself."

She touched a bandage on Lanny's face. Her voice softened. "How does Jake McIntosh look?"

"Kind of beat up."

Harper Teal stepped onto the porch in time to hear, his reddish eyebrows meeting each other in a scowl. He said severely, "I've told you boys over and over, I disapprove of you fightin'." He moved down for a closer look at his son. "But if you can't go around it, be damned sure you win. Did you?"

Lanny loosened up and answered with pride, "Sure did. Whipped him fair and square, Pa. On the way home, they ganged up on me, but I think I put a hurt on a couple of them."

Harper nodded with satisfaction. "Always remember, never go lookin' for trouble, but if it comes, don't let nobody tread on you."

Carrie fixed an accusing gaze on Andy. "Where was the law when the McIntosh bunch was trying to beat him to death?"

Andy admitted, "Asleep, I'm afraid. After the fight at the dance, Sheriff Seymour and I made sure Lanny took the road home. We didn't think Jake was in any shape to follow him."

Angrily she turned to her father. "We've got to put a stop to this trouble, or people are going to die. Some of us, maybe."

Harper declared, "It's up to Ethan McIntosh and his brood. That damned old Yankee has got his mind set on runnin' the whole county."

She said, "Listen to yourself, throwing out the word *Yankee.* The war's been over for more than twenty years."

"Not everywhere. We're still standin' up for the little people."

Carrie braced her hands on her hips. "We're all little people, even the McIntoshes and their kin. Compared to the big ranches, none of us amounts to a hill of beans."

"And we never will unless we fight for what's ours." The old man tromped back into the house.

Carrie stewed. "Come on in, Lanny, and let me check you over."

Lanny said, "The doctor patched me up fine."

Her voice lashed at him. "I said come in this house!"

Lanny followed her, his shoulders drooped.

Bud mused, "I pity her next husband. He'd better have a hide like that old brindle bull."

Andy asked, "Does she have any prospects?"

Bud glanced up at Daggett. "Everybody around here knows her too well. They know the red in her hair ain't just for looks." He pointed his chin toward the bunkhouse. "You'll stay all night, won't you, Ranger?"

"It's too late to go back to town."

"Don't expect too good a supper. The mood Carrie's in, she'll burn the biscuits and oversalt the beans."

Daggett had stood on the porch, leaning on his cane, observing the scene without comment. When Bud went into the house to see about his brother, Andy asked Daggett, "How's the leg?"

"Healin'. Thought you went to town to keep the peace."

"I'm afraid I didn't do a good job of it."

"Next time, knock some heads together. You'd be surprised how sensible people get when they see a little blood. Especially if it's theirs."

"You can do it yourself when you're ready to ride."

Daggett seated himself on the bench. "I kind of hate to leave. I like the cookin'."

"Or maybe the cook?"

Daggett almost smiled. "She grows on you."

At the table, Andy found the Teal family in better spirits than he might have expected in view of the beating Lanny had taken. The patriarch did not bellow at anyone. Carrie's biscuits were just right.

Harper said, "Pass me the gravy, Lanny, and tell me again how you whipped Jake McIntosh."

"Wasn't much to it, Pa. Me and Lucy was dancin' along right fine till he come in drunk, itchin' for a fight. So I gave it to him. Then a couple of Jake's friends messed in."

Carrie glanced at Andy. "What was the law doing?"

"The Ranger pulled them off of me like a pair of whimperin' pups. When Jake hollered that he'd had enough, Pickard offered to let them take me on one at a time. But they both acted like they needed to go somewhere."

Carrie looked to Andy for corroboration. He said, "That's about the size of it."

She said, "We're beholden to you."

Harper said, "Lanny could've whipped the whole bunch without help. He eats nothin' but beef, like the Lord intended when He gave us cattle. Them McIntoshes have got chickens runnin' wild all over their place. That's what makes them weak, eatin' so much chicken." He cut off a square of steak and dipped it in a gob of gravy on his plate. "The only trouble with beef is that when it's on the hoof, you've got to watch all the time that somebody don't steal it. They're always tryin'."

Andy said, "Are you accusin' the McIntoshes?"

Harper's eyes narrowed. "I will, when I find the proof."

Bud Teal had listened without comment. He said, "You

know, Pa, half the people around here are convinced that *we're* doin' it."

Harper's face reddened. "Let them accuse me to my face. There ain't a man in this county that I can't whip."

"That won't convince them. They still remember Vincent Skeen."

Carrie stiffened, staring darkly at her brother across the table. She arose and quickly left the room.

Harper frowned. "That was the wrong thing to say, son."

Bud looked chagrined. "It just popped out of my mouth. But it's the truth. People ain't got over blamin' us for what he did."

Harper grimaced at the memory. "It was an awful sight for your poor sister to see."

"Yeah," Bud said, "terrible." He pushed back from the table and went outside, leaving half the food on his plate uneaten.

Lanny reached over with a fork and speared a biscuit Bud had taken but had not bitten into. He said, "No use lettin' the last biscuit go to waste."

His father gave him a critical look. Lanny said, "I've got to keep up my strength. No tellin' when Jake McIntosh may come lookin' for some more."

Harper warned, "If you see he's wearin' a gun, you better go way around him. Even Carrie can shoot straighter than you."

Andy found Bud sitting on the barn step, patching a bridle. He said, "You kind of shook up your sister."

"Didn't mean to. We tried to keep her from seein' him layin' there shot to hell, but nobody could hold her back. She'd have killed every McIntosh that came in sight that day, but we wouldn't let her have a gun."

"Now she's talkin' about makin' peace."

"She doesn't want to lose anybody else."

"Have the McIntoshes ever said anything about the jail-house killin'?"

"They don't talk about it. Neither do we." Bud accidentally punched his thumb with the awl. He flinched. "I've never understood how a sensible woman like Carrie got herself wrapped up in a son of a bitch like Skeen. The rest of us saw through him almost from the first."

Andy said, "Lanny told me he beat her."

Grimly Bud said, "Just once. She floored him with a chunk of stove wood. Hand me that leather string, would you?"

Andy knew the subject was closed.

Harper Teal stomped into the bunkhouse. It was still dark, but he thundered, "You boys get up. You're wastin' daylight."

Someone lighted a lamp. The cowboys and two of the Teal brothers crawled out from beneath their blankets. Lanny did not move. His father strode over to Lanny's cot and roughly shook the boy's shoulder. "Come on. We've got no room here for layabouts."

Lanny groaned. "I'm too stiff to move. There ain't a place on my body that don't hurt."

"Best thing for that is exercise. If you ain't off of that cot by the time I get to the door, you'll have no breakfast." Harper left without looking back.

Lanny made two unsuccessful tries to rise to his feet. He sat back on the cot, his face twisted. "What makes Pa so damned mean?"

Bud said, "Too bad you can't remember Grandpa. He was worse. They had to be tough to survive in his time. They had no easy life like we've got now."

"Easy?" Lanny gingerly pulled a shirtsleeve over a sore arm, then repeated with the other. "There's got to be a better way to make a livin'."

"But after a good day's work you go to sleep knowin' you've earned your keep."

"I've heard other people say that. Usually they're the ones who hire somebody else to do the work for them."

Harper nodded satisfaction upon seeing Lanny take a chair at the table, but he wolfed down his breakfast without comment. Finished, he pushed to his feet and said, "Carrie, you always fix too much coffee. It gives these boys an excuse to dawdle instead of gettin' out to work."

When he was gone, she said to the others, "I hope you-all set him a pace today that he can't keep up with. Bring him home walkin' on his knees."

Bud said, "I don't think it can be done. I've never seen a man who can get drunk on hard work like Pa does."

Lanny said, "The trouble is, he always wants us to be with him when he does it."

The men stood up and prepared to leave the table.

Daggett turned a fierce gaze upon them. "Ain't you-all goin' to carry your stuff to the pan so the lady doesn't have to?"

Shamed, the men carried their cups, plates, and utensils to the cabinet. Daggett thanked Carrie for the meal. The other men followed suit and straggled out toward the barn. Andy pushed his chair back and arose. He said, "Thank you for the breakfast. I'll be gettin' to town."

Daggett told Carrie, "I think it's time for me to go too. It's been a real pleasure gettin' to know you, ma'am."

She frowned. "Are you sure that leg is well enough?"

"The longer I stay here, the harder it'll be to leave."

Andy was aware of a regretful look that passed between them. He felt he had witnessed something that should have been private.

Daggett handed her the cane he had been using. "Thanks for lettin' me have the borry of it."

"It'll be here the next time you need it." She smiled. "I don't mean that I want to see you get hurt again."

"Next time I see that brindle bull, I'll let Pickard wrestle with him."

They saddled their horses. Daggett still limped. He struggled to mount up, but Andy knew better than to offer help.

Andy said, "We need a good look at the McIntosh family. I thought we might circle over to their place before we go back to town. While we're there we can give Jake a talkin'-to."

"What he needs isn't talk. A smart tap on the head with the barrel of a six-shooter would do him a world of good."

"You've been listenin' to the Teals. I expect the McIntoshes see things different."

Daggett grunted. "It complicates things when you've got to look at both sides. You're not sure who to shoot."

One of the cowboys had told Andy that to find the McIntoshes' place he had only to follow the creek. The Teals had settled on the upper part, where the springs brought it to life. The McIntoshes had come along later, taking a long stretch of the creek farther downstream. For a while Andy saw cattle bearing the Teals' T Cross brand. Then he began coming across the Bar F of the McIntosh family. After a time he heard yelling and reined his horse in that direction. He found several men herding cattle into a crude brush corral. Among them he recognized Jake and his father.

The McIntoshes saw Andy and Daggett but did not acknowledge them until the cattle were penned and the gate closed. Gray-bearded Ethan McIntosh stared hard at Andy as if trying to remember where he might have seen him before.

"I'm Andy Pickard," Andy said. "My partner and I were at the Hawkinses' place when you came by."

The old man extended his hand hesitantly, as if he might change his mind and jerk it back.

Jake said, "He's a Ranger, Papa. He was at the dance." Jake had no bandages on his face, but he showed several dark bruises and some abrasions still inflamed.

Ethan's eyes narrowed. "Were you one of them that beat my boy up so bad?"

Andy said, "No, sir. Lanny Teal did that all by himself."

"Just Lanny? That is not quite the way I heard it." Ethan cast an accusing glance at his son. Jake looked away. Ethan said, "I doubt that it is a mortal sin to improve upon the truth in a modest way. We have all done it. Look, Rangers, we have these weaned calves to brand. If we wait much longer, somebody is likely to maverick them. Somebody like those Teals."

"Go on ahead. We didn't come to disrupt your work."

Andy was not one to stand around and watch. He pitched in and helped one of the McIntosh sons to flank calves and hold them down for the branding, earmarking, and cutting. Daggett assumed responsibility for the fire that heated the irons. His sore leg would permit little more.

Ethan said, "You appear to have had experience at this."

Andy said, "Some."

"I'd think you'd want to forego your Ranger job and do something for yourself."

"My plan is to have cattle of my own when I can buy some more land."

"Buy it?" Ethan was dismissive. "There is still vacant state land to the west of here that you could use for nothing. If you don't own it, you don't have to pay taxes on it. You pay only on your cattle, and only on as many of them as you allow the assessor to see."

"The state's sellin' off land as fast as it can."

"It will never be able to sell land that has no water on it. Besides, out past the Pecos, there is more land than cattle."

"Have you ever seen it?"

"No, but I know it's there, free for the taking."

Andy frowned. "For good reason. Some of it's so sparse that a cow has to graze in a run."

Ethan asked, "Have you met Old Man Harper Teal?"

"Yes, sir."

"When Harper begins buying dry land, I will too, if only to prevent that old thief from getting what should be mine."

Andy thought about it before saying, "What makes you think he's a thief?"

"It's common knowledge. Ask anyone."

That was essentially what Andy had heard from the Teals except that they were describing the McIntoshes. The two old men had a lot more in common than they knew, he thought. He said, "If you have any proof, I'll get out a warrant."

Ethan pondered. "Not yet, but when I get it I'll shout it from the rooftops."

The cattle branded and turned out, the McIntoshes mounted their horses and started toward their headquarters. Ethan invited Andy and Daggett to go along. As they rode, the old man pointed out several varieties of grass. "It's strong and puts the pounds on them. Of course, there's brush here that cattle don't eat. I've thought it would be good for goats, if there was any market for them."

Andy said, "I've seen some white goats with long, silky hair. Owners shear them like sheep."

"I'll look into it one of these days. A man with a family

needs to ring every bell he can reach. If he does not, some-one else will."

In the conversation Andy found that Ethan's family consisted of a wife, three sons, a daughter named Patience, and a son-in-law named Barstow, on whom Ethan bragged at length. "He works as hard as any man I know," he said. "My daughter had her head on her shoulders when she married him."

If so, Andy thought, Ethan was luckier than Harper Teal had been with his late son-in-law.

Riding toward the ranch headquarters, Andy contrived to pull his horse beside Jake's. He asked, "How are the battle wounds?"

"The heart still pumps all right."

"I've wondered why you keep fightin' with Lanny Teal. They say he always beats you."

"Why does a man keep gettin' back on a bronc that throws him off? He hopes to wear him down."

"Lanny doesn't really want to fight you."

"What business is that of the Rangers?"

"We were sent here to try and keep things peaceful."

"Run the Teals out of the country. That'll do it."

"Funny. They said pretty much the same thing about you-all."

Jake's voice sharpened. "The day'll come when we'll have to burn them out like a wasp's nest."

Andy warned, "Do, and the Rangers will come after you."

"Sounds like you've taken sides already."

"We haven't, and we won't unless somebody forces us to."

Nearing the headquarters, Ethan said, "It is late. You Rangers are welcome to eat supper with us and stay the night."

"We'd be obliged," Andy said. Ranger protocol would have called for him to defer to Daggett, but the older Ranger might have declined the offer. Andy wanted to spend time with the McIntoshes as well as the Teals and become better acquainted with both families.

Ethan said, "In spite of anything Harper Teal may have told you, we have no tails nor horns, nor do we breathe fire. All we ask is to be able to scratch out an honest living and remain in the good graces of the Lord."

"That doesn't seem like too much to ask."

"Some people won't leave us alone, though. They accuse us of things we never did, more than likely trying to cover their own transgressions. Are we supposed to lie down and let them walk over us?"

"You're supposed to obey the law."

"That we do. You can't blame Jake if he faces off against that Teal boy once in a while. He can't be expected to stand still against Lanny Teal's provocations."

"I was at the dance. I didn't see Lanny provoke him."

"He knows Jake considers Lucy to be his girl. He took her to the dance to goad Jake into a fight."

"Has anybody asked Lucy whose girl she wants to be?"

"Jake staked his claim. That should be enough to keep everyone else away."

Andy was a bit put off by McIntosh's strong sense of family entitlement. He argued, "A woman's not like a piece of land. She's got a mind of her own."

"Not a very bright one if she chooses Lanny over Jake. Any McIntosh is worth a dozen Teals."

The McIntoshes' headquarters did not look greatly different from the Teals'. Andy saw two frame houses, one newer but smaller than the other. He assumed it was where the daughter and son-in-law lived. A bunkhouse stood halfway between the smaller house and the barn. The corrals were of upright cedar stakes, fitted closely together so no animal larger than a rabbit could work its way through. Chickens scratched around the barn. Farther away, Andy could see a hog pen. It was a more diversified operation than the Teals'.

Though the creek ran nearby, a windmill stood just behind the larger house, its wheel turning slowly. The sucker rod clanked with each stroke.

Ethan swept a wide arc with his callused hand. "It's nothing fancy like the English dukes and earls who come over here with disgraceful amounts of money, but everything you see was built piece by piece with our own hands and the sweat of our brows. A hardworking man can do well for himself."

*He can if he doesn't have to pay to use the land,* Andy thought. But he could foresee an end to that. It would be the end of free range people like the McIntoshes and the

Teals. Changes were overtaking them whether they acknowledged it or not.

Andy asked, "What if somebody buys all this out from under you?"

"They can't. I have bought the land where the headquarters sits, and the land along the creek. I need not be concerned about the rest of it. Without water, no one else can use it."

Ethan noticed that Andy was intrigued by the windmill. He said, "It furnishes house water for drinking and cooking. With so many cattle upstream, we don't trust the creek to be clean. It's a marvel how much mud one cow can stir up. Horses are even worse."

Andy saw something more in the mill. Up to now, ranchers who staked their claims on rivers, creeks, and springs could claim by default outlying areas worthless without access to water. This had the effect of choking out latecomers who found no watered land. But in other parts of Texas, Andy had seen a trend toward drilling wells and erecting windmills that could bring up underground water where there was none on the surface. In time the free range operator would no longer be able to hold settlers at bay simply because the land was dry.

McIntosh's windmill foreshadowed his eventual defeat unless he adapted.

The son-in-law loped ahead to open the gate and hold it for the other riders to pass through. Jake joked with him. "Barstow, when are you goin' to make uncles of us?

You've been married long enough to give her two babies by now."

Embarrassed, Barstow tried to string along. He said, "I'm bashful."

"When I want somethin', I jump right in," Jake said.

Jake's brother Harvey intervened. "That's how you got those bruises. You jumped in over your head."

"I'll whip him the next time. You can bet on it."

"I'll bet on it the day I see that red rooster lay eggs."

Critically Ethan said, "Jake, you should be ashamed, making crude suggestions about your own sister."

Jake shrugged. "She didn't hear it."

Ethan muttered to Andy, "I hope I can keep that boy alive till he's thirty. Perhaps by then he'll grow up."

Andy found that the McIntosh cowboys had their own cook, operating in a small kitchen at one end of the bunkhouse. The family members ate in the main house, where Ethan's gray-haired wife ruled over the kitchen with the stern authority of a top sergeant. She was assisted by her married daughter, a short, plump little woman of perhaps thirty, whose pleasant smile seemed locked in place. Andy wondered idly if she kept it while she slept.

Ethan called his wife Agatha. Like her daughter, she was short in stature, broad in the hips. Unlike her daughter, she did not smile much but issued a lot of orders. She said, "Jake McIntosh, you'll not eat at my table until you wash your face and hands and comb your hair. We may live in the country, but we do not have to be countrified."

Jake protested that soap burned the lacerations on his face. She said, "All the better. You'll know to keep your hands in your pockets the next time you're tempted to fight."

Andy soon decided he liked these people, just as he had come to like the Teals. He also realized that this was a dilemma in the making. Sooner or later he might have to act against one of the families, or both.

Leaving the McIntoshes' ranch after breakfast, he asked Daggett, "What do you say now that you've seen them all?"

Daggett frowned. "I say *damn it!*"

# CHAPTER

## 5

Logan Daggett sat on a bench in front of the general store, his hurt leg stretched straight. He did not arise as Andy walked up. He asked, "Where you been?"

"Around. Listenin' to talk."

"Figured out yet who to blame for the trouble?"

"Some say it's the McIntoshes. Some say it's the Teals."

"I could've told you that without talkin' to anybody."

"It's all I've got."

Daggett had been whittling on a scrap piece of pine. It was beginning to take the form of a pistol. He said self-consciously, "The blacksmith's boy has been followin' me around. I'm makin' a little somethin' for him."

This show of generosity took Andy by surprise. "We're here to keep the peace, and you're givin' him a gun?"

"I don't know how to carve him a Bible." Daggett brushed pine shavings from his legs. A small, hungry-looking dog sniffed at them and turned away disappointed. Daggett said, "I haven't seen either of those two young fightin' roosters in town."

"I hear the Teals and the McIntoshes have been busy workin' cattle."

"I hope they're workin' their own, and not somebody else's."

Andy asked, "Any reason to think otherwise?"

Daggett's voice softened. "The time I spent with the Teals gave me a chance to look them over. They don't seem like the outlaws some people say they are. Carrie told me their family history."

"Do you think she told you all of it?"

"It ain't in her to lie."

The firmness of Daggett's voice told Andy he had best tread lightly. It had occurred to him that Carrie might remind Daggett of his wife of times past. He considered before he asked, "Does she resemble somebody you used to know?"

Daggett thought about it. "Nope, not a bit."

The barking of a dog led Andy's attention to a horseman coming up the street. Tall and gaunt, he was dressed in black, like a preacher, with blankets and a war bag tied to his saddle. A rifle rested in a scabbard beneath one leg. His coat bulged over a pistol on his hip. Andy said, "Here's one I haven't seen before."

Daggett's face fell. "Oh, hell. You don't know who that is?"

"I don't think so."

"You've heard of Nelson Rodock, ain't you?"

The name was familiar to Andy, though the face was not. Rodock had a reputation as a lethal troubleshooter who usually brought a quick end to whatever problem he was hired to solve. He managed to stay within the letter if not the spirit of the law. At least he managed not to get caught.

Andy said, "He looks like he could walk into the church and preach a sermon."

Daggett shook his head. "If he did, it would be at a funeral."

Andy suggested, "Maybe he's just passin' through."

Daggett said, "He wouldn't travel around for the fun of it. He's here because somebody's paid him, or is goin' to." He jerked his head. "Come on, back me up." He limped out to intercept the rider. Andy hastened to join him.

Daggett stopped, his right hand resting near his pistol. He said, "Howdy, Rodock. It's been a while."

Rodock drew up on the reins and stared with flint-gray eyes. Recognition brought a grim smile devoid of humor or warmth. "Howdy yourself, Logan Daggett. I figured somebody sent you to glory years ago."

"You tried once. I've got the scar."

"I was having an off day. I am a better shot now."

"So I keep hearin'. They say an undertaker has gotten fat, followin' you around."

"My reputation far exceeds my record. I have not killed half as many men as some people believe. And those I *have* killed deserved it."

"You spent a couple of years as a guest of the state for tryin' to kill me."

"The time was not wasted. I learned much while I was there, for which I have you to thank."

The two men stared coldly at each other in the loudest silence Andy had experienced in a long time. At length Rodock asked, "Do you have any business with me here today?"

Daggett said, "You're not in the fugitive book. But I'd be glad to put you there if you give me any reason."

"I am much more careful than in my younger days. I intend to grow a long gray beard and die in bed." Rodock gave Andy a quick glance, but it was Daggett who held his attention. "Good day, gentlemen."

Daggett's eyes were squinted as he watched Rodock move on toward the hotel. He said, "Things were touchy enough around here before he showed up. I'd save everybody some trouble if I shot him here and now."

"But bein' a Ranger, you can't."

"Not in town, with people watchin'. But if we were out in the country with nobody around . . ."

"You'd shoot him?"

"Like a rabid dog. How else do you think a handful of Rangers managed in those bad years after the Reconstruction? We couldn't make them fear God, but we damned sure made them fear us."

Two heavily laden freight wagons lumbered up the street, cutting deep tracks in the dirt. One was loaded with spooled barbed wire, the other piled high with posts. Somberly Daggett said, "Here comes some more trouble, like Rodock wasn't enough."

Proprietor Babcock stepped out onto his store's porch.

Smiling, he braced his hands on his broad hips while he watched the wagons' approach. He shouted, "It's about time you got here!"

The lead teamster pulled his mules to a stop and said, "Here's your order, Mr. Babcock."

Babcock said, "Been expecting you for a couple of days. Where have you been?"

The teamster said, "You can get only so much out of a mule."

Babcock pointed down the street. "It's too late to start for the Hawkinses' place today. Pull over by the wagon yard. You can deliver these goods to him tomorrow."

"The sooner we get away from here, the better we'll like it."

Daggett pulled a long strip of bark from a cedar post and gave it a moment's serious study. Tossing it aside, he said, "There'll be bloodstains on this wire before Hawkins gets it strung."

The teamster said, "It wouldn't be the first time. Me and Shorty got shot at over in Brown County. We tried to tell them it wasn't our wire. We just haul whatever the public pays us to."

Daggett said, "You ought to charge extra for carryin' this stuff."

"I do. This is the only hide I've got, and I place a high value on it. If I'm to risk losin' a piece of it, I expect to get paid."

Babcock's voice carried a hint of resentment. "You certainly charged enough for this job."

Daggett said, "We tried to talk Hawkins out of fencin' his land, at least till some of the bigger operators broke the ground."

Babcock appeared defensive. "It's a free country. A man has a right to do what he wants to with his own property."

Andy said, "There's been wars fought over that proposition."

Babcock flared. "Hawkins has a right to build a fence, and I have a right to sell him the wire and posts. As Rangers, it's your responsibility to uphold those rights." He retreated inside his store.

The teamsters had not moved. One said, "So you two are Rangers. Me and Shorty bleed easy. We'd be obliged if you'd stay around close. We'll even buy you both a drink."

Andy said to Daggett, "Why don't you go with them? I'll watch the wagons and see who-all takes an interest."

A great many people did. By ones and twos, they drifted down to the wagon yard once the teamsters had parked their wagons and turned the mules into a corral for a fill of grain. Andy watched Harold Pearcy and Sonny Vernon walk up. Pearcy foolishly tested a barb, then jerked his hand back. A tiny bubble of blood rose on the tip of his finger. He tried to suck it away.

Andy said, "I could've told you those barbs are as sharp as the devil's horns."

Pearcy rubbed a remnant of blood onto his trousers leg. "It was the devil that invented them."

Sonny said derisively, "Harold don't believe nothin' till he gives it a try."

Andy said, "Like jumpin' on Lanny Teal? Someday you boys'll learn there's some things you can't get away with."

Soon after Pearcy and Sonny left, Mason Gaines sauntered over to frown over the wire. He said, "I wonder if Hawkins talked to the Teals or the McIntoshes before he ordered this?"

Andy said, "I don't see any reason that he has to."

"I doubt they'll be happy about it. Once Hawkins gets his fence up—*if* he does—others will follow his example."

Andy said, "It's a free country."

"It's freer if you're big. Hawkins isn't."

Judge Zachary strolled over from the courthouse, chewing on a half-smoked cigar that had lost its fire. "I see that the rumors were correct," he said. "I am afraid this means some unpleasant days ahead."

Andy said, "I don't see any legal way somebody could stop Hawkins from buildin' his fence."

"No, but there are illegal ways. They usually end in court. Mind you, I respect August Hawkins, but he is a stubborn man. When he makes up his mind to something, he refuses to consider consequences."

"This part of the country seems to have more than its share of stubborn men."

Bud Teal was the first of his family to inspect the wire. Leaning from the saddle, he tested a barb between two fingers without cutting himself. "Wicked," he said. "I'll bet this stuff would even turn that brindle bull."

Andy said, "You haven't caught him yet?"

"Haven't seen him. Maybe he got tired of our ugly cows." He turned his attention back to the load of wire. "Hawkins is takin' a big risk with this."

"He wants to save his grass for his sheep. What's wrong with that?"

"Only that he's startin' somethin' a lot of people won't like."

"Your family for instance?"

"Lots of families." Bud reined his horse around. "I'll need to be tellin' Pa about this. I don't think he'll take kindly to it."

Jake McIntosh showed up an hour later with his father, Ethan. Jake's expression revealed nothing about his feelings. Perhaps he had none, one way or the other. Ethan was blunt, however. Fists clenched, he said loudly, "Satan's tool, it is. Any place that wire touches, the land is poisoned forever."

Andy had heard the same charge against steel plow points. He said, "It's Hawkins's own land."

"But this could spread like smallpox. The best thing is to stop the contagion before it starts."

"How do you figure on doin' that, Mr. McIntosh?"

"Even a hardheaded sheepman can be persuaded."

"You'd best not go against the law. It'd be our job to stop you."

Ethan's face twisted with indignation. "You, who've broken bread with us at our table?"

"I'd hope to break bread with you again, but we have

to enforce the law. We have to protect people's property rights."

Face flushed, Ethan turned away. He said grittily, "Come on, son. We're leaving."

Jake lingered a little. He kept looking at the wire, but his mind was on something else. He asked, "Seen Lanny Teal in town lately?"

Andy said, "Not since he got waylaid on his way home from the dance."

Earnestly Jake said, "You can believe me or not, but I had no hand in that. After the fight at the dance, I was too stove up to tangle with Lanny again."

Andy said, "I'd like to believe you."

"There's been too many lies told about us McIntoshes. I'd like to move someplace where nobody ever heard of us. I'd change my name to Smith or Jones or somethin'."

Orphaned by Indians when he was a boy, Andy was sensitive to the importance of blood kin. He said, "A man shouldn't ever turn his back on family."

Jake said, "I'm proud of my family, but I hate the reputation some folks have stuck us with. We're God-fearin' people."

"Seems to me that the Teals are too."

"They'd like you to think so. It wouldn't surprise me none if they put Hawkins up to this."

Andy knew better, but it would be futile to argue the point with Jake.

The jail cell cot seemed harder than ever tonight. Dozing fitfully, Andy kept turning, trying to find a soft spot.

There was none. Sleeping in the jail saved money and provided a roof for shelter, but he had not seen a drop of rain since he had been here. Shelter be damned, he thought. From now on he would sleep on a cot at the wagon yard.

He was startled fully awake by the clanging of a church bell. A bell in the middle of the night was not a call to services. He grabbed for his hat, then his trousers and boots. Still buttoning his shirt, he burst through the jail door and broke into a run. Ahead of him, men were shouting, moving toward a huge blaze near the wagon yard. Panicked horses and mules squealed and raced in circles inside the corrals.

The wagonload of fence posts was enveloped in flames.

# CHAPTER

## 6

One of the teamsters futilely dipped water from a trough and threw it on the fire a bucketful at a time. His efforts made no showing against the blaze. Rapidly losing ground, he gave up and stood back disconsolately to watch his wagon and its cargo go up in smoke.

Stable owner Scanlon ran excitedly back and forth, beseeching the onlookers to help save his property. Townsmen threw water on the wooden fence to prevent its loss. Others raked loose hay away from the blaze lest it catch fire and take the barn with it.

The teamster slapped at smoldering black spots on his shirt. Recognizing Andy, he said resentfully, "Kind of late showin' up, ain't you?"

"I wasn't expectin' this," Andy admitted.

"There goes half of my rollin' stock. Good freight wagons don't come cheap."

Daggett was slower getting to the scene. He still limped despite claiming that his injury had healed. He held silent. At this point there seemed to be nothing to say.

Unlike many others, Deputy Salty Willis was fully dressed. He had probably not bothered to take his clothes off when he went to sleep. He picked up a large metal container at the fence and brought it to the Rangers. He said, "Smells like coal oil."

Andy took a whiff. "That tells us how they did it. It doesn't tell us who they were."

Daggett nodded grimly. "I smell the McIntoshes behind this."

Andy asked, "Why the McIntoshes? There's lots of free range people that wouldn't be happy about Hawkins's fence. And what about the Teals?"

"Just the same, I'd bet my money on the McIntoshes."

"Don't you think you're makin' too fast a judgment?"

"Experience has taught me to play my first hunch. It generally proves out."

Sheriff Seymour came up in a trot, his shirt and trousers not yet buttoned. His boots were on the wrong feet. Breathing hard, he said, "They didn't wait long."

Andy asked, "Any suspicions?"

"I suspicion just about everybody but the old and infirm. And even some of them."

Storekeeper Babcock was trailed by his daughter. He quickly sent her home when he saw that some of the men had run to the fire in their underwear. His first comment to the Rangers was defensive. "That's Hawkins's loss, not mine. The posts belonged to him."

Andy was mildly irritated by the merchant's quick evasion of responsibility. He said, "You hadn't delivered them to him yet."

The teamster demanded, "What about my wagon? Who's responsible for that?"

Babcock was defensive. "Not me. You were paid to haul the goods, that's all. The wagon is yours."

"Was," Andy said. It and its load slumped into a smoky, smoldering heap, sending up a massive shower of sparks. The wheels lay flat on the ground.

The teamster glared at Babcock. "Nobody's paid me for the haul yet."

Babcock said, "You didn't complete it. You were supposed to deliver all the way out to the Hawkinses' place."

For a minute it appeared that the Rangers might have to break up a fight, but Babcock stopped the argument by briskly walking away.

Andy told the freighter, "Maybe you can sue whoever lit the fire. That's if we're ever able to find out who it was."

Tracks would be of no help. Too many people had added their own, hurrying to the fire, trying to fight it. Nor was the oil can likely to yield any information, for most people kept coal oil to fill lamps and lanterns, and to light stoves and fireplaces.

Andy told Daggett, "Looks to me like we're up a stump."

Daggett shook his head. "We'll keep an eye on the McIntoshes. Sooner or later one of them will make a wrong step."

Andy frowned. "She sure took ahold of you, didn't she?"

"She? Who you talkin' about?"

"Forget I said it."

"Carrie's got nothin' to do with it. I've suspicioned the McIntoshes all along."

Andy said, "We'd better get to know more about the lay of the land before we make up our minds. The first guess is wrong, often as not."

"Yours, maybe. Not mine."

Newspaper editor Tolliver was talking to the teamsters and making notes on a pad lighted by the flames.

Daggett poked Andy with his elbow and jerked his head toward a man who stood alone, watching the fire with no evident emotion. Andy recognized Rodock. He said, "Do you reckon . . ."

Daggett said, "I wouldn't be surprised."

There was no question of going back to sleep. Andy studied faces, especially those of people who seemed pleased by the conflagration. As daylight came, he found that some of the wooden spools that contained the wire were scorched. Whoever burned the posts had made an attempt against the wire as well, but the flames had consumed the coal oil, then died out.

The freighter and his helper hitched a team to the remaining wagon. He said, "I'm gettin' this load of wire off of my hands as quick as I can. Whichaway's the Hawkinses' place?"

Andy looked at Daggett. "Might be a good idea if we went with him. He could run into trouble."

"He's already had trouble," Daggett replied. "You go. I'll stay around town. If Rodock wiggles a finger, I want to see it."

Andy had breakfast, then went to the wagon yard. The freighters had already left. It did not take long to catch up to them on the road, for the wagon and its load were too heavy to make much speed.

"You were in a hurry," Andy said to the wagon's owner.

"It don't take me long to see when I'm not welcome. From now on I'm haulin' nothin' but dry goods and groceries."

"Fences are comin', like it or not."

They met a couple of travelers along the way but no one who offered any overt threat. Late in the afternoon Andy saw the Hawkinses' ranch house ahead. Starting and stopping, the wagon picked its way through a scattered band of sheep. A large wether grazed along out front. Around its neck a small bell clanged pleasantly with each step the animal took.

The teamster said, "That bell would drive me crazy, but I guess the sheep was crazy to start with. Most of them are."

Andy expected him to add "along with the men who own them," but he didn't. That was a common attitude in much of Texas.

Hawkins had half a dozen sheep in a small pen, most freshly shorn of their wool. Under a shed and on a spread-out tarp, he was shearing one with a pair of hand clippers. The wool was dusty gray on the surface, but next to the skin it was creamy white. Looking up and wiping sweat from his face onto his sleeve, Hawkins acknowledged the wagon's arrival with a nod. He finished the job and untied the sheep's legs. The animal struggled to its feet and leaped over a shadow before running out to join the others.

Hawkins rolled the fleece and pushed it down into a long burlap bag before coming out through a wooden gate.

"Hello, Ranger," he greeted Andy. His extended hand felt slick from the greasy wool. He gave the wagon a moment's attention. "There ought to be another, with the posts."

Andy gave him the news. Hawkins took it solemnly. He said, "I should have expected something like that. I came out onto the porch this morning and found a message on the wall. It was not a love letter."

Andy asked, "What did it say?"

"It said, 'No fences.' It was signed, 'the Regulators.' Had a noose drawn with it. Poor artist, but a clear message."

Andy knew of groups elsewhere calling themselves regulators. Usually they were secretive about their membership, often masked or hooded and acting under cover of darkness, enforcing their version of law and proper behavior. They might begin as vigilantes, augmenting local peace officers, but power tended to corrupt them, leading them to support private grudges and vendettas, take on political aspirations, and drive away or even kill those who might oppose them.

Andy said, "Looks to me like you've run up against a mob."

"A mob is just a gathering of people who don't have the courage to act on their own."

"But put them together, and they can hurt you."

Hawkins stared at the wagon. "A load of wire isn't worth

much without posts to string it on." He said to the teamster, "How long would it take you to bring me another wagon-load?"

The teamster shook his head. "Mister, I ain't haulin' no more posts. Not for you, not for nobody. Show me where to dump this wire."

Hawkins pointed. "Over there by the barn. And stack it, don't dump it." He turned back to Andy. "I'll see if Babcock can find me some more posts."

Skeptical, Andy said, "Are you sure? Might be smart to stand back a while and see how the wind blows."

Hawkins frowned. "You were too young to go to the war, but I wasn't. We fought for what we thought was right. Those on the other side were sure *they* were right. I don't think we really proved anything, but we stood up for what we believed in. That's what I'm doing now."

"But you had a whole army on your side. This time you're standin' out here all by yourself."

"I'm standing up for my rights."

Andy felt pride in the man's strong principles, but he also felt impatience. He remembered Bethel recounting a story from a book about a proud but foolish old warrior who rode into battle against a windmill, thinking it was a dragon.

The so-called regulators might indeed be a dragon.

Hawkins said, "As soon as I finish the shearing, I'll take the dog and bring in my sheep. You'll be staying the night, won't you?"

Andy thought he should, for whoever burned the wagon

and left the message might return. "It's too late in the day to go back to town."

"I'll ride in with you tomorrow. I have to talk to Babcock about another load of posts."

Hawkins stuffed the final fleece into the sack. The two teamsters were unloading the spooled wire. Andy had no wish to join them at it. He said, "I'll help you bring in the sheep." That might be useful experience. Someday, when he became a rancher instead of a Ranger, he might want to keep sheep as well as cattle. Lots of hill country people seemed to prosper by owning both.

He admired the way the dog handled the sheep with little coaching. Hawkins said, "They've bred his kind in Scotland for generations. The herding instinct is part of his nature. Take him away from sheep and he'll herd hogs or chickens or whatever else he can find."

It seemed to Andy that some people were born with that herding instinct, constantly trying to control others. These nameless regulators were a case in point. Logan Daggett was another.

He asked, "What happens if a sheep fights back?"

"They never do. That's why they're called sheep." Hawkins's brow furrowed. "I'm a sheep*man*, Ranger, but I'm not a sheep."

After supper they sat a while on the porch, Hawkins smoking his pipe. They talked of weather and wool prices and other subjects but avoided what was uppermost in their minds.

Andy stretched and said, "I see the teamsters have

bedded down out by the barn. I think I'll take my blanket and join them."

Hawkins pushed to his feet and tapped his pipe against a porch post. "Bring them to the house with you for breakfast. After I turn the sheep out to graze, we'll start for town."

So many things were running through Andy's mind that he could not go to sleep. He relived the burning of the posts. He kept seeing in his mind's eye the penciled warning from the regulators. He sensed that the threat was not idle. A lot of people had a stake in keeping the range open and free.

Hearing horses, he sat up and listened. He had remained in his clothes, except for his boots. He quickly put them on and strapped his gun belt around his waist. In the dim light of the moon he counted half a dozen men on horseback. As they neared, he realized that all wore hoods over their heads. One fired a pistol into the air and shouted, "Hawkins, come out here!"

The riders' attention was focused on the front of the house. They did not see Andy standing in shadow. The man brandishing the pistol shouted again for Hawkins to come out.

Andy shouted, "Hawkins, you'd better stay where you're at!"

The horsemen reacted with surprise. The one holding the pistol swung it toward Andy. Andy fired a shot that struck between the horse's feet. The frightened horse jumped. Its rider fell from the saddle, losing his hood and the pistol.

On his knees, he felt around desperately, trying to find the weapon.

Andy fired again, the bullet raising dust just in front of the fallen man. He shouted, "Everybody back off! I'm a Ranger!"

He stepped up close to the man on the ground and said, "Let me get a look at you." The face was familiar. Andy had seen him hanging around a saloon in town. He had also been at the fire, watching but not joining others who attempted to snuff out the flames. He had seemed to enjoy the spectacle.

Andy held the muzzle of his pistol an inch from the man's nose and said for all the riders to hear, "You-all drop your guns so I won't be forced to kill this upstandin' citizen."

Several pistols and a rifle hit the ground. Andy knew that even if the men were unarmed, he could not long control so many still on horseback. He could not stop them if they turned and ran, so he gave them permission. "Now turn those horses around and git."

"What about our guns?" one man asked.

Andy said, "You can pick them up at the sheriff's office. I expect he'll have a few questions to ask you."

The fallen man started to arise. Andy tapped his chin gently with the pistol's muzzle. "Not you. We're goin' to have a little talk about the majesty of the law."

The riders began to pull away. The ostensible leader held back to say, "Ranger, we don't see where you have any call to mix in this. It's a community matter."

The voice was muffled by the hood the speaker wore. Andy thought he might have heard it before, but he could not be certain. He said, "It's a matter for the law when you burn up people's property and threaten their lives."

The man said, "Just the same, you tell Hawkins that if he strings any of that wire, he's liable to get hung with it."

Andy cringed at the grisly image of Hawkins strangling on a barbed wire noose. He motioned with the pistol. "Get away from here, or I'll find out how many of you I can shoot before I run out of shells."

One rider had not dropped his pistol, for he turned and fired a shot. It was not clear whether he was shooting at Andy or at the man on the ground. Andy put a bullet near the horse's feet. The animal began to pitch. The rider dropped his pistol and grabbed at the horn. He managed to stay in the saddle and ride off after the others.

The two teamsters had stood back, avoiding entanglement. Now they edged closer but kept their distance from Andy's kneeling prisoner. The wagon owner said, "I wouldn't want to walk in your boots, Ranger. You won't know those men if you meet them on the street. One of them could step up and blow your head off."

Andy shook his head. "Every Ranger in Texas would be lookin' to kill him. A man would have to be stupid to take that chance."

"I've known a lot of stupid people in my time." The teamster waited to be sure his point had soaked in. He added, "If it's all the same to you, we'd sooner not have you ride back with us. We don't want to be anywhere close when lightnin' strikes you."

Andy smiled in spite of himself. "Fine with me. Your wagon travels too slow anyway. I would appreciate it, though, if you'd haul these guns to the sheriff."

Hawkins had come out onto the porch in his underwear. Andy asked him, "Is this man a neighbor of yours?"

Hawkins studied the face. "Bigelow, I didn't think you had the stomach for a thing like this. I thought you were all bellow and no bite."

Andy said, "It doesn't take much guts when you cover your face and ride with a mob."

Bigelow was trembling. In a breaking voice he said, "That last shot was aimed at me."

Andy asked, "What makes you think so? I figured it was aimed at me."

"They were afraid I might tell who the rest of them are. We're not supposed to get ourselves captured."

Andy said, "Then you ought to've stayed at home." He retrieved a set of handcuffs from his saddlebag and fastened Bigelow's wrist to a spoke in a wagon wheel. Bigelow complained, "Sittin' here this way makes me an easy target. And it's liable to throw a kink into my back."

Andy said, "You'd have gotten a kink in your *neck* if you'd killed Hawkins."

"We just figured to throw a scare into him, is all."

Accompanied by Hawkins, Andy reached town with his prisoner. He found Daggett before he found the sheriff.

Daggett's eyes were grim as he stared at the prisoner. He said, "Why didn't you shoot him when you had the chance? There's nothin' gets a mob's attention like killin' the foremost."

"Killin' is the last resort."

"Sometimes it takes a strong dose of salts to flush the bowels."

Andy delivered the frightened prisoner to Sheriff Seymour's office in the jail. The lawman seemed not surprised. "Oscar Bigelow," he said, "I've been waitin' for you to stumble over your own feet. I always figured you for a member of Skeen's outfit, but I couldn't prove it."

Bigelow mustered up a moment's defiance. "You can't prove it now, either."

Andy said, "He won't need to. I'll file charges on you for attempted murder."

Bigelow went slack-jawed. "Murder? We didn't kill nobody."

"You fired into the house. You could've killed Hawkins or his wife. Now, if you'd like to tell who else was with you last night, I might whittle the charge down a little."

Bigelow looked at the floor. "I can't. They'd kill me."

"A few days on bread and water might change your outlook."

"I can't. I taken an oath. Anybody talks, he dies." Bigelow's voice tightened with desperation. "You won't get nothin' out of me, so you'd just as well turn me loose. I promise I'll be gone from this country before sundown."

Daggett said, "Let's sit on him a while. If he doesn't

tell us what we want to know, we'll give out the word that he spilled his guts, then turn him loose. I'd bet he never gets to the county line."

Bigelow cried, "You wouldn't do that."

Daggett said, "We sure as hell would. You're no good to us if you won't talk."

Andy suspected that Daggett meant it. The idea disturbed him, but he played along. "Sounds all right to me."

Bigelow shook like a man in the throes of a bad hangover. "I just can't. You know what happened to Callender."

Seymour explained, "That's the man who was murdered a few days before you got here. I was fixin' to arrest him on suspicion when somebody shot him in the back. I figure he knew too much, and they were afraid I'd make him tell."

Bigelow said, "They gave him a day to leave the county, but he didn't want to go without his cattle. I wouldn't be that foolish."

Andy said, "You keep sayin' *they*. Who is *they?*"

"If I was to tell you, I could kiss my ass good-bye."

Daggett's face was severe. "Pickard, bein' raised with the Indians, I expect you know some ways to make him talk."

"I do, but I don't believe in usin' them."

"When you've handled as many criminals as I have, you'll change your way of thinkin'."

The teamsters brought the night riders' weapons to town in their wagon, dumped them at the sheriff's office, then left after a heated argument with storekeeper Babcock over who should stand the loss of the burned wagon. Babcock held firmly to his contention that he bore no responsibility for the fire, though he condescended to pay for the hauling. Thus all concerned gained some and lost some.

Babcock was reluctant to accept Hawkins's order for another load of posts, citing the trouble the first shipment had caused. Hawkins said, "I'll need several more loads of wire and posts before I can fence my place all the way around. Don't you want the business?"

The promise of additional profit brought Babcock around to Hawkins's way of thinking, though with reluctance. He insisted on payment in advance, one order at a time. He said, "You may not live to see the last load delivered."

Andy watched the sheriff inventory the captured weapons in his office. Seymour said, "I doubt anybody's goin' to claim this artillery."

Andy said, "It would be like writin' a confession."

They took Bigelow to the judge's office, but the judge was not there. A clerk said he was at his ranch. Bigelow sat handcuffed in a chair. Andy could almost smell the man's fear.

Seymour said, "Skeen's rustler gang had three or four killin's charged against them. I always suspicioned that Bigelow was one of the outfit, along with Callender, but I never had any proof. They—or somebody—has been back at it lately."

Andy said, "Bigelow talked about takin' an oath. When members have to swear an oath, it generally means the group is prepared to snuff out anybody who breaks the vow."

"What if they was to break into my jail? I wouldn't want Bigelow on my conscience, like Skeen."

Bigelow protested, "The jail is a death trap. You've got to take me someplace else."

The sheriff said, "Maybe we would, if you told us what we want to know."

Bigelow hung his head. "They'd hunt me down like a dog."

Seymour shrugged. "Then there's nothin' to do except lock you up."

Bigelow trembled. "You'd just as well shoot me now."

Daggett declared, "We're thinkin' about it." He took a firm grip on Bigelow's arm and lifted him from the chair. "I've got a sore leg, and I'm awful easy aggravated, so don't aggravate me."

Cradling a rifle across his left arm, Andy looked down the courthouse hall but saw no one. He led the way to the front door and down the steps, warily studying the light horse and wagon traffic on the dirt street. "Looks about as clear as it'll ever be," he said.

The jail and the sheriff's office were in a separate stone building adjacent to the courthouse. It was a walk of only about thirty yards in the open. They were halfway across it when a bullet struck the jail wall and ricocheted, singing. Andy swung the rifle around in reflex, searching wildly for the shooter.

A second shot brought a yelp of pain from Bigelow. The sheriff and Daggett lifted the prisoner between them and hurried him into the jail. Andy walked backward, following them and watching for rifle smoke. The shots could have come from anywhere across the street. He quickly entered the jail and closed the door.

Seymour and Daggett supported Bigelow until they could get him into a chair. The prisoner's ear was bleeding.

Seymour gave the wound a quick examination. "A couple of inches over and you'd be dead. As it is, you've just been earmarked."

Daggett offered no sympathy. He said, "A swallowfork, I'd call it."

Sobbing, Bigelow touched a hand to his ear and looked at the blood. "They want to kill me. They'll do it yet."

Fists hammered against the jail's outside door. A voice called, "Pete, let me in. It's Salty."

Seymour nodded at Andy. "My deputy. Open the door."

The lanky deputy rushed inside, carrying a rifle. Andy closed and bolted the door behind him. The deputy said, "I heard the shootin'. Anybody hurt?"

Daggett said, "Nobody that matters."

Andy studied the trembling prisoner a moment, then looked about the jail. He had not noticed before that every cell was vulnerable to a gunshot from one of the windows. An assassin would not even have to break in.

The sheriff said, "I know what you're thinkin'. That's why I put curtains over all the windows. Nobody can see in from outside."

Andy said, "Just the same, this jail would be like a shootin' gallery if somebody pulled one of those curtains

down. Kerrville has got a jail that would hold a bull elephant."

Seymour put up no argument. "After dark. One of you
Rangers ought to take him. The minute I cross a county
line, I'm out of my jurisdiction. You know how these slick
defense lawyers can use a thing like that."

Daggett said, "Every last one of them ought to be taken
out and hung."

Andy said, "I'll go."

Seymour ordered his deputy to patrol the jail from outside, preventing anyone from approaching the windows.

Andy tried to sleep, but the big railroad clock seemed
to try shaking itself from the wall. Each movement of
the heavy pendulum sounded like the cocking of a gun.
When the lamp's faint glow showed one o'clock, he
arose from the cot and fetched his rifle from a rack on the
wall.

The sheriff was already up and moving about. "Salty's
got two horses for you out back," he said. "Ready?"

Andy nodded and fetched the keys from the sheriff's
desk. He unlocked Bigelow's cell. "Come on," he said. "We
got some travelin' to do."

Suspicious, Bigelow sat up on the edge of his bunk but
did not move toward the door. "I want to know where we're
goin'."

"Someplace where you'll be safer. Roll your pillow up
in your blanket. If anybody manages a look through the
window, it'll appear like you're still sleepin'."

Bigelow complied. He touched a hand to the bandage on his ear. "It burns like hell."

That sounded like a call for sympathy, but Andy could not summon any.

Daggett was on his feet. He asked, "Sure you don't want me to go with you?"

Andy said, "Three men would attract more attention than two. Besides, if somebody takes a shot at this jail, you'll be here to help catch him."

Andy handcuffed Bigelow and led him by the arm toward the back door. He said, "Somebody blow out the lamp."

He gave his eyes time to become accustomed to the darkness, then opened the door and led Bigelow out. As Seymour had said, two horses were tied outside. He motioned for Bigelow to mount up. In barely more than a whisper he said, "If you try to run, I'll shoot you myself."

Bigelow whined, "You treat me like I'd killed somebody."

"For all I know, you may have."

The moon was but a sliver and cast little light. The shadows between the town's buildings were dark as ink. Andy held to them as much as he could. Bigelow started another complaint, but Andy cut him off. "Why don't you just holler out and tell everybody where you're at?"

Bigelow said no more. The last building was just ahead. Soon after passing that they would be among live-oak trees and cedars. He would avoid the road a while, then cut back into it when he felt they were on safe ground.

Four horsemen pushed out from behind the last building.

Though the light was poor, Andy saw that they wore hoods over their heads. He tried to bring his rifle into position, but one of the riders pushed his horse into Andy's and almost jarred him out of the saddle. The man, little more than a dark shadow, shoved the muzzle of a pistol into Andy's face.

He said, "Drop the rifle. The six-shooter, too. We don't want to kill a Ranger, but we'll do it if we have to. All we're after is your prisoner."

Andy said, "You can't have him." It was a hollow statement. Though he still held the rifle, he knew he would not live long enough to bring it into play.

The rider said, "Bigelow, we don't like the company you're in."

Bigelow's voice broke. "I ain't told nobody nothin'. I ain't *goin'* to tell them nothin'. I swear."

"That's what Callender said, but we knew he'd break. He'd talk like an old widder woman."

Bigelow begged, "I won't. You know me."

"Yes, we know you." The horseman's pistol flashed fire. Bigelow doubled over, clutching at his stomach. A second shot cut off his cry.

Andy tried to bring the rifle up. A gun barrel knocked his hat off. A second blow was like an explosion in his brain. He slid from the saddle.

Through a loud roaring in his ears he heard a voice say, "Bigelow's still wigglin'."

A third shot seemed to echo for minutes. Another voice said, "Not now, he ain't."

Dogs were barking all over town. Andy heard hoof-beats receding into the night. He tried to push himself up but had no strength for it. His last thought before he sank away into darkness was that he had failed. He had lost his prisoner.

Regaining consciousness, Andy realized he was lying on a cot in the jail. He raised a hand to the place where his head throbbed most and felt a thick bandage. Blinking, he recognized the doctor leaning over him.

"Don't make any sudden moves," the physician warned. "Your brain may be like scrambled eggs after the blows you took."

Daggett's coarse voice penetrated Andy's pain. "I doubt that. There couldn't be more than a spoonful."

Andy struggled to remember what had happened. It came back to him in fragments. "They didn't let us get very far."

Daggett said, "They were layin' for you."

"But we didn't tell anybody."

"This is a tough town to keep a secret in."

Andy knew but had to ask anyway. "What about Bigelow?"

"He's about the deadest man you ever saw."

Andy felt crushed by the heavy weight of failure.

Daggett said, "The minute you found out who he was, he was a danger to the others. They figured he'd break. What they did to him and to Callender is a warnin' to any-body else who might know more than is good for him."

Andy lamented, "It'll be extra hard now to get people to talk to us."

The sheriff and his deputy came along in a while. Seymour said, "Me and Salty went over every inch of the ground out there. Never found even a cartridge shell."

Daggett asked, "What about horse tracks?"

"They're all over the place, and they all look about the same."

Daggett said, "Even if we could find the right ones, they'd probably lead us in a circle and scatter. Whoever shot Bigelow may never have left town."

Andy said, "So we have to suspect everybody we see?"

Daggett nodded. "I've been doin' that all along. As far as I know, Pickard, you're the only honest man in town besides me, and I've even got some doubts about you." A tentative smile flickered and was quickly gone.

Andy had difficulty in keeping his concentration. He said, "Soon as this headache lets up, I'm ridin' out to see August Hawkins. I'll try to talk him into waitin' a while on his fence. The mob may not warn him anymore. They're liable to just shoot him."

Dubious, the sheriff said, "He's a hardheaded man."

"So am I, when I have to be."

Daggett said, "Yeah, or they'd have busted your skull like a watermelon."

Andy raised up a little, then dropped back onto the pillow. He felt as if a blacksmith were using his head for an anvil. "After I talk to Hawkins, I think I'll pay a visit to the Teals and the McIntoshes. They might let somethin' drop."

Daggett said, "The Teal family came to town yesterday evenin', all but the old man. They're still here. I'll go talk to them."

Andy blinked. "They were here when Bigelow was shot?"

"You're always tellin' me not to jump to conclusions. Lots of folks were in town last night."

Andy said dryly, "I suppose you'll question Carrie."

"I like to be thorough."

"Maybe I ought to go help you."

"I can handle this without help. You stay here and rest, or your brain is liable to go to clabber."

Daggett cut off discussion by walking away. The sheriff's gaze followed him out of sight. Seymour said, "Even if the Teal boys know somethin', they won't tell it."

Andy said, "Daggett knows that. It's not the boys he really wants to talk to, anyway."

The sheriff caught on. "Carrie? I'm surprised. I thought there wasn't nothin' in his veins except ice."

"There's a side to him that he doesn't show much. He's surprised me, too, once in a while."

# CHAPTER

## 7

By noon, Andy felt recovered enough to go outside and sit on a bench. He saw Daggett escorting Carrie into the hotel restaurant. Most people considered it the best in town, though he had visited cow camps that served better fare. Andy had seldom seen a full-blown smile on Daggett's face, but he was smiling now. So was Carrie.

There's no accounting for a woman's taste, he thought.

In a while he saw Rodock enter the restaurant. He wondered if Daggett's smile left him.

Early in the afternoon the Teal family left, Carrie and Lanny in a supply-laden wagon, the others on horseback. Daggett stood on a corner and watched until they were gone, then returned to where Andy sat.

Andy asked, "Did they tell you anything?"

Daggett shook his head. "Never got much chance to talk to the boys."

"I doubted that you would."

"Carrie said her brothers were asleep at the wagon yard when the shots were fired."

"She was with them?"

"Of course not. They wouldn't let their sister sleep in a wagon yard. They got her a room in the hotel."

"So she can't be sure they were asleep."

"They wouldn't lie to her."

It was useless for Andy to belabor the point. "I think I'll go back in and lay down a while."

"You'd just as well. I can handle anything that comes up."

Andy knew it was true, and it grated like gravel in his craw.

He was on his way to the Hawkinses' ranch soon after daylight. His head still ached and was sore to the touch. He could not pull his hat down tightly, but it was good to be up and moving. He had lain abed about as long as patience would allow.

He came upon the Hawkinses' sheep. The dog loose-herded them while they grazed, turning back any that strayed far from the flock. Andy noticed that the dog limped. The hair on one leg was matted. Evidently he had been licking an injury. Noticing small splotches of blood on several sheep, Andy felt a sense of alarm.

As he rode up to the corral, he rough-counted about thirty sheep lying dead. Hawkins bent over one, shearing its fleece with hand clippers. Hearing Andy's horse, Hawkins jumped to his feet and grabbed a rifle that leaned against a fence. With recognition came relief. "Andy, I thought one of those night riders had come back."

"It looks like you were all set to shoot somebody."

"Anyone who would kill a bunch of helpless sheep deserves to be shot."

Andy dismounted and entered the corral. Flies were already buzzing around the dead animals. Hawkins said, "I have to salvage the wool while I can." He bent back to the shearing.

Andy asked, "Anything I can do to help?"

"Just find the hood-wearing sons of bitches who did this."

Hawkins's eyes smoldered with anger as he described the attack. "They called for me to come out of the house. Said they'd burn the place down if I didn't, so I went out. The leader reminded me what happened to the fence posts and said I'd be a dead man if I tried again. I managed to haul off and hit him once in the face. One of the others clubbed me down." Hawkins rolled the fleece. "They're probably the same ones who shot up the house the other night."

"Minus one." Andy explained about Bigelow.

Hawkins took satisfaction from the news. "So now they're killing their own. If I were a member of that bunch, I'd watch my back."

"You'd best watch it anyway. They meant it when they told you to give up the fence. Next time they won't stop with your sheep."

Hawkins tied the fleece and forced it into a burlap bag. "I suppose you've come out to try and persuade me."

"That was my intention. This trouble won't last forever. Your fence can wait."

"I swore I wouldn't let them control me."

"Just for a while. Sometimes a man has to retreat so he can live to fight another day."

Andy saw reluctance in the sheepman's eyes, but Hawkins gave in. "Tell Babcock to cancel my order. One lone sheepman can't fight the mob. Or one Ranger, either."

"I promise you, we'll do our best, me and Daggett."

Jake McIntosh and his brother Ike had roped a heifer missed in the earlier branding. They had her feet tied and were heating a steel ring in a small mesquite fire when Andy happened upon them.

Jake still showed a bruise from his fight with Lanny Teal. He said, "Don't worry, Ranger. She's one of ours. Her mammy is right over yonder, carryin' our brand."

"Never thought different," Andy replied. When the ring was hot, Jake picked it up with two sticks and methodically drew a Bar F brand on the heifer's side. One of the brothers had already notched her ear.

Andy asked, "I don't suppose you've seen a stray brindle bull around here?"

Jake said, "We have. We've chased that old hellion from one end of this place to the other. I wouldn't be surprised if the Teals ran him over here to bedevil us."

"If you fenced your land, you could keep him out." Andy hoped he was planting the seed of an idea.

"Papa hates fences like he hates rattlesnakes."

"Some others do, too. I don't suppose you heard that night riders hit Hawkins's sheep last night."

Jake appeared surprised. "Did they hurt the old man?"

"No, but they killed thirty or so head."

The news left Jake troubled. "I suppose you've come

over here to find out if we had anything to do with it. I swear to you, we didn't. No matter what some folks think of us, we don't go around killin' people's livestock. Not even sheep."

Andy sensed that Jake was sincere. He said, "I didn't think you-all were responsible. I just had to make sure."

Jake dropped the hot ring into the sand to cool it. "We heard about your bad luck with your prisoner. We had nothin' to do with shootin' him." He paused. "Have you talked to the Teals?"

"Daggett has. They didn't own up to anything."

"And never apt to." Jake picked up the hot ring with his fingers but quickly dropped it again. "Changin' the subject, have you seen anything of Lucy Babcock? I ain't had time to go to town."

Andy did not want to admit that he had seen Lucy hanging on to Lanny Teal's arm. "I've seen her helpin' her daddy at the store."

"Pretty as a spotted pup, isn't she?"

That was not the way Andy would have phrased it, but he said, "She is, for a fact." The little he had seen of Lucy had given him the impression that she was like an autumn leaf, swept one way, then another by whatever wind happened by.

Jake said, "I can't figure what she sees in Lanny."

"What man can ever understand a woman's mind? I don't, and I've been married a while."

"But that redheaded Lanny of all people . . . he's as ugly as a mud fence."

"He's not a bad feller when you come to know him. You could be friends if you'd get past the bad blood between your family and his."

"Damned unlikely, the way Papa and Harper Teal feel toward each other."

Andy said, "They're two stubborn old men who've carried a grudge way too long. You're too young to remember the war, and so is Lanny."

"I have to respect Papa's feelin's. Anyway, my quarrel with Lanny is personal."

"Why don't you stand back and let Lucy make her own choice?"

"She might choose wrong. I'd feel bad about lettin' her make a mistake."

Jake untied the heifer. She jumped to her feet and pawed the ground with one forefoot, looking for somebody to fight. Jake tossed his hat at her. She flipped it over her back, then trotted away, shaking her head. Ethan McIntosh rode up with his son, Harvey. He was in the same belligerent mood as the departing heifer. He studied her a moment, then said critically, "That is not the prettiest brand I ever saw. Did I not send you to school to learn your letters?"

Jake said, "Puttin' a brand on a hairy hide ain't like writin' on a slate. The main thing is to let everybody know that heifer is ours."

McIntosh scowled. "Some don't care whether they're ours or not. We're missing a bunch down on the south side. Harvey and I are sure they have been run off." He turned upon Andy with an angry challenge. "Instead of sitting here indulging yourself in gossip, Ranger, you should be doing something about it."

Andy said, "Show me where they were at. Maybe they left enough tracks that I can follow them."

"From what I heard, you can't even take care of a prisoner."

The old man's prickly attitude got under Andy's skin, but he tried not to let it cloud his judgment. He asked, "How did you hear about it?"

"One of those infernal wagon peddlers dropped by yesterday. He sold my wife and daughter a lot of worthless doodads. It was a waste of money, but that's womankind for you. They are drawn to anything that glitters or shines."

Jake said, "Me and Ike were ridin' down on the south end yesterday. We didn't see nothin'.'"

Ethan's face contorted. "You wouldn't see an elephant in the kitchen unless it stepped on your foot. Someone is determined to steal us blind and push us out of this country. I see the fine hand of Harper Teal."

Andy pointed out, "The Teal place is to the north of you, not the south."

"But Mexico is not. If they drive those cattle into the South Texas brush, I had just as well scratch them out of my tally book."

Jake said, "You don't reckon Vincent Skeen has risen from the grave, do you, Papa?"

"Not likely, with the heavy load of lead he carried. But his old gang of thieves may have reunited." Ethan jerked his head at Andy. "Come on, Ranger. You, too, Jake and Ike. Get your minds on your business."

Andy wished Daggett were here. He had a keener eye for tracking. But to circle by town and pick him up would cost too much time. There was no way to know how much head start the thieves had.

Harper said, "I hope you have sufficient ammunition, Ranger."

"My cartridge belt is full."

"If we catch up to the rustlers, I want to see every one of them carry lead enough to sink him to the bottom of the deep blue sea."

"In that case, you'd better send somebody to town to fetch my partner Daggett. He prefers to shoot first and then ask questions, if he's got any."

Harper nodded. "Harvey, you go. If I sent Jake, he would stop to spark that storekeeper's daughter and forget what he went for." He jerked his head again. "Let's be gone from here."

Jake said, "But we've got no grub with us, and no blankets."

Harper's answer was fierce. "You can sleep with your saddle blanket. As for grub, you ate enough supper last night to carry you for a week. If you'd fought through the war as I did, you'd know to punch extra notches in your belt and persevere. Live off the fat of the land."

Jake still had reservations. "When you go south from here, the land gets awful skinny."

"So will we all if we let them steal everything we have." Harper started off in a stiff trot.

Jake muttered, "Papa's got a way of endin' a conversation in a hurry. Especially when it goes against his thinkin'."

Andy said, "Lots of people are like that." He thought of his Ranger partner, who had little patience for argument. Daggett took it as a matter of immutable truth that he was always right.

They reached a narrow valley where Ethan and the boys had placed a set of young cows and their calves some days earlier. Ethan said, "They would not have left here on their own volition. It's some of the best grass on the ranch, and the creek furnishes all the water they would want. The tracks indicated that they were driven south."

Andy pointed out, "That's away from the Teals' ranch."

Ethan declared, "They would not keep Bar F cattle on their own land. They had just as well go to the sheriff and sign a confession. But if old Harper is out to break us, he could pass the cattle on to accomplices to be driven out of the country."

"I don't know why you're convinced that Harper Teal is behind it."

"That old Johnny Reb hates Union men. There is little he would not do to gut me."

"I thought the war got settled at Appomattox."

"Not until every one of those old rebels is dead and buried. Help me get the evidence and I'll bury Harper myself."

Andy glanced at Jake and Ike. Both were looking away, staying out of it.

They found a few tracks too badly windblown for certainty about the direction of travel. Andy said, "I'd say they were goin' south, but it's hard to be sure."

Ethan said, "South makes more sense than north."

Just at dusk, Andy shot a deer. That would be their supper, without salt and without coffee to wash it down. They followed the tracks until dark, losing them frequently and spending a lot of time searching.

Ethan chided his sons, "If you had been paying attention, we could have joined this trail a day sooner. By the time we catch up—if we do—our cattle will be speaking Spanish."

He had Andy and his sons up before daylight. They roasted more venison on sticks above the coals while they waited for sunup so they could see the tracks. Ethan dropped his meat on the fire but brushed away the ashes and ate it anyway. He was every inch an old soldier. He caught his sons exchanging glances of disapproval and said, "If you had gone hungry as many times as I have, little things like ashes and dirt would not bother you."

Jake replied, "We didn't say anything."

Ethan shook his head. "The younger generation! I'm afraid there is scant hope for the world."

Andy went out to check on the horses so he could grin without risking the old man's anger.

They had been underway about an hour and had proceeded only a couple of hundred yards when they saw

Daggett, Harvey, and Sheriff Seymour catching up. Ethan growled, "I don't know why they brought Seymour along. Without his glasses he couldn't even see a cow, much less her tracks."

Reining up, Daggett said, "We smelled the smoke from your campfire. It don't look like you've got very far."

Andy said, "A crow in flight would've left a better trail than this."

"It's too bad the Indians didn't teach you a lot more."

The mention of Indians aroused Ethan's curiosity. Andy had to explain that as a boy he had been stolen by Comanches and had lived among them for several years.

Ethan said, "At least the Comanches were honest thieves. They made no pretenses about their intentions . . . not like some people who go to church every Sunday. On Monday they will steal your socks without taking your boots off."

Daggett and the sheriff had brought the Ranger pack-mule along. Jake said, "I hope you got some coffee in that pack."

The sheriff said, "Coffee, bacon, some flour and salt."

Jake grinned. "Come the next election, you've got my vote."

Ethan cut him a glance that told him to shut up.

Daggett was not long in finding the trail of the cattle. Though he sometimes lost it, he usually found it again more quickly than Andy could. By the third day the all-meat diet had become monotonous, but the tracks were fresh. Daggett said, "You can't get but so much travel out of a cow-calf herd."

Ethan said, "Cows are the factory. If you steal enough of them, you drive a man out of business. I am sure that is what Harper is thinking. He would love to lay his hands on my land."

Andy had given up trying to argue that the only way Ethan could protect his hold on the land would be to buy it. He hoped the three sons were more accepting of a new idea.

Daggett rode out in front, the others trailing behind to prevent compromising the trail should Daggett lose it and have to circle back to hunt for it again. Late in the day the big Ranger halted abruptly, then signaled the others to come up.

He pointed and said, "Yonder they are."

A strung-out herd of cows plodded along at a slow, footsore pace. Their calves, of all sizes from babies to short yearlings, struggled to keep up. Most were in the dusty drags, behind the main herd.

Andy counted four riders with them. He considered the possibility that a fifth might be somewhere ahead, marking the route.

Andy looked to Daggett. "What do you think?"

Ethan spoke up sharply. "Charge into them. Kill every man and hope Harper Teal is among them."

Andy had little concern that he would be.

Daggett said, "Mr. McIntosh's got the right notion. Slam into them hard and fast. Maybe they'll be too rattled to put up much of a show."

Andy cautioned the McIntoshes, "You know that recklessness can get somebody killed."

Ethan was not moved. He said, "If you're scared, stay back and let my boys and me handle this. These are our cattle."

Andy said, "I'm talkin' about bein' cautious. You don't want to make an easy target. And remember that it's hard to hit what you aim at from a runnin' horse."

Daggett remained in the lead, holding the riders to an easy trot as they closed the distance. They were within two hundred yards before one of the herders looked back. He shouted a warning, and two of the men quickly turned their horses around. The other, up at point, was too far ahead to hear.

The thieves fired a couple of shots, then decided escape was the best option. They spurred their horses into a hard run, sweeping past the startled point rider. He followed but could not catch up.

Waving a pistol, Ethan leaned forward and let out a furious screech as he applied his spurs. Andy thought he felt a puff of wind as the old man raced by him. Then two Rangers and four McIntoshes were in full pursuit. The sheriff trailed a little.

Ethan drew up beside the point man and fired. The rider threw up his hands and tumbled from his running horse. Looking back, Andy saw the sheriff dismount beside the fallen rider. Daggett managed to pass Ethan and pull in beside another of the thieves. The rider fired at him but missed. Daggett put a bullet into him and brought him down.

The other two fugitives managed to draw more speed from their horses and gradually widened their lead. Daggett began slowing his horse. Andy followed suit as he felt his mount tiring. The three McIntosh sons had not been able to keep up with their father. Like the Rangers, they gave up the chase.

Ethan did not stop until he realized he was far out in front all by himself, losing ground to the remaining two thieves. He reined around and came back, cursing. "We could have gotten them to the last man if you hadn't all quit."

Daggett removed his hat and wiped a sleeve across his sweating forehead. "They were outrunnin' us. You'd've been in a fix if they'd turned about and come at you out there all by yourself."

"I would not," Ethan protested. "I would have killed them both."

Andy said impatiently, "We brought down two of them, and we got your herd back." He turned to look at Ethan's sons. "Anybody hurt?"

Ike's sleeve showed a streak of blood. He said, "Just nicked me a little. It was a lucky shot."

Daggett led the way back to examine the two fallen outlaws. He spent only a moment with the first, dismissing him with a motion that said he was dead. Sheriff Seymour stood beside the one Ethan had shot in the side.

Andy dismounted but saw that this man, too, was dead. He asked, "Did he say anything?"

Seymour said, "I hoped to ask him some questions, but he just groaned a time or two and died."

Ethan drew his horse close. His eyes were wild with lingering excitement as he leaned down to look at the fallen man. "Are you sure we can't make him talk?"

Andy gritted his teeth. "It's hard to get a man to tell you much after you've killed him."

Ethan was disappointed. "Damn the man for dying too quickly!"

Daggett said gruffly, "It was you that shot him."

Ike broke the tension by saying, "Papa, our cattle are scatterin'. Let's go see about them."

Ethan and his sons rode off to gather the herd.

Andy closed the outlaw's glazed eyes. He asked the sheriff, "Do you know him?"

"Yeah. I've had to jail him for fightin'. He's agreeable when he's sober, but he's a mean drunk."

"Did you look at the other one?"

"I know him. He's finished off many a Saturday night in a cell. He's a singin' drunk."

Daggett said, "Too bad those other two got away. I don't suppose you were able to see who they were?"

The sheriff grimaced. "With these old eyes of mine? All I could do is guess."

Andy asked, "And if you were to guess?"

"I'd guess Harold Pearcy and Sonny Vernon. But don't tell Ethan. He might hunt them down and shoot them without waitin' for judge and jury."

The McIntoshes brought the cattle together. Jake caught the two loose horses and led them to where Andy and Daggett waited. He studied the outlaw's face. "I've seen that man in town."

Seymour nodded. "Did you ever happen to notice who he palled around with?"

"Never paid that much attention. When I'm in town, I've got better things to do."

They hoisted the dead man onto one of the horses and rode to where the other lay. In his pocket Andy found a crumpled letter addressed to Colley Lamkin. He scanned the letter, written to remind Lamkin that he owned the writer money.

Ethan joined them shortly and said he knew neither of the men. "I do not waste my time becoming acquainted with lowlifes." He pointed toward the herd, and his eyes brightened. "They're mostly ours, all right, but a few of Harper Teal's are in there too. That's quite a joke on Harper. He sends thieves to steal my cattle and they take some of his as well."

Andy stifled a sudden impulse. There was probably some fool law against choking an old man, no matter how much he might deserve it.

The little posse had gone through the provisions Daggett and Seymour had brought. They found a bag of coffee beans and a small slab of bacon in an outlaw's blanket roll. Andy had no compunctions against eating a dead man's food. In this case it would otherwise be left for the coyotes. To hell with the coyotes, he thought. Let them catch a rabbit.

Daggett stared over a cup of coffee at the two men tied facedown across their horses. "They won't last long if we stay with the McIntoshes and this slow herd. We'd best carry them back to town as quick as we can."

Seymour said, "They had friends among a certain element. I'm afraid shootin' them won't make any of us popular with that crowd."

Daggett replied, "We wasn't sent here to be popular. We came to bring peace and quiet. That means if you have to kill some people, you do it."

Andy said, "Maybe these two are the last."

The sheriff grunted. "I wouldn't bet a plug of tobacco on that. At least old Ethan got his cattle back. I won't have to listen to him bellyache about me bein' too old for this job."

Andy asked, "Have you ever thought about sittin' in a rockin' chair on the porch and lettin' the world handle its troubles without you?"

"I think about it all the time, but I've got nothin' to retire on. Spent most of my life protectin' other people's property but never had a chance to get my own. Damned little money, either. So here I am, wore out like an old pair of boots. My eyesight is fadin', and I've got nothin' much to show for my life. There's old Ethan McIntosh with ranch and cattle that I've helped protect for him, bitchin' because I haven't done more. You watch, he'll soon holler for me to arrest Harper Teal."

Daggett pointed out, "Don't it strike you strange that the Teals would have somebody steal their own cattle?"

"It could be a way of coverin' up."

Andy said, "Or maybe neither family is implicated. Maybe somebody *is* tryin' to break both families."

The sheriff asked, "To what purpose?"

"So when the smoke clears, they can pick up the leavin's. Mason Gaines hinted as much."

"Gaines?" Seymour rubbed his chin. "I never did cotton to that carpetbagger. Never could trust a man who was always right."

Andy said, "He could be fannin' up trouble for his own reasons. Then again, it might not be him at all."

Seymour said, "There's aplenty of free rangers that have got no love for either family. My jail ain't big enough to hold them all."

Andy said, "If we can find the right one or two, maybe that'll put the quietus on what's left."

Daggett looked at the bodies tied over two horses. "Let's lope up and get them to town before they turn ripe. We've got no shovel."

Andy attended the funeral, not to mourn but to see who-all came. Among that group, he thought, might be some of the people responsible for the troubles. The crowd did not amount to much, however. Aside from the sheriff, Deputy Willis, and the two Rangers, the gathering numbered fewer than a dozen. Even the minister was reluctant, for he had never seen the two in church and knew little to say in their behalf. Instead he preached a sermon on the wages of sin and mentioned no names.

As the attendees dispersed, Andy and the sheriff watched two county employees begin shoveling dirt into the graves. Andy asked, "Did you see anybody you suspect?"

Seymour said, "I suspect just about everybody who

was here, not countin' the minister. He showed how little he knows about sin."

Editor Tolliver waited until the sheriff was gone before he approached Andy at the cemetery gate. "Might I trouble you for a few questions?" he asked.

"I don't know as I've got any answers."

"I am interested in how these two thieves came to their end."

Andy told of trailing the cattle and almost taking the culprits by surprise. "Ethan McIntosh shot the first one. Daggett got the second. We couldn't catch the others."

"Did anyone recognize the two who got away?"

Andy chose not to mention the sheriff's guess. "Never got close enough."

"And the two who were shot . . . did either of them say anything?"

"One lived a few minutes. The sheriff stopped to see about him but told us he was too far gone to talk."

"So you learned nothing about who might have been behind the taking of the cattle?"

"That's the size of it."

Tolliver's heavy mustache quivered. "Quite convenient, wouldn't you say, for anyone who might be a party to the trouble around here? The only identifiable thieves died without answering any questions."

Andy frowned. "If you're tryin' to say somethin', speak straight out."

"I hear that Ethan McIntosh has made some interesting accusations against Harper Teal."

"He's obsessed with an old grudge, and his mind is slippin'."

"I have long suspected that Sheriff Seymour has leaned more toward the Teals than the McIntoshes. He was Confederate, too. And you have only his word that the wounded outlaw said nothing. What if our esteemed sheriff did not want him to say anything?"

"Are you accusin' him?"

"Not at all. I am simply weighing the possibilities. Our sheriff is no longer young, and he faces an uncertain future. Lesser men in his position have succumbed to the temptation to profit from others' misfortunes."

"Whatever you print in your paper, you'd better be ready to back up with the evidence."

"That I shall, when and if the time comes. You may not recognize it, Pickard, but you and I are working in the same vineyard. We are both seekers after the truth."

Watching Tolliver walk back down toward town, Andy weighed the man's words. Yes, Seymour had been alone with the dying thief. If he had reason not to want the man to talk, he could easily have rushed the dying process.

Andy tried to dismiss what Tolliver had said, but the seed of doubt was germinating.

Andy and Daggett were having a late breakfast in the little hole-in-the-wall café, listening to proprietor Kennison propose solutions for the world's problems, when a rider swept by at a speed too reckless for a town street. Daggett exclaimed, "That's Carrie." He jumped up and rushed for the door. "Pay the man!" he shouted as he hurried out.

Andy dropped a handful of change on the table. It was too much, but he did not have time to wait for a count. He caught up to Daggett as Carrie jumped down from her sweat-streaked horse in front of the jail. Daggett's shout stopped her as she reached for the door. She turned, her face flushed with excitement.

The words tumbled out without allowing time for her to catch her breath. "Thank God, Logan, you're here. Our place got shot up in the wee hours this morning. We fought them off, but now Pa is on his way to the McIntoshes' ranch. He intends to have it out with Ethan McIntosh."

Daggett asked, "Are your brothers with him?"

"Yes. Somebody is going to be killed if you don't stop them."

Andy asked, "Anybody hurt?"

"One of our cowboys cut his arm on a broken window glass, is all. It was too dark for good aim, but we poured as much lead into them as they poured into us."

Daggett said, "Let's grab our horses. We'll have to ride hard to get to the McIntoshes' place first."

Andy said, "I don't think we can."

"We'll try, even if we kill two horses doin' it."

Editor Tolliver walked down the courthouse steps, attracted by Carrie's breathless manner. He said, "May I ask the occasion for all this excitement?"

Daggett said, "You tell him, Carrie. We ain't got time."

She protested, "I'm going with you."

"You've nearly killed that horse already. Best thing you can do now is to find the sheriff. Tell him what you told us, then go home."

The two Rangers hit a long trot toward the wagon yard.

# CHAPTER

## 8

Riding hard, Andy began hoping he and Daggett would reach the McIntoshes' ranch headquarters before the Teals. Sporadic gunfire told him they had not.

Daggett said, "Damned knotheads have already opened the ball."

Andy said, "Maybe nobody's dead yet."

He saw that the Teals were spread out afoot, taking refuge behind a wagon, behind a shed, beneath the windmill tower. Lacking clear targets, they fired at the main family house and the bunkhouse. Occasional answering shots came from the shattered windows. The invasion had taken the McIntoshes by surprise, without time to pull together in one defensive position.

Daggett did not hesitate. He held his horse to a hard trot and rode into the line of fire, waving his hat. His shout was like thunder. "Put those guns down! Stop this goddamned foolishness right now!"

Surprised by the older Ranger's audacity, Andy swallowed hard and followed him, his spine tingling in anticipation of a bullet.

Harper Teal rose up from behind a wagon. He lifted his

rifle and yelled, "Git out of the way, Daggett! You want to get shot?"

Daggett's stern voice resonated with authority. He said, "Harper Teal, you lay that rifle down." He turned toward the main house. "Ethan McIntosh, you get yourself out onto the porch. I want to talk to you. Right now!" He turned a fierce gaze back at the scattered Teal forces. "Anybody fires a shot, I'll kill him."

The combatants were so taken aback by Daggett's forceful presence that no one raised a protest. Most lowered their weapons, though they did not lay them down.

The front door opened slowly. Ethan McIntosh poked his gray head out and paused as if expecting to be shot.

Daggett said, "Come on out. There ain't nobody goin' to hurt you unless it's me. You hear that, Harper Teal? The same goes for you."

Teal did not reply, but he stepped from behind the wagon, holding his rifle at arm's length. Daggett told him to lay it on the ground.

Teal said, "First I want to see that Ethan's not heeled."

McIntosh, now farther out on the porch, raised both hands to his shoulders. "I've no weapon on me. But lest you take that as an opportunity for treachery, Harper Teal, there are more inside. They can cut out what little heart you have."

Teal put down his rifle and stepped into the open. "You Rangers have got no business here. This is a private matter."

Daggett said, "It stopped bein' private when the first shot was fired. It's you who've got no business here, Harper. You're trespassin' on McIntosh land."

"Ask Ethan about the trespassin' he did when him and his bunch raided our place after midnight."

McIntosh looked surprised. "Us? Not a soul left this place save for my son Jake. He sneaked off to town."

Lanny Teal left his refuge behind the windmill. He shouted, "Damn you, Jake, I've told you to stay away from Lucy!"

Jake burst out onto the porch. "You go to hell, Lanny. I'll see whoever I want to, whenever I want to."

McIntosh ordered his son back into the house. "There are matters of far greater importance here than your shallow infatuation. Take up your station in case they begin shooting again."

Jake obeyed resentfully, but only after declaring, "Someday, Lanny."

Lanny replied, "How about now?"

Harper Teal glared at Lanny. "Boy, I don't know what I'll ever do with you. We've come here to set things right, and all you've got on your mind is that scatterbrained schoolgirl. I'll bet she's never scalded a hog or wrung a chicken's neck."

Red-faced, Lanny came up with no suitable reply. He muttered under his breath and looked at the ground.

Daggett said to Harper, "Ethan McIntosh swears that whoever raided your place, it wasn't him or his outfit."

Teal flushed. "If you believe that, you're a bigger fool than I thought you was. He's been tellin' folks that me and my boys are behind the cattle stealin' and other such around here. Anybody with a lick of sense knows he's a liar. That wily old scoundrel's been tryin' for years to get my scalp. He'd do better to worry about his own."

Andy said, "The fight between you two is so old, I'll bet you don't even remember what started it."

"You'd lose the bet. It was over a nice piece of creek land. Him bein' a Yankee, the carpetbag government seen to it that he got it instead of me."

"You got yourself a good ranch in spite of that."

"With Ethan workin' against me all the way. He figures if he can run me off, he can grab what's mine. But I ain't goin' noplace. I'll still be here when he leaves, or when he's lowered into the ground. Either way would suit me fine."

McIntosh had gradually moved down from the porch, scowling. "You'll have to live to be a hundred before you see either event come to pass."

Teal no longer talked to Daggett or Andy. He turned his anger directly on McIntosh. "You damned old land hog, you ain't got nothin' I want, and you ain't gettin' anything I've got. If you don't quit accusin' us or sendin' night riders to shoot up our place, I'll put a couple more holes in you than the Lord intended."

Daggett faced Teal. "Everybody's said enough. Harper, I want you to take your boys and go home. Now!"

Teal seemed torn, but after trying to stare Daggett

down, he said, "All right, we'll go, but this thing ain't over. It looks to me like you've chosen who to crawl in bed with, so I'll thank you to never come back onto our place. As for Carrie, she's already had hurt enough in her life. I don't want you to ever speak to her again."

Andy started to intervene. "But it was Carrie—"

A dark look from Daggett stopped him from saying more.

Teal said, "You tell your McIntosh friends that the next time they come shootin', they'd better bring along a minister. They'll need him to preach the funerals." He made a sweeping motion with his arm. "Come on, boys. There'll be another day."

The Teals mounted up. All three of McIntosh's sons came out onto the porch, guns in their hands. The old man stood in the yard, where he and Teal had faced each other. He complained, "Is that all you Rangers are going to do? Look what they've done to my house. Look at the bullet holes."

Daggett was trying hard to keep his emotions under control. He gave the old man a look of disgust but choked down whatever he was aching to say. Andy said it for him: "Be glad there's no bullet holes in any of you. Or are there?"

Ethan said, "Not a scratch. It will be a cold day in July before the Teals ever get the upper hand over us. We'll wipe out the whole bunch someday."

Andy said, "You ought not to talk like that. People might get to thinkin' you mean it."

"Hell, I do mean it."

Andy had come to regard Ike as the most sensible of the McIntoshes. He turned to him. "Maybe you can talk to your father."

Ike was still on edge. He said, "They had no call to come down on us like they done, hollerin' and shootin'."

"Somebody raided them. They thought it was you."

Ike shook his head. "It wasn't, and that's the truth. We were all here last night except Jake, and Papa told you where he was."

"Then maybe you'd better give some thought to who it was, and the reason they did it."

Ethan declared, "It wasn't anybody but that old boar hog and his litter. He was lying through his teeth."

Andy heard the impact of a bullet on human flesh a split second before he heard the crack of a rifle somewhere out in the brush, in the direction the Teals had taken. Ethan doubled over, clutching his side and gasping for breath. Ike rushed to him.

"Papa!" Easing his father to the ground, Ike turned an anguished gaze toward Andy and Daggett. "He's been hit."

Daggett wheezed, "Damn! I didn't think Harper would do it." He dropped onto his knees beside the old man as two women came rushing from the house. He looked up at Andy. "Let's get him inside before they fire again. Let's get everybody inside."

Quickly they carried Ethan into the house and placed him on his high-backed bed. The bullet's impact had knocked the breath from him. He struggled to regain it. McIntosh's wife Agatha tore his shirt open and unbuttoned the front of his long underwear. The bullet had cut a gash across the ribs. It was bleeding.

Ike asked frantically, "Do you think it went into his lung?"

Such a wound was often fatal, if not immediately, then more slowly through pneumonia. Agatha examined the damage. "I don't think so. It appears to me that he might have a broken rib or two, but nothing he's apt to die of."

At the moment she was the calmest of the McIntoshes. She said, "The Indians couldn't kill him. Rebel bullets couldn't do it. He's not about to leave us now because I won't stand for it." She pointed to the door. "Patience and me will get him ready. Ike, don't you and the boys just stand there. Go hitch up the wagon so we can take him to the doctor."

His face grim, Daggett motioned to Andy. "Let's catch up to the Teals. We'll see if they can explain that shot."

Stepping out onto the porch, Andy said, "We don't have to catch up. Bud and Lanny are comin' back."

The two Teal brothers stopped their horses a little short of the porch. They were clearly agitated. Bud said accusingly, "I thought you Rangers were goin' to see that nobody shot at us."

"Nobody did. Not here."

"Somebody fired a shot. Lucky it didn't hit any of us."

Daggett's voice was severe. "It hit Ethan."

Bud's jaw dropped. "Ethan? I swear, Ranger, it wasn't none of our bunch done it. We figured one of the McIntoshes fired at us."

Daggett's fists were clenched. "You wouldn't lie to me, would you?"

Bud said, "Lyin' is against our religion. I'll swear on the Bible in front of all the McIntoshes."

Andy said, "Maybe another time and place. Right now the McIntoshes wouldn't believe you if you swore on a whole stack of Bibles. You'd best be goin' before they decide to take up their guns again."

Bud hesitated. "How bad is the old man hurt?"

"He'll live. But this won't improve his disposition any."

Watching them leave, Daggett muttered, "I wish I could believe them, but who else would take a shot at Ethan?"

Sheriff Seymour came along shortly. He said, "I met the Teals out yonder a ways. Is the trouble over with?"

Andy said, "For today, it looks like."

"Anybody hurt?"

"Ethan took a bullet across his ribs. They're fixin' to haul him to town. Naturally he blames the Teals. He's talkin' crazy."

"Nothin' new there. Him and Harper both talk crazy when it's about each other. Sometimes I'm tempted to go off on a long huntin' trip and let nature take its course. Things might get quiet around here afterward."

Andy said, "A graveyard is quiet, too, but who wants a big graveyard?" He considered the shot that came from the brush. He asked Seymour, "Did you see anybody besides the Teals as you rode in?"

"Nary a soul."

Andy reluctantly thought of editor Tolliver and the suspicion he had aroused about the sheriff. Seymour could have fired that shot before he showed himself. He tried to push the thought from his mind, but it would not leave him.

Daggett brooded. "There was a time when I wouldn't take a cussin' like the one I got from Harper Teal. I must be gettin' old."

Andy said, "He was mad. Maybe when he cools down, he'll see things different."

Seymour said, "Old men can be awful stubborn. I know, because I'm gettin' there myself."

*Just getting there?* Andy thought.

Daggett's eyes widened as a new idea struck him. "I wonder where Rodock was, him and that rifle."

Andy, Daggett, and Seymour accompanied Jake and Ike as they and the two women carried Ethan to town in a wagon. The doctor gave the old man a preliminary examination and declared, "You probably don't deserve it, Ethan, but you could live to be a hundred. After I treat your wound, it would be a good idea for you to stay around town a few days. We will want to be sure you'll not develop blood poisoning."

Ethan roared, "Stay in town? Hell no. We have no intention of throwing away good money on a hotel room. The boys and the womenfolks are taking me right back home where I belong."

The doctor said, "It is obvious that the bullet did no damage to your lungs. I am giving you my best advice."

"And at no bargain price, I'll wager. What this town needs is another doctor, a good one."

The doctor said, "It would also need patients with judgment enough to listen to him."

Agatha said, "Ethan hasn't listened to anybody but me in all these years, and not always me. Many's the time I've considered divorce, but there's my family to think of. So I just let him rant and pay no attention to him. We'll stay in town like you said, Doctor."

Movement was painful for Ethan. He indulged in heavy profanity as his sons helped him get up and out to the wagon. He complained as they placed him on spread-out blankets and was still complaining as the wagon rolled down the street toward the hotel.

Watching, the doctor commented to Andy and Daggett, "I thought you Rangers came to bring peace. I believe I have seen more bullet wounds, bruises, and abrasions since you got here than before you arrived."

Sheriff's Deputy Willis put down a whittling stick and pushed to his feet from a bench outside the saloon as Andy and Daggett approached. He said, "The sheriff asked me to keep an eye on Rodock." He jerked his thumb toward the saloon door. "He's in there."

Daggett asked, "Has he been there long?"

"Not very. He just came out of the hotel a little while ago. He headed straight for here."

"Can you say for sure that he was in the hotel all night?"

"Well, pretty certain. He was playin' poker in the saloon early in the evenin'. I got tired of watchin' him clip a couple of farmers, so I went home about ten, eleven o'clock. I figured he wasn't goin' nowhere."

"You might've figured wrong. He could've left right after you did."

Rodock was sitting alone at a table when Andy and Daggett walked in. He was playing solitaire and appeared only marginally interested in the cards. He yawned as Daggett approached him. He said, "Pull up a chair and set yourself down. You can choose the game."

Daggett remained standing. "Where have you been all day?"

"I indulged in a game of chance till the wee hours. I've spent most of the day in bed."

"Alone?"

A wry smile crossed Rodock's face. "You don't think I'd sully an innocent woman's name by using her for an alibi, do you?"

"If she was with you, she couldn't be too damned innocent."

"The fact is, there wasn't any woman. I was by myself. Is there a reason I need an alibi?"

"The Teal ranch got raided last night. Considerin' your line of work, I thought you might've left some boot tracks out there."

Rodock betrayed no reaction. Calmly he declared, "One unfortunate result from my so-called line of work is that any time something happens, people jump to the conclusion that I was involved. Why should I raid someone's ranch? What would be in it for me?"

"That's a question I'd like the answer to."

The solitaire game went against Rodock. He shuffled the cards and said, "My horse is in the wagon yard. He was there last night and has been there all day. You can ask that hay shaker, Scanlon. He'll tell you."

"Somebody could've lent you a horse."

"Do you intend to arrest me?"

"If I get some proof."

"In the meantime, I assume that you do not care to join me in a game?"

"I think we've been playin' one right along."

Rodock gave him a cold smile and began laying out the cards again. Daggett motioned for Andy to follow him outside. Andy said, "You're figurin' he could've been part of that raid on the Teals."

"Not for fun. I'm bettin' somebody paid him. Maybe Old Man McIntosh."

Andy argued, "He swore that nobody except Jake was away from his ranch last night."

"That could be the truth, as far as it goes. But the first year I went to school, I learned that two and two add up to four. Ethan vowed revenge right in front of us when we got his cows back. You heard him. He could've hired Rodock and some others to do the job for him. That way the only dirt on his hands would come from countin' out the money."

Andy could not stop thinking about the sheriff. "It could be somebody else entirely."

"It could, but right now my money's on Ethan."

"If it was Rodock, and Ethan paid him, how come he took a shot at Ethan?"

"Maybe he missed his target. He might've been shootin' at me."

"Does he hate you that much?"

"Only half as much as I hate him." Daggett lapsed into a thoughtful silence. He brushed aside some wood shavings and sat on the bench the deputy had vacated. He stared off at nothing in particular. Finally he said, "That damned Rodock. I've got half a mind to walk in there and shoot him."

"You don't know it was him. You're only guessin'."

"Even if it wasn't, he's earned a good killin' twenty times over. The old-time vigilantes had the right idea. Hang them quick and hang them high."

"You're not talkin' like a lawman."

"I'm talkin' like a lawman who's brought in more than my share of bad men, only to watch pettifoggin' lawyers and judges turn them loose. Put enough lead in one of them, and you're shed of him for good."

"The Rangers don't do it that way."

"No? Have you never seen a Ranger tell a man to run, then shoot him and claim he tried to escape?"

Andy had, a few times. The incidents had left him shaken, though he understood the frustrations that led to them. He said, "Maybe we've moved past that kind of thing. Maybe we've come into a better time."

"Not till they shut down the last jail for lack of business."

Toward sundown, Carrie Teal came up the street in a buckboard. She had a couple of carpetbags under the seat. Spotting Daggett and Andy on a bench in front of the general store, she reined the horses toward them. Daggett arose quickly, taking off his hat and walking out to meet her. He said, "I thought you went home."

She was plainly distressed. "I did, but I couldn't stay."

"How come?"

"Pa figured out that I sent you Rangers to the McIntosh place. He raised a terrible row. My brothers took up for me, and I saw that there was about to be a fight. I had to get away."

"What do you plan to do?"

"Take a room in the hotel until he calms down."

"What if he doesn't?"

"Then I'll try to find work here in town."

"I don't think he'd stand still for that. He's liable to come roarin' in here to drag you home."

Her voice was stern. "Then there *will* be a fight."

Daggett took hold of her hands. "If you need any money . . ."

"I have a little. It wouldn't look right, taking money from you. People would talk."

"Let them talk." Daggett turned to Andy. "I'll escort her over to the hotel and see that they give her a decent room."

Andy said, "People *will* talk, sure enough."

"It'll give them somethin' to do with their idle time."

Editor Tolliver stepped out of the saloon and watched the buckboard moving away with Carrie and Daggett on the seat. He said, "It appears to me that Daggett has chosen his side."

Andy said, "Rangers don't take sides."

"Almost everybody takes sides. I thought by his reputation that Daggett was made of cast iron, but I see he has a soft spot in his armor. It will not sit well with the McIntosh faction."

"He's just tryin' to be a gentleman, that's all."

"Daggett a gentleman? That challenges credulity."

Andy was not sure he understood what Tolliver had said, but he chose not to ask. Tolliver would probably tell him at considerably more length than Andy chose to hear.

Tolliver said, "What more can you tell me about events at the Teals' and McIntoshes' places?"

Andy had told him nothing, but he knew the sheriff had. He said, "Nobody got killed." He was used to filing terse reports that wasted no words. He saw no need to give Tolliver more. The man would probably fill out the story from imagination anyway. Reading his newspaper, Andy had noticed that his writing was not handicapped by facts.

Tolliver said, "It would appear that events are building toward a violent climax. I suspect I shall soon have much to write about."

Andy began to anger. "Is that what you're hopin' for? More killin' so you can have a bigger story?"

"Most great literature is grounded in violence and tragedy. This situation could yield a book that would rank my name up there with Irving and Twain. It has Rangers, vigilantes, gunfights, everything but Indians. I might put in a few of those for extra color."

Andy had not read many books. He had never heard of Irving or Twain. "If I was you, I wouldn't start countin' the money just yet."

He did not see Daggett until he was about to bed down on his wagon yard cot. Daggett was silent as he walked into the little circle of lantern light, his mind on matters far away. Andy waited for him to say something, then asked, "Did you get Carrie settled in the hotel?"

Daggett was jarred back to reality. "Yes, and took her to supper. We had us a long talk afterward."

"Has she decided what to do?"

"She has, me and her together. What would you think about standin' up with me in the mornin' while I get married?"

"Married!" Andy blinked in surprise. "I'd think you were movin' way too fast. Are you sure you've thought this through?"

"I've thought on it a right smart. Her comin' to town just brought things to a head sooner than I expected."

"Where would you take her, and where would you live? Rangers travel around an awful lot."

"You're married."

"I don't get much time to spend with my wife."

Daggett was not moved. "Maybe I've been a Ranger long enough. Maybe it's time I find somethin' else to do. I could run a ranch for somebody, or open a store in town."

Andy could imagine Daggett on a ranch, but not running a store. He said, "Have you thought how Harper Teal will take this? You know what he said about you and Carrie, and about not settin' foot on the Teal ranch again."

"Once we're married, there won't be much he can do."

"Except maybe shoot you. He's already had one son-in-law that he hated."

"He can't hold a grudge forever."

"He's had a grudge against Ethan McIntosh ever since the war. And what about the McIntoshes? They'll figure you've thrown in with the Teals."

"I can't help that. It's high time they put their damnfool feud aside."

"They've got too much invested in it to quit."

Andy was not convinced that Daggett realized what he was getting himself in for. He said, "You told me you were married once. What makes you think it'll work out this time if it didn't before?"

Daggett seemed to retreat back in time. His face creased, and his eyes seemed to be looking at something far away. "It would have worked the first time if I hadn't been away too much. There came a day when I was gone, and an outlaw I was huntin' for decided to hunt for *me*. He didn't find me at home, but he found my wife."

Andy guessed the rest from the savage expression on Daggett's face. "What did you do?"

"What any man would do. I hunted him down and killed him." Daggett looked away. "But it didn't bring her back to life."

# CHAPTER

# 9

Daggett had intended that the wedding be private, that it not be noised about. He did not consider the drawing power of his name, however. The minister was a jovial sort who loved a crowd and saw to it that the word was spread around town. By ten o'clock in the morning more people had gathered than his little church could comfortably seat. Daggett grumbled about not wanting it to turn into a spectacle.

Sheriff Seymour was there, his expression dour as he watched the McIntosh family gathering. They had remained in town until the doctor was convinced that Ethan's wound would not become life-threatening. Seymour said, "I don't see a happy face amongst the whole bunch. They're figurin' you Rangers have crawled into the blankets with the enemy."

*Just one of us,* Andy thought. He knew Daggett had been leaning in that direction almost from the first. He said, "I haven't taken sides, and I don't intend to."

"But if worst comes to worst, are you strong enough to stand up to a man like Daggett?"

Andy answered honestly, "I don't know."

Editor Tolliver walked from his office to the church. He

wore a tailored suit. A pair of leather gloves covered the ink stains on his hands. He said jovially, "Too bad there's nobody in the McIntosh family for *you* to marry, Pickard. That would help balance the equation."

"Even if there was, I doubt that I could get my wife to agree to it."

The minister's wife sat down at the piano and began to play. Daggett looked as if he had indigestion. Andy said, "You're supposed to smile."

"I didn't figure on this bein' a show."

Andy walked up the aisle alongside Daggett, pondering the possibility that Daggett might break and run. Carrie appeared from a side room at the rear of the church. In lieu of her father, storekeeper Babcock walked with her, holding her arm. Her dress was plain, probably one she customarily wore to church. But Andy gave no thought to that. It was the woman herself who caused his jaw to drop.

He had not considered Carrie beautiful, but she was radiant now, her smile bright as sunrise. Daggett's hand shook as he grasped her fingers and the minister began the ritual.

The ceremony was mercifully short. Self-consciously Daggett kissed the bride, then hurried her out through a side door to escape the crowd. A few people shouted congratulations, and a couple offered off-color suggestions that might have prompted Daggett to turn and administer punishment had he been less eager to get away.

Turning toward the door, Andy saw Rodock. He immediately looked for a firearm. Rodock said, "Don't worry. I am not carrying. I respect the solemnity of an occasion such as this."

"I'm surprised to see you here at all."

"I like to attend weddings. They remind me not to repeat my most unfortunate mistake, marriage."

"It didn't work out?"

"My way of life was incompatible with hers. She did me the great favor of running away with a dry goods drummer. I fear that Daggett is in for a longer sentence than mine was. Unless I kill him."

"Why would you do that?"

"At the time we had our set-to many years ago, I was hired to do a job. It was strictly business, nothing personal. Unfortunately, I underestimated his instincts for self-preservation. Then it became personal."

Andy frowned. "He thinks you're here on business now."

"My business, young friend, is always confidential."

As Rodock walked away, Judge Zachary approached, smoking a black cigar. He said, "Andy, I hope you know that Rodock is a dangerous man. I would give him room if I were you."

"How do you come to know him?"

"As county judge, it is my business to keep an eye on dangerous men who come into my community. He may stand before my bench one day."

*If he and Daggett don't kill each other,* Andy thought.

The judge said, "I've been expecting you to drop in for a

visit at my ranch some evening. I would like to hear about your years as a captive of the Indians."

"I never felt like a captive. I was just one of them."

"All the more interesting."

A small group of well-wishers surrounded the newly married couple. A nervous Daggett beckoned Andy with a subtle crooking of a finger. "Would you bring my stuff over from the wagon yard to the hotel? Me and Carrie will stay there a few days till we find somethin' a little more permanent."

"There won't be no place permanent as long as you're a Ranger. I hope you explained that to her. She's lived in one place all her life."

"It'll be a big change for both of us, but we're strong."

"Right now, you don't look like you could whip an old man with a broken arm."

"You want to try me, Pickard?"

Andy grinned. "It's too pretty a day for a fight." His grin faded as he realized that Harper Teal might come to town before the day was over, looking for his daughter. There might indeed be a fight.

He looked around for Sheriff Seymour but could not see him. The lawman had mentioned the possibility of leaving town for a long hunting trip. Right now, Andy had rather be with him wherever he was than to be waiting here for the unpredictable.

The Teals arrived in the middle of the afternoon, Harper flanked by his sons and two cowboys. Andy heard the commotion and walked out into the street to meet them. Harper reined up and faced Andy with narrowed, flinty eyes that could kill cotton at thirty paces. He demanded, "Do you know where my daughter's at? I'm here to take her home."

Andy tensed. "I don't believe she'll want to go."

"That's none of your business. She'll do what I tell her to."

"Yesterday, maybe. Things are different today."

"What do you mean, different?"

"You'll have to ask her."

"I will. Where's she at?"

Andy pointed. "The hotel. She's probably expectin' you. I was."

Harper rode around Andy. His sons and the cowboys followed but let him ride a couple of lengths ahead. Andy walked alongside Bud's horse. He said, "Your daddy is fixin' to get a surprise. I don't know how he'll take it. You'd better stay close and not let him do somethin' he'll be sorry for."

"I don't think he's ever been sorry about anything. Except maybe not shootin' Ethan McIntosh back when it was legal to kill a Yankee."

By the time Harper reached the hotel, several bystanders had fallen in behind to watch. One was Jefferson Tolliver, with the eagerness of a man awaiting a show.

Andy thought, *Whatever happens, he'll write it up twice as big as it really is.*

Harper stopped just short of the hotel steps and shouted,

"Carrie! I know you're in there. Come on out. You're goin' home."

Carrie did not answer. Harper shouted again.

Andy muttered to Bud, "With all due respect, your daddy's got the manners of an Arkansas mule."

Bud took no offense. "And the stubbornness."

Carrie appeared in the doorway, a dour Daggett at her side, his arm locked with hers. He was unarmed. She said quietly, "Hello, Pa. You didn't have to arouse the whole town. You could have come in and knocked on my door like a gentleman."

"I'm gentleman enough to know that my daughter doesn't belong in a town like this. It's time you went home."

She said, "You drove me away yesterday. You said things I never thought I would hear from you."

"You sicced the Rangers onto us. I was mad."

"So was I. You're still mad, but I'm not."

Harper turned his anger on Daggett. "Ranger, I told you to stay away from my daughter. It appears like you didn't hear me."

"You were plenty loud. I heard you."

"But here you are with her, and in a hotel! I've got every right to kill you."

"You've lost any rights you had over her. Carrie and I are married."

Harper's face froze. Slowly and deliberately he dismounted. Daggett motioned for Carrie to remain where she was, then moved down the steps and faced Harper on the ground. He said, "She's still your daughter. But more than that, she's my wife."

A screeching sound escaped from Harper's throat. He brought up a hard fist and drove it into Daggett's chin. Daggett staggered backward, falling on the steps. He arose quickly, his eyes wild and dangerous. He knotted a fist and drew it back. But somehow he called up enough control to stay his hand. His voice crackled. "You're her daddy, so I'll grant you that one. But don't you try for a second."

Bud and Cecil were on the ground immediately, holding their father's arms. "Pa," Bud said, "you don't want to make a show of yourself, fightin' in the street. Besides, he can whip you."

"He'll play hell." Harper tried to shake loose, but his sons held him firmly.

Bud argued, "Daggett's a good man. It won't be like it was with Skeen."

Harper seethed. "Don't you mention that name ever again."

Andy said, "You boys had better get him home."

Harper quit struggling. He lifted his gaze to Carrie, still up on the porch. His voice dropped back to a normal level. "All right then, you've made your bed. Now lay in it. I don't ever want to see you again."

Carrie stood straight and proud. "Pa, you don't mean that."

"I never say what I don't mean."

Her face grim, Carrie folded her arms. "Then, so be it."

Harper said, "Come on, boys, let's go. I don't have a daughter no more, and you ain't got a sister." He climbed into the saddle.

Bud hung back to speak to Carrie. "Sorry, sis. Maybe he'll change his mind once he's got past his mad."

She stood firm. "How many times did you ever see him change his mind?"

Daggett climbed the steps and gently put his arms around her. "Come on back inside. We've got a lot to talk about." They disappeared inside the hotel. Andy watched the Teals ride down the street and out of town. Anger welled up inside of him over Harper's bullheadedness. It gave way after a bit to sorrow for Carrie. He wished he could say something to comfort her, but that was for Daggett to do.

He looked up to the hotel's second story. He saw Ethan McIntosh and his wife Agatha, watching from a window. They had witnessed the whole event. Likely as not, Ethan had reveled in it.

Tolliver held a stub pencil and scribbled on a pad of paper. Angrily Andy said, "Ain't you bein' awful nosy?"

Tolliver kept writing. "A newspaperman has a special dispensation to be nosy. The people deserve to know all the news."

Andy had pondered over Judge Zachary's invitation to come out to his place for a visit. Stableman Scanlon told him how to find the Zachary ranch. "It's just a couple of miles out on that trail yonder." He pointed.

The ranch was not large by Teal or McIntosh standards. The house was a small and simple frame dwelling with a little gingerbread trim around the front but little other ornamentation. The judge sat in a rocking chair on the porch. He probably had not been home long.

He bade Andy to dismount and come up on the porch to join him. "I have some Kentucky bourbon inside if you care to indulge."

Andy declined. "I hardly ever drink anything stronger than coffee."

"I can fire up the stove and fix that."

"It's too warm for coffee. I just wanted to see this place. The sheriff has been tellin' me about it. He says you're a lucky man."

"I am. This little ranch has been a refuge to me, a real treasure."

"Doesn't it get lonely?"

"For someone else, perhaps, but not for me. No matter how tiresome the day has been, I can sit here and watch my cattle grazing. Evenings I often see deer venturing out of the thickets to browse. And listen to the birds sing! They are infinitely more pleasing than the idle chatter of so many foolish people."

Andy said, "I don't think they're always singin'. They're warnin' each other to stay away from their territory. Just like people."

"I like to think they are singing. I have always hated strife."

"Bein' a judge, I guess you've seen a lot of that."

"Far too much. There have been some who have said my court has been too strict, longer on punishment than on mercy. But sometimes it is necessary in the interest of law and order. There is right, and there is wrong. The line between them is as stark as a stone wall, but there are still those among us who do not recognize it. That is why I like this place so much. No arguments, no strife." He smiled. "Except perhaps among the birds."

Andy thought of Bethel, and how much he wanted to give her a place like this. He mentally calculated how much he had saved in a bank in Austin. Maybe that place was closer than he thought.

He asked, "How come you never got married?"

Zachary pondered a moment. "I answered my country's call and went off to war. By the time I came back, the girl I wanted had married someone else. For a long time I shied away from likely women. Then one day I looked in the mirror, and an old man looked back at me. I realized I had waited too long. But the bachelor life has its own compensations. Were I married, I would probably have to live in town instead of here in this place of rest and solitude."

Andy had been wondering about Sheriff Seymour. He had not seen him since yesterday. He found Deputy Willis sitting in the sheriff's chair, his feet on the desk. The deputy was whittling on a stick, letting the shavings litter the floor. Willis seemed startled at the sound of footsteps, then relaxed when he saw that they were not made by the sheriff.

"Oh," he said, "it's you. I thought maybe Pete was back."

Andy asked, "Back from where?"

"A settler south of here reported losin' some stock. He couldn't be sure when they were taken. Might've been the McIntoshes, or it might've been the Teals that took them."

Andy said, "It's hard to believe either family was responsible."

"I can see how you might not want the Teals involved, now that your partner is a Teal in-law. You're lettin' your feelin's get in the way of your judgment."

"I've eaten at both families' tables and slept in their bunkhouses. Have you?"

"No, personally I've never had much use for either side. They're too rich, and got too much land. The way I see it, everybody ought to have about the same, nobody rich and nobody poor."

"The world doesn't work that way."

"It sure as hell don't. What have you got, Ranger, besides a job and a wage? No more than me, I'll bet. I've shoved a poor man's boots under the supper table as long as I can remember. If things don't change, I'll still be doin' it when I'm an old man."

"You can't take it out on the Teals and the McIntoshes. They've got their good side, like most people."

"Billy the Kid must've had a good side, too. I'll bet he was kind to his horses." Willis cursed suddenly and jerked his right hand away from the stick. His thumb was bleeding. "Damn! I was lookin' away and cut myself." He sucked on his thumb and spat blood at a spittoon but missed. He said, "That's a lesson for both of us. When you're doin' a job, don't look away."

The sheriff had not returned by dark. Andy visited the saloons and found people still talking about the confrontation between Daggett and Harper Teal. Their conversations dried up quickly when Andy came within hearing.

Editor Tolliver was engaged in a poker game. He had the largest stack of chips on the table. He gave Andy a sly smile. "I don't suppose you have seen your partner tonight, Ranger. I suspect that he is rather busy with his new duties."

Sarcastically Andy said, "I suppose you intend to write all about it?"

"No, in regard to certain matters, silence is best. I would not wish to shock elderly ladies or confuse our youngest readers."

Andy fantasized about forcing Tolliver to eat several copies of his newspaper, though he restrained himself from any effort to bring the dream to reality. He read the cards in Tolliver's hand and said, "I hope you don't expect to bluff your way through with two queens."

He left Tolliver red-faced and trying too late to hide his hand.

Sheriff Seymour limped into town toward noon the next day, dusty, droop-shouldered, and near exhaustion. He stopped at a horse trough and pumped fresh water into his cupped hands to drink, then removed his hat and doused his head. The water cut trails through the dust on his face.

Andy trotted to meet him as Seymour turned back

toward the open street. He asked, "What's happened to you? Where's your horse?"

Seymour seated himself on the edge of the trough. "Got him shot out from under me." He scowled. "Ain't there nobody travelin' today? I never met so much as a freight wagon all the way in. I could've used a ride."

Looking tired enough to fall, he drank more water, then explained. "I was lookin' for some stolen cattle. Caught up to them south of here. There was four men drivin' them."

"Recognize any?"

"Never got close enough to be sure. I was two maybe three hundred yards away when one of them leveled a rifle at me and killed my horse. Pinned my leg under him. I managed to work my saddle gun free and take a shot at them, but I don't know if I hit anybody. I was half the night workin' my leg out from under my horse."

"Any idea whose cattle they were?"

"Never got close enough to see any brands except for one cow that dropped off and shelled out a baby. She was wearin' the McIntosh Bar F. That made me figure the Teals might've been responsible."

"Except that the Teals were in town yesterday."

Seymour shook his head. "Damn! I thought I had it all figured out."

Andy said, "I'll bet you're hungry. It's just a few steps over to the chili joint."

Seymour nodded. "Ain't eaten since breakfast yesterday. A pox on them boys."

"You say you don't know who they were?"

"Not for certain. Two of them took off arunnin'. The two who hung back and shot at me could've been Harold Pearcy and Sonny Vernon. Like I say, my eyes are none too good anymore."

While the sheriff put away two eggs and a slab of steak, Andy told him of the events he had missed. Seymour listened intently to the account of the wedding and the confrontation with Harper Teal. He said, "If I was Daggett, I'd ask Ranger headquarters to give me a different assignment, away from here. When Harper Teal gets really mad, he loses all sense of judgment. He could've shot Daggett. For that matter, he might've shot his own daughter."

"He wouldn't do anything that crazy."

"He's capable. They say in the war he killed two Yankee cannon crews, turned the cannons around, and fired them at the bluecoats. They say he got shot twice but was too stubborn to bleed."

Andy had long since learned to take war stories with a grain of salt. He said, "So you've got no idea who was stealin' the cattle?"

"If it wasn't the Teals, I haven't got the slightest notion. I'd almost swear that Vincent Skeen had come back to life, if I hadn't seen him layin' dead in his cell."

Andy said, "Maybe it's Skeen's ghost, come back to bedevil you for lettin' a mob kill him in your jail."

Seymour snorted. "A ghost?"

"Indians believe in them. Who can say for sure that they're wrong? The Comanches were afraid of dead men's spirits. They thought they came back to do mischief."

"I don't believe in anything I can't see, and I've never seen a ghost."

"You've never seen the wind, but you've felt it. You know it's real."

"All right, you look for a ghost. I'll look for a live human bein' with no compunctions about other people's property."

Andy said, "I don't really believe in ghosts, either, but I lived with the Indians long enough to know there are things out there that we can't see or understand. Maybe one of Skeen's accomplices has taken up his idea."

"That makes more sense than some ghost spirit."

Andy nodded. "But you can't see an idea, either."

"You stayed with the Indians too long."

Andy had dropped off to sleep on a cot under the wagon yard's hay shed when someone shook his shoulder. He came awake reaching for the pistol beneath his blanket. An unfamiliar voice whispered, "Ranger, come with me."

Andy could see only a vague shape in the darkness. "Who are you?"

"Harold Pearcy. You know me. Come on, we need you."

"In the middle of the night?"

"It ain't my choice, either. I'll saddle your horse for you while you get dressed."

"I'm dressed now except for my boots, and I'll saddle my own horse. Where are we goin'?"

"To the doctor's house first. He won't come with me unless you do. Sonny Vernon needs him real bad."

Andy remembered them. The hapless pair had jumped on Lanny Teal while he was fighting with Jake McIntosh. The two had impressed Andy as potential candidates for the penitentiary. Saddling his horse, he asked, "What happened to Sonny?"

"I'll tell you about it while we travel. There's too many ears around here, and everybody don't need to know."

They rode side by side to the doctor's house. The doctor had just finished harnessing a horse to his buggy. He said, "Thanks for coming, Ranger. I could not get this young man to tell me much, and I had no intention of leaving town with him unless I had the strong arm of the law by my side."

Andy said, "I don't think either one of us ought to go anywhere till he tells us what this is about."

Reluctantly Pearcy said, "Sonny's wounded. I thought he'd get better, but he's worse. I'm afraid he's fixin' to die without he gets proper doctorin'."

Andy asked, "How did he come to get wounded?"

Pearcy hesitated. "We was drivin' cattle when somebody come chasin' up from behind us like he meant business."

Andy asked, "Who?"

"We didn't go back and ask him. There was a little shootin', and Sonny got hit. I snuck him away so nobody would see he was hurt. I didn't want the regulators comin' after him."

"Why should they?"

"Truth is, me and Sonny been ridin' with them some.

They're hell on secrecy. You know what they done to Callender and Bigelow. They'd do the same to Sonny and me. I decided the best thing was to leave the country with him. But we didn't get very far."

Andy asked, "How far?"

"To that sheep outfit of Old Man Hawkins's. Him and his wife, they done what they could for Sonny, but it's not enough."

Andy suspected that Pearcy had been with the night riders who had struck the Hawkinses' place some nights earlier. He asked with sarcasm, "Are you sure you know the way in the dark?"

Pearcy was not sharp enough to catch the irony. He said, "Sure, I been there before."

Andy asked, "Which one of you killed the sheriff's horse?"

Pearcy grunted. "The sheriff? Is that who was after us?"

"It was."

"I didn't want to have no killin' hangin' over me, so I shot at his horse. We thought he might keep after us afoot, but he didn't."

"The horse pinned him down. When he got free, he had to walk all the way back to town."

"I'll bet he's mad at us."

"He is, except he doesn't know who you are. Yet."

Pearcy worried, "He'll figure it out, and the regulators will, too. Me and Sonny took those cattle for our own selves, without askin' anybody. The regulators warned us against goin' out on our own."

They reached the Hawkinses' place at daybreak, the doctor following close in his buggy. The sheep were still in the corral where Hawkins kept them at night for safety from predators. The dog came off the porch, barking.

The front door opened a couple of inches. A man peered out cautiously, then moved onto the porch, a rifle in his hands. Hawkins said, "Andy Pickard, is that you?"

"It's me. The doctor is right behind us."

Hawkins watched the buggy come to a stop. He said, "Pearcy, you better help the doctor with his bag and anything else he may need."

Pearcy dropped the reins. Andy half expected the horse to run away, but it was trained to stand ground hitched. Andy suspected it was stolen, for Pearcy was not bright enough to school a horse.

Hawkins held the door open until the doctor and Andy entered the house. Pearcy carried the bag in, then went back outside to take the horses to the barn. Hawkins's wife was in the kitchen, poking wood into the range and setting a coffeepot on to boil. Hawkins pointed to a small bedroom. "The boy's in there, Doctor. The bullet's too deep for us to get at it. Maybe you can do better."

Sonny was unconscious. Without even feeling his forehead, Andy knew he was running a high fever.

Hawkins said, "I tried to get Pearcy to fetch you right after they got here, Doctor, but he was afraid. These boys are in over their heads."

Andy said, "They've put you at risk by comin' here. The regulators may be afraid they've told you too much."

Hawkins said, "They haven't told me a thing. I've always tried to keep to myself and avoid being entangled in any of the troubles around here. But they have landed on my doorstep nevertheless. As a Christian I could not turn these boys away. Who knows? I may be entertaining an angel unaware."

The doctor said, "Hardly an angel. But he may become one if I don't get that bullet out of him."

Andy held a lamp close while the doctor probed the wound deep in the young man's shoulder. Though still unconscious, Sonny stirred restlessly. Hawkins and Pearcy held him as still as they could. The doctor brought out the slug and pitched it to Pearcy. He dropped it as if it were a horseshoe just out of the forge. It left a smear of blood on his hand.

"Goddamn it!" he exclaimed.

Hawkins cautioned, "You boys are in too precarious a position to be using the Lord's name in vain. You may be meeting Him sooner than you think."

Pearcy asked the doctor, "How soon do you think Sonny'll be able to travel?"

"Travel?" The doctor looked at him askance. "Are you trying to kill him?"

"I'm tryin' to keep somebody else from doin' it. If they get the idea we might talk too much, they'll squash us like bugs. They've never liked us much in the first place. They just tolerated us so they could use us."

Andy said, "I don't see where you owe them anything. Tell me who they are. Me and Daggett will take care of them."

"I don't know all of them. Even if I told you about the ones I know, there'd be others. I wouldn't stand a snowball's chance in hell. For all I know, the doctor here could be one of them."

The doctor said, "If I were, that boy would already be dead."

Andy said, "If you won't tell us who they are, maybe you can at least tell us who they aren't. Were any of the McIntoshes in on that raid at the Teal ranch?"

Pearcy considered. "No, they had nothin' to do with it. But Jake McIntosh is a friend of ours. We thought he'd like it if we got a shot at Lanny Teal."

"You did that for Jake?"

"That's what friends are for. Only we never saw Lanny. Never saw anybody, really. It was too dark."

"The Teals naturally thought the McIntoshes had raided them, so they rode over to pay them back. You could've gotten Jake and some others killed."

The idea disturbed Pearcy. "Never thought of it like that."

The doctor finished bandaging Sonny's wound, then sat back and stared at the unconscious young man. "Sooner or later," he said, "someone will start looking for these two. The longer they stay here, the more they jeopardize Mr. Hawkins and his wife. The doctor in me says this boy should not be moved. The realist in me says he ought to be taken away from here as soon as possible."

Andy said, "It's plain that he can't leave on horseback. Mr. Hawkins, could you let me have the borry of your wagon?"

"Certainly. Where do you intend to take him?"

Andy thought it best to keep that information to himself. "You'll be better off not knowin'." He turned to the doctor. "When you get to town, will you tell Logan Daggett that I've taken two material witnesses to a safe place? I'll be back in a few days."

"I'll do that."

"Don't tell anybody but him. Nobody."

Sonny moaned as they carried him out and laid him atop two folded blankets in the bed of Hawkins's wagon. Andy asked Pearcy, "You know how to handle a wagon?"

"Sure. I ain't no fool."

Andy could argue with him about that, but he didn't. He said, "You can tie the horses on behind, yours and Sonny's."

Pearcy was ill at ease. "You takin' us to town? That ain't such a good idea."

"I'm takin' you where you'll be safe. You, anyhow. The shape Sonny's in, I can't guarantee that we won't have to stop and bury him."

"Sonny's my cousin. I ain't lettin' him die, not even if I have to wrestle the devil to the ground and bob off his tail."

Andy mounted his horse in the early morning light and bade good-bye to the Hawkinses and the doctor. Pearcy sat on the wagon seat, trembling, looking back toward town as if he expected pursuit.

When Andy had freed Bigelow from his cell, it was his intention to take him to a strong jail in Kerrville, beyond the regulators' home ground. He considered Kerrville now but decided instead to take the two to Fort McKavett. The town had a doctor, and the Ranger camp was nearby. The Rangers could hold Pearcy and Sonny as witnesses until they were needed.

Besides, Andy might get a chance to see Bethel.

Pearcy asked, "Where are we goin'?"

"Straight up," Andy said, "and a little to the left."

# CHAPTER

## 10

The wagon was built for work, not for comfort. The rough terrain shook Sonny back to consciousness. Andy told him, "Sorry, but you'll have to put up with this for a while. After a while we'll get to a better road."

Pearcy said, "You call this a road?"

It was nothing more than a wagon trail, and a poor one at that.

Andy said, "It's the best way to get us out of the county without runnin' into a bunch of nosy people."

For the fourth or fifth time, Pearcy asked, "Where we goin'?"

As before, Andy said, "You'll see when we get there." If Pearcy knew they were going to a Ranger camp, he might abandon his cousin and run. Andy hoped some time in confinement might prompt him to share what he knew.

By the time they camped for the night, Sonny was exhausted. His fever was down, however. Andy told him, "We brought a shovel, but maybe we won't have to use it after all."

Weakly Sonny asked, "Was I in that bad a shape?"

Pearcy said, "The angels were already singin'."

"All I heard was sheep."

Andy made stew from a piece of mutton Mrs. Hawkins had put in the wagon. He took it as a favorable sign that Sonny ate all Pearcy gave him. Sonny was still confused. He remembered the bullet striking him. He had patches of memory about Pearcy holding him in the saddle and taking him to a ranch house. He remembered almost nothing about his time at the Hawkinses' place or about the doctor removing the bullet. He did not understand the reason for their flight now.

Pearcy said, "Remember what happened to Callender and Bigelow? It could happen to us. Them fellers are awful afraid somebody will tell their secrets."

Sonny looked at Andy with frightened eyes. "You won't let them get to us, will you, Ranger?"

"No, I won't, but you owe me."

"We ain't got any money."

"It's not money I'm after. It's information . . . names."

Sonny glanced at Pearcy. "We can't do that. They *would* kill us."

Andy asked, "If you knew how dangerous they are, how come you to ride with them in the first place?"

Pearcy said, "We never had nothin', me and Sonny. It stuck in our craw, seein' other people have so much, and us with nothin'. We was told that if we took enough cattle from the Teals and the McIntoshes, we could end up with a piece of their land."

"I thought the McIntoshes were your friends."

"Jake is. He treats us like we're somebody. We never cared for the old man, though."

Sonny put in, "Nothin' we ever done suited that old fart. Anyway, friendship ends when there's money on the table."

Pearcy said, "Me and Sonny figured to go partners when we got some land of our own."

Andy said, "*If* you got any land. Don't you know they would squeeze you out? When you pitch a piece of meat into a bunch of dogs, the strongest will grab it all."

"Never thought of it thataway."

Andy doubted that they had thought much at all.

They had been on the trail an hour the next morning when they rode over a stretch of rising ground and suddenly came upon a horseman. Pearcy sucked in a sharp breath and said, "Oh, my God."

Andy asked, "What's the matter?"

"I know this man. I think he's a regulator."

Andy had seen him in town. It was too late now to avoid him. The man stopped his horse in one rut of the trail so that Pearcy had no choice but to pull up on the team. He gave Pearcy and Sonny a quick glance, then asked Andy, "I know these boys. Looks like you've got yourself a couple of desperate outlaws, Ranger."

Lying was not one of the things Andy did best, but he grabbed at the first idea that came to mind. "Sonny's horse fell with him and broke his shoulder. We're takin' him to his granddaddy's house till he heals up."

"Where does his granddaddy live?"

"Uvalde." That was a long way from Fort McKavett.

"Odd job for a Ranger, doin' escort service."

"I thought so myself, but an order is an order."

The man rode on. He appeared satisfied, but Andy wondered.

By the second night's camp, Sonny was strong enough that they lifted him out of the wagon and let him lie on the ground. Sitting up, leaning against Andy's saddle to eat supper, he said, "This ride has churned my innards into buttermilk."

Andy said, "The old wagon's springs are tired, like us, but we've put the worst of it behind us."

Pearcy said, "I hope we've put the regulators behind us. That bunch would hang the likes of me and Sonny without botherin' to say grace."

Pearcy almost jumped from the wagon when he saw the Ranger camp just ahead. He whirled around on the seat, his eyes wild. "What's this? What've you brought us to?"

Andy dropped his hand to the butt of his pistol to discourage Pearcy from doing something foolish. He said, "I promised I'd bring you to a safe place. I doubt there's a safer place anywhere than a Ranger camp."

"We're under arrest?"

"You've been under arrest ever since the Hawkinses' place."

Pearcy's voice quavered. "I've heard what the Rangers do to people."

"Only to people that misbehave. You ain't goin' to misbehave, are you, Pearcy?"

Pearcy lowered his head but did not answer. Andy said, "If you don't like it here, there's an easy way for

you and Sonny to go free. Just give me the names I'm
lookin' for.''

"You know I can't do that."

"You will, when you get tired enough of this place. I
hope you enjoy hard labor."

He accompanied the wagon to the sergeant's tent. Sergeant Ryker stepped out and surveyed the prisoners. He
said, "Have you and Daggett already taken care of the
trouble back yonder?"

Andy said, "I'm afraid not, but these two have had a
hand in it. I hope I can leave them here for safekeepin'.
One is goin' to need a doctor's attention."

The sergeant nodded, looking at Pearcy. "We can use a
swamper to do heavy liftin' around camp. We just sent the
last one off to the pen."

While a couple of Rangers took Pearcy and Sonny in
hand, Andy explained briefly to the sergeant what had
happened. He said, "These two boys are little fish in a lake
that's too big for them."

The sergeant said, "I think we can make life miserable
enough that they'll be glad to give us chapter and verse."
He changed the subject. "Seen your wife?"

"Not yet. I thought I'd drop by and say howdy."

The sun was still high in the west. The sergeant said,
"Your horses look tired out after the trip. Why don't you
give them a day's rest before you start back?"

Andy had intended to do that anyway, but this made it
official. "Sergeant, heaven must have a special place prepared just for you."

The sergeant grinned. "I'm willin' to wait." He turned his gaze toward a man approaching the tent. He said, "That's a gun salesman. Just sold me a new pistol. I'll bet he'd oblige us in puttin' on a little show for your prisoners." The sergeant went out and talked to the salesman, who smiled as he listened to Ryker's proposition. Ryker returned and said, "That buggy yonder is his. If you'll take it a little piece down the road, out of sight, we'll give your boys somethin' that'll keep them awake tonight."

Andy followed directions. In a little while he saw Sergeant Ryker and the salesman walking toward him. The sergeant paused to fire a couple of pistol shots. He shook hands with the salesman, who then climbed into the buggy.

Andy asked, "What was that all about?"

The salesman grinned. "Ryker pretended that I was a prisoner and walked me by the boys you brought in. He let them hear him say that since I wouldn't talk, I wasn't of any more use to him. Soon as we got out of their sight, he fired his pistol."

Andy whistled to himself. "I'll bet they wet their britches."

"It'll give them somethin' to chew on besides those hard biscuits. Looks to me like the Rangers could afford to hire a better cook."

In camp, Andy found Pearcy badly shaken. Pearcy declared, "He shot that man. Walked him out yonder and shot him like a dog."

Andy tried to keep a solemn face. "He wouldn't talk.

There wasn't any point in lettin' him laze around and eat at the state's expense from now to Christmas."

"How long had he been here?"

"The sergeant said they brought him in yesterday."

"They didn't give him much time."

"Sergeant Ryker is not a patient man."

The sergeant walked up to Pearcy, carrying a shovel. "I want you go out yonder and dig a grave. Three or four feet is deep enough. That feller won't be diggin' out."

Pearcy broke into a cold sweat. His eyes were desperate as he turned to Andy. "You promised that me and Sonny could go free if we told you what you want to know."

"That's what I said."

"We don't know hardly any of the regulators. We were part of a little bunch that was drivin' off cattle. They used to be members of Vincent Skeen's outfit."

"Who else is left?"

Pearcy wiped a sleeve across his sweating face. "There's just a couple that we know, Miley Burns and Ed Granger. They never did think much of me and Sonny. They just took us along when they couldn't find nobody else. And when Sonny got shot, they ran off and left us to take care of ourselves."

Andy remembered seeing Granger's name in his fugitive book. Burns might be there, too, under a different name. He asked, "Are they the ones who took Bigelow away from me and killed him?"

"I don't know. Till that happened, I never knew that

Bigelow belonged to the regulators. Him or Callender either."

Andy said, "We'll want you to sign a statement about what you've told us."

Pearcy trembled. "I ain't much at writin', so you put it on paper. I'll sign it."

After Andy hugged Bethel hard enough to squeeze the breath from her lungs, she stood off at arm's length and studied him critically. "No bullet holes this time?"

"Sorry to disappoint you." He did not tell her about being clubbed unconscious when the regulators killed Bigelow. That had left only a small scar, hidden by his hair. It hurt only when he put on his hat or took it off.

She helped him unhitch the horses from the wagon and lead them to a pen. Watching him feed them, she said, "I guess you'll be going right back, as usual."

"I'm under orders to give the horses a day's rest first."

She was pleasantly surprised. "A whole day together? What will we do with so much time?"

"I suppose there's a lot of work needs doin' around here."

"A lot. But it can wait. If we've just got a day, let's don't waste it all out here with the horses."

Her arm around his waist, she led him to the house.

She made breakfast the second morning but ate little of it herself. Staying within reaching distance of him, she mused, "I suppose it would break a dozen Ranger rules if I went with you."

"At least that many."

"What if I did it on my own, without asking you? It wouldn't be your fault then, would it?"

"You're thinkin' like a lawyer. Besides, we don't know what may happen over there. It could get dangerous. I wouldn't want you caught in the middle of it."

"There are other women in that town, aren't there? Daggett's new bride, for one."

"She was born there." He kissed her. "Best forget it. Maybe this thing will be over with before long, and I'll be back."

"They'll just send you someplace else. It'll go on this way as long as you're a Ranger."

They had been down this road many times. Andy had no fresh arguments. He said, "Can you spare some bacon, and maybe a few eggs? Eatin' gets kind of chancy on the trail."

She soon presented him a couple of sacks, both heavy, and a small basket of eggs. He said, "You must figure I'm goin' to eat a lot."

"You've got to keep up your strength for when we're together again."

He lingered with her until his conscience troubled him. This was not what the state was paying him for. He kissed her fiercely and climbed into the wagon. He said, "I'll see you as soon as I can." The team made a quick start. Andy looked back to be sure his saddle horse was still tied on behind. He saw Bethel standing with her hands clasped in front of her. She went into the house just as the trail made a bend, and he lost sight of her. He kept seeing her in his mind's eye for a long time. Someday . . .

He made better time on the return trip. He could push the team for more speed without worrying about jolting Sonny Vernon. He had time to think about the situation to which he was returning, to do some guessing about who might be involved in the trouble. He eliminated first one, then another from his list of possibles, then reconsidered and reinstated them as suspects.

Of only one thing was he nearly certain: that someone was trying to steal enough cattle from the Teals and McIntoshes to leave them in financial straits. They were also trying to manipulate the two families into a crippling fight that would leave them vulnerable to the free range advocates.

Toward dusk he found a creek and decided to camp. He unhitched the team, staking them and his saddle horse where the grass looked greenest, then started a small fire. He lifted out the sack of groceries Bethel had given him and waited for the fire to burn down to smoldering coals. He saw the horses lift their heads and look back in the direction from which they had come. Turning, he saw a woman riding sidesaddle. He recognized her on sight.

Bethel reined up and asked, "What's for supper?"

He blurted, "What in the hell are you doin' here?"

She smiled. "A woman's place is with her husband."

"Not this woman, and not this husband, not where I'm goin'."

She dismounted without help and removed her saddle. She said, "I don't suppose you have another stake rope?"

"No, but I've got a pair of hobbles. I ought to've put them on *you* this mornin'."

She led the horse to the creek and let it drink its fill, then held out her hand. "The hobbles," she said.

"I'll do it," he said stiffly. He tied the hobbles to her horse's forefeet. It would not stray far with that kind of restraint. It was likely to remain close to the other horses.

She was still smiling. "Did anybody ever tell you that your nose flares out when you get mad? It's not a handsome sight."

"You've got to go back."

"In the dark? I'd wander like a child in the wilderness. You wouldn't want that to happen to your wife."

He saw that she had him. He said, "You'll go home in the mornin'."

"Maybe. Right now, you put the coffee on and I'll see what I can fix for our supper."

He had never been able to remain angry at Bethel for long. She hummed a happy tune while she busied herself around the cook fire. As he watched her, his impatience faded. Come morning, he would put his foot down. She would have to go back. But tonight he enjoyed sharing the blankets and feeling her warmth.

Bethel asked him about the town, the trouble, about Logan Daggett. She said, "He has a severe countenance."

Andy admitted, "He doesn't smile much."

"How did he attract a woman like this Carrie Teal?"

"I ain't even figured *you* out yet. How can I understand a woman I barely know?"

Bethel speculated, "Maybe she didn't realize what it's like, being the wife of a Ranger who never gets to stay home."

Daylight brought him awake, momentarily disoriented to find Bethel lying close beside him. He listened to birds announcing the dawn and a cow somewhere, calling for a wayward calf. Gently he nudged Bethel. "Time to get up," he said. "We'll have breakfast, then I'll get you started on the road back to McKavett."

She yawned and turned aside the blanket that covered her. Wearing only a thin shift, she looked beautiful to Andy, even with her hair disheveled and sleep in her eyes. He was tempted to say there was no hurry about fixing breakfast.

She said, "How can I go back? I don't see my horse."

The hobbles lay on the ground, but her horse was gone. She said, "Now, how do you suppose he managed to get the hobbles off? That's a smart horse."

Andy felt a little of yesterday's anger rising. "Maybe he had a smart woman to help him."

"Well, there's nothing to be done about it now. He's probably halfway home."

"Not quite." Andy saw Bethel's horse a couple of hundred yards away, grazing peacefully. "I'll go fetch him while you fix breakfast."

Bethel's shoulders drooped in disappointment. "If anybody ever makes you a good offer for that horse, sell him."

By the time he returned, leading the horse at the end of a rope, Bethel seemed to have accepted the situation. At least, Andy hoped so. He said, "No tricks this time. You go on back home where you'll be safe." He knew there was a chance she would wait for him to get out of sight, then follow.

She promised, "All right. No more tricks. But you'll have to admit that it's nice to have me around."

"There's never been any question about that. But if worst comes to worst, I don't want you gettin' caught in the cross fire."

They lingered a while after breakfast, then Andy saw Bethel on her way back to Fort McKavett. He already missed her before she was out of sight.

August Hawkins was penning his sheep as Andy pulled up in front of his house. Mrs. Hawkins came out onto the porch, speaking Spanish. Andy did not understand the words, but he understood the gestures. She was beckoning him to come inside.

Andy said, "I'll go see if Mr. Hawkins needs help with his sheep."

The dog provided all the help needed, but Andy was ill at ease in a situation where he did not understand what was being said. He shut the gate behind the sheep and told Hawkins, "I'm a little later than I figured in gettin' the wagon back to you. Got delayed some."

He explained about Bethel.

Hawkins said, "My late wife was like that. She listened politely to everything I told her, then went ahead and did what she pleased."

Andy asked, "Anything happen while I've been gone?"

Hawkins frowned. "A couple of men came by here yesterday and inquired about those two young fellows you carried away."

"What did you tell them?"

"I told them I had not seen anyone answering the descriptions they gave."

Andy said, "Did you recognize them?"

"By face. One is named Granger. If I were given to speculation, I would hazard that they were associated with your prisoners in some sort of mischief."

"I guess they were worried about what the boys might tell us."

"Did they tell you anything?"

"Sergeant Ryker is a persuasive man. Pearcy told what he knew. It wasn't much."

Hawkins frowned. "I've heard of some Ranger methods that go beyond the pale."

"The sergeant didn't hurt them. He just scared them to death."

"Your friend Daggett strikes me as someone who would do more than that."

Andy conceded, "He might. It doesn't take much to touch him off. That's why I didn't send for him to help me with Pearcy and Vernon."

"He may not be pleased that you took the full task upon yourself."

"That won't be anything new. He hasn't been pleased with much else I've done. I've found that it's best to do things my own way and ask him afterward."

At breakfast Hawkins announced that he would accompany Andy to town. "I've been waiting for the wagon so I could fetch some things from Babcock's store."

Andy said, "I'd be pleased to have the company." Exchanging talk with Hawkins along the way helped keep his mind from Bethel.

Hawkins stopped the wagon in front of Babcock's store. Andy shook his hand and thanked him for the several days' use of the wagon.

Hawkins dismissed the gratitude with a wave of his big hand. "Who knows? I may make a sheepman of you yet."

Rubbing his hands on an apron, the storekeeper stepped out onto the porch to greet Hawkins.

Andy said, "I've been gone for several days. Any excitement?"

Babcock shook his head. "Not since that set-to between Harper Teal and Ranger Daggett. The town has been so quiet that someone claimed to have seen a mountain lion sleeping in the street. I put little stock in that, of course."

Andy knew the story. The same yarn was being told about Fort Worth. He asked, "Have you seen Daggett around?"

"He's out in town somewhere. He never comes into the store except to buy some tobacco."

Andy turned, intending to take his horse to the wagon yard and turn it loose. He almost bumped into Daggett. He looked for welcome in the Ranger's eyes but saw none. Daggett declared, "You should've reported to me as soon as you got to town."

"I just now got here. Had some delay on the trip." He explained about Bethel.

Daggett frowned. "A man ought to keep a tight rein on his wife. It's his place to set the rules and hers to follow."

Andy doubted that Daggett held any such rein on Carrie.

Daggett said, "I never quite understood where you went. The doctor just told me you were takin' two prisoners to a safe place."

Andy told him about escorting Sonny and Pearcy to the Ranger camp. "Sergeant Ryker put the fear of God into Pearcy. He spilled all he knew."

"Good. Now we're gettin' somewhere."

"Not far enough. The trouble is, he just belonged to a little bunch of cow thieves who took orders from the regulators." He related the names Pearcy had given him. "Burns and Granger were go-betweens. They never let him get close to anybody higher up."

Daggett mulled over the names. He said, "I've heard the name Ed Granger, but I can't tie a face to it."

Andy said, "If we take out Burns and Granger, that'll bust up the theft ring. But it doesn't help us deal with the regulators."

"One job at a time."

\* \* \*

Andy was not sure he had done the right thing in sending Bethel home. He missed her, especially when he
saw Daggett and Carrie together. He could not help making comparisons. He was convinced that Bethel was the
prettiest of the two, though Daggett would have disagreed. Carrie was half a head the tallest and a few years
the older. Bethel had grown up as the daughter of a well-
to-do farmer on the lower Colorado River, though some
of the farm had been lost in the bitter Reconstruction
years after the war. Carrie's strong-willed family had
struggled and sacrificed to build a modest ranch here in
Central Texas, amid feuds and political fighting. Only a
person who had nothing would consider them well-to-do.
Now Carrie was estranged from her father. Bethel had lost
hers years ago.

Daggett and Carrie took their meals in the hotel's din-
ing room. Andy ate in Kennison's chili joint down the
street, where the food was cheaper and just as filling, even
if not so fancy. Eating in the hotel was a quick way to
shrink a wallet.

Finished with his meal, Andy walked back to the hotel
and waited for Daggett. The big Ranger had not told Andy
his plans, and Andy had not asked. He knew how badly
Daggett disliked answering questions. Their first stop was
the sheriff's office. Seymour and his deputy were both
there, the sheriff taking his after-lunch nap, Deputy Willis
looking at pictures in *The Police Gazette*. The sheriff
opened one eye, then the other, as he heard the Rangers'
boots tromping across the pine floor, their spurs jingling.

Yawning, he said, "Andy, we were thinkin' about sendin' a search party out for you."

Daggett cut straight to the guts of the matter. "Do you know where we might find Miley Burns and Ed Granger?"

Seymour rubbed sleep from his eyes and put on his thick-lensed glasses. "They stay out with the owls and the coyotes. I hardly ever see them in town. What do you want them for?"

"Pickard brought back information that they're a little careless with other people's cattle."

Seymour did not seem surprised. "Granger has a squatter's shack back in the hills. He has a brother here in town. Works as a clerk at the hotel."

Daggett said, "Oh, him. I didn't connect the name. He sure don't look like a cattle rustler. He looks like a clerk."

"I don't think him and his brother see much of each other."

Andy told the sheriff, "I found out who shot the horse from under you. Like you guessed, it was Pearcy and Vernon."

The sheriff pulled out his shirttail and rubbed his glasses on it. "I suspicioned that, but I wasn't close enough to see for sure."

Andy said, "You may not've known it, but you shot Sonny in the shoulder."

"With these poor eyes of mine? It had to be the devil's own luck. Where are those boys now?"

"In a safe place. It was them—Pearcy, anyway—who

told me about Burns and Granger. He was sore afraid they'd
come after him to shut him up. Or the regulators would."

"What did he know about the regulators?"

"I'd better not say, not till me and Daggett have a
chance to check on all of it." Though Pearcy had been
able to tell him little, it might be useful to let the impression spread that he had indeed given Andy some useful information.

The sheriff's face settled into a deep frown. "In the beginnin', we needed the regulators. Things had got out of
control. I looked away because they were doin' work that
the law wouldn't let me do. They hung some bad men,
and they ran some others out of the country when I didn't
have any legal basis to do it myself. Even horsewhipped a
few wife beaters and whiskey-soaks who wouldn't support their families."

Daggett nodded grimly. "I've seen it happen in other
places. After a while people went to usin' the vigilantes
for their own purposes. They accused innocent men
they wanted to get rid of. They went to takin' whatever they
wanted because folks were afraid to fight back, or even to
say anything."

Seymour nodded. "That's about the way it played out."

Daggett said, "Up at Gainesville early in the war, a mob
came together, supposed to be good Confederates. They
got to accusin' first one man, then another, of havin' Union
sympathies. Some did, I suppose, but others just had somethin' somebody wanted bad enough to bear false witness.

They wound up with a mass hangin' that folks up there are still ashamed to talk about."

Seymour said, "There was a time I could've stopped it but didn't want to. Now I wouldn't even know where to start." He took a whiskey bottle from a desk drawer and silently offered it to the Rangers. They declined. He took a long swallow, then asked, "Want me to go with you after Burns and Granger?"

Daggett said, "We can handle it. It's better if you stay here in case the Teals and the McIntoshes all come to town at one time."

"You're a Teal in-law. Can't you keep that from happenin'?"

"You know what Harper Teal said to me. I don't have any more say in that family than"—he broke off as a tall man stepped through the office door—"than that newspaperman comin' yonder."

Jefferson T. Tolliver was dressed in a white suit that contrasted with the black ink stains on his fingers. His confident stride carried him up to the officers. He said, "I am preparing to go to press with this week's edition. I wonder if you gentlemen have anything of interest to tell my readers."

Andy would not have told Tolliver what time it was, but Daggett said, "We're goin' out to try and find two men. We've got it on good authority that they're cow thieves."

"On what authority, may I ask?"

"A couple of other thieves. It takes one to know one."

Outside, Andy said, "I don't see why you had to tell him that. He'll blab it all over town."

"I want him to."

"But if we don't reach Burns and Granger first, we're apt to find them shot dead or hung from a tree."

"Either way, the job gets done. The regulators would save the county the cost of a court trial."

"That's too rough for my taste."

Daggett shrugged. "Rough or not, it's justice. We're not talkin' about Sunday school teachers here; we're talkin' about a pair of cow thieves." His frown returned. "Speakin' of thieves, don't you think you were too lenient with Pearcy and Vernon?"

"I got what I wanted from them. They're not much more than a couple of kids."

"They've already set the pattern. They'll wind up decoratin' a rope or bleedin' to death through holes the Lord didn't put there. In the long run, you haven't spared them much."

"At least I've given them a chance. Maybe they'll decide to go straight."

"And maybe coyotes will quit stealin' chickens." Daggett stopped and pointed down the street. "You trot to the wagon yard and get our horses. I'm goin' over to the hotel and accidentally let the word slip that we're goin' after Burns and Granger. I'm bettin' that all we'll have to do then is to follow that clerk."

Andy saw the logic. "You've got the mind of a Comanche."

"I take that as a compliment."

# CHAPTER

## 11

The wait was not a long one. The hotel clerk, wearing his suit, left through a back door and trotted toward the wagon yard.

Andy asked, "What did you tell him?"

Daggett said, "Nothin' directly. I just made sure he could hear me when I told Carrie we were on our way out to find Burns and Granger. I told her I hoped we could get to them before the regulators do."

Shortly the clerk left the wagon yard through a back gate, spurring a dun horse into a brisk trot. Daggett said, "We don't want to spook him. Let him get a long head start. If we lose sight of him, we can follow his tracks."

Andy said, "You might. I wouldn't want to bet on me doin' it."

"Maybe you need to go back and live with the Indians for a while. You didn't finish your education."

They let Granger reach a distant stand of cedar before Daggett touched spurs to his horse. Andy said, "It doesn't look like he's followin' a trail. He's cuttin' across country."

"It's just as well. He won't get his tracks mixed up with somebody else's."

Andy wished for Daggett's confidence. He said, "What'll we do with them if we catch them? You know that jail isn't safe if somebody is bound and determined to get at a prisoner."

"Do you know how the Mexicans trap a mountain lion that's been into their flocks? They stake out a kid goat in an open place and wait for the lion to show up."

"So we'll use Burns and Granger for the goat?"

"Might catch us some regulators."

"The goat usually gets killed, doesn't it?"

Daggett dismissed the argument. "Two thieves. Their lives ain't worth a bucket of spit."

It became clear to Andy after a while that the beeline direction the clerk was taking would cross over land claimed by the Teal family. The man knew where he was going and was in a hurry to get there. Andy considered mentioning it to Daggett but knew it would make no difference to the older Ranger. His course was set.

The Rangers came suddenly and unexpectedly upon Bud and Lanny Teal. No one spoke for a minute, getting over their surprise. Bud broke the silence. "Daggett, what're you doin' here? Pa is just over yonder, beyond that thicket. You know what he said about you not ever comin' onto this place again."

Daggett said, "We're on Ranger business. We're followin' a man who doesn't care whose land he crosses over."

Bud nodded. "We saw a rider a little bit ago." He paused. "How's Carrie?"

"She's fine. Just fine."

"Glad to hear it. We worry about her, but Pa won't abide us even speakin' her name. Tell her we said hello."

"I'll do that."

Bud frowned. "When you catch up to that feller, do you expect any trouble? Me and Lanny will go with you if you'd like."

Andy could only imagine Harper Teal's reaction if two of his sons rode along to help Logan Daggett.

Daggett said, "Thanks, but I doubt it'll amount to much. Just a couple of two-bit cow thieves not worth the rope it'd take to hang them."

"Do any of them answer to the name of McIntosh?"

"Sorry to disappoint you. They don't."

"I'm not disappointed, but Pa would be. He still thinks the McIntoshes are tryin' to steal us blind."

Andy said, "You don't believe that, do you?"

"Old Man Ethan is a bullheaded Yankee, but I doubt that he's a thief. Nor his boys, either."

Lanny said, "Jake is. He's been tryin' to steal my girl."

Bud said, "She's not hard to steal."

While the two Teals argued about Lucy Babcock, Daggett put his horse into a long trot to make up for lost time. Andy spurred up even with him and said, "If it wasn't for the two old men, I think the family feud would die out like a spent match."

Daggett said, "It looks to me like Ethan and Harper will live forever, unless they kill each other."

The clerk stopped occasionally, probably to give his horse a rest. The Rangers came dangerously close to riding up on him. They managed to pull into screening brush so they were not discovered. Andy said, "You might not think so, seein' him in that town suit, but he knows to take care of a horse."

"Like as not, he took to the clerk's job because it was easier than runnin' off other people's cattle. Safer, too."

"You've got to give him credit for tryin' to warn his brother."

"No credit. If he wasn't an outlaw before, this makes him one."

Late in the afternoon the Rangers rounded a chalky hill and saw a small frame house, unpainted, faded to near the color of the ground around it. Several rough cedar-post corrals and a small barn stretched out in the rear. Andy could hear cattle bawling in the pens.

He said, "What would you wager that the brands aren't theirs?"

"That would be a sucker bet."

The clerk's dun horse was tied outside the corral, alongside two others. Andy could see three men inside, among the cattle. They seemed to be arguing.

Daggett said, "This is a good time to go among them, while they're not lookin' our way."

By the time the men discovered they had company, the Rangers were within pistol range. Daggett said in a gravelly voice, "Now, boys, I wisht you'd shuck any guns you've got and pitch them into that trough yonder."

One of the men demanded, "Who the hell are you?"

Dismayed, the clerk said something Andy could not

hear. Evidently he identified the two visitors as Rangers. One of the men seemed for a moment to toy with the idea of fighting it out, but caution countered his instincts. He pitched a pistol into the dry trough as ordered. The other man had already done so. Andy assumed from a facial resemblance that he was the clerk's brother. The clerk did not appear to be armed.

Daggett said, "I won't waste my breath tellin' you you're all under arrest. You can see that."

"What for?" the clerk's brother demanded.

Daggett jerked his head toward the cattle, bunched in a corner of the pen, staying as far from the men as they could. They were range raised and not accustomed to seeing people afoot. "We've got testimony from one Harold Pearcy that the two of you are engaged in the unlawful takin' of cattle that belong to somebody else. The brands on these tell me that he did not lie."

Andy sensed that Daggett was toying with the men now that he had them in custody. Cat and mouse. Usually that game ended with the cat eating the mouse.

He took a quick look at the brands. They were T Crosses. Not one was the McIntoshes' Bar F. He said, "If the Teals ever catch you stealin' their cattle, they may make short work of you."

Sweating, Ed Granger said, "These strays were on our range, eatin' our grass. We just gathered them up and was fixin' to drive them back where they belong."

Daggett said, "I'd like to see you tell that yarn to a jury.

They'd probably give you five years extra for bein' such a bad liar."

Granger's nervousness was infecting his partner. Burns asked, "What're you goin' to do with us?"

"Turn you over to Sheriff Seymour. He'll keep you in jail till the court convenes."

Burns argued, "A prisoner got lynched in that jail last year. The regulators never even took him out of his cell."

"How do you know it was the regulators?"

"Who else would it have been?"

"Tell us who they are and we'll arrest them before they can touch you."

Burns pleaded, "We don't know all of them. Even if we told you about the ones we know, the others would kill us for sure."

Daggett showed no sympathy. "You boys have done a poor job of choosin' friends."

It was too late in the day to take the prisoners to town. They could too easily make a break in the darkness. Andy said, "I hope there's enough grub in that shack to feed all of us."

Daggett said, "Two of us, anyway."

Resentfully Granger said, "We bought and paid for that grub with our hard-earned money."

Daggett said, "We're confiscatin' it in the name of the State of Texas. Pickard, handcuff these men to a couple of fence posts. I'll go see what I can find to eat. Catchin' cow thieves stirs up my appetite." He turned to the hotel clerk. "Can you cook?"

The clerk hung his head like a whipped dog. "Some."

"Then you come with me to the shack. I don't like to see a man's talents go to waste."

Andy counted the cattle and made a note in his fugitive book in case he was called upon to testify. He opened the gate and drove the animals out to find their way back to their home ranges or wherever else they chose to go. He led the horses into the corral, removed bridles and saddles, and put out some grain he found in the barn.

Ed Granger asked plaintively, "You goin' to leave us out here like this all night? What if it comes a rain?"

Andy had not seen rain in weeks. He said, "We'll cover you with a wagon sheet." He realized that, like Daggett, he was playing cat and mouse with the prisoners. He had not intended that. "We'll let you sleep inside if you'll behave yourselves."

Granger said, "You're not a bad sort, but I can't say as I like your partner much."

Andy replied, "Sometimes I don't either, but if I want him to know that, I'll tell him myself."

Smoke rose from the metal chimney. After a while Daggett came out of the shack and shouted, "Supper's ready!"

Andy released the prisoners from the fence posts, then handcuffed them together to impede their mobility.

Daggett approved. "Sometimes you surprise me, Pickard."

"I learned from good teachers." He thought of Rusty Shannon and Len Tanner.

Daggett and the clerk had cooked a big supper. Ed Granger complained about the waste. Daggett said, "We'd just as well use it up. You're not comin' back here."

The two prisoners sat on the floor to eat, plates in their laps. Andy was not concerned that they would try to escape. They were having a hard time coordinating their movements enough to eat supper. Granger used his left hand, Burns his right. The hands were locked together with only a short chain between them.

The clerk was free to move around. Andy whispered to Daggett, "He didn't do anything but try to warn his brother. I have to credit him for that."

"He's got bad blood in him."

"You can't hold a man for what his kin have done. I say we ought to let him go."

"If we did, he might rouse up some friends to deliver the prisoners from us. I say we'd better hang on to him a while."

Andy argued, "A man is supposed to be considered innocent till he's proven guilty."

Daggett grunted. "What idiot said that? Everybody's guilty of somethin'."

The shack's furnishings were sparse: a small iron stove, two steel cots, the table and a couple of chairs. The stove was still too warm for comfort. Andy and Daggett handcuffed the pair together. The chain between them was looped around the frame of a cot. Daggett said, "You'd have a hard time draggin' that cot out the door, and a harder time tryin' to get on a horse with it. Was I you, I'd settle down and try to get a good night's sleep."

The clerk had said little. Now he protested, "They can't stretch out and get comfortable that way."

Daggett said, "They'd just as well get used to bein' uncomfortable. They're goin' to have a lot of it. Now, you lay down on that cot they're hooked to and see how quiet you can be."

"What're you goin' to charge me with?"

"We'll think of somethin'. Pickard, you take the first watch. I'll stand the last one." Daggett laid himself down on the second cot and soon was snoring peacefully. Andy pulled a chair out from the table. With his pistol in his lap, he settled down for some long, dark hours.

Daggett awakened sometime after midnight to relieve Andy. He asked, "The boys give you any trouble?"

"No, but they've been restless. I don't think they've slept much."

"Maybe by the time we get to town they'll be wore down enough to answer questions."

The handcuffed prisoners awoke with complaints about sore backs and aching shoulders. Daggett ignored them. He ordered the clerk, "Get over to that stove and stir us up some breakfast. The mornin' is half over with."

It was still dark outside.

Soon the clerk had made up a tall stack of flapjacks. Andy found a jar of syrup. Granger complained, "This syrup's got ants in it."

Daggett said, "A few ants are probably healthy for you."

Andy tried to remove as many as possible from his own breakfast, though he could not get them all. The blackstrap molasses was strong enough to overwhelm any flavor the ants might add.

Breakfast finished, Daggett sacked what foodstuffs remained and said, "Time to saddle up."

Granger grumbled, "If they kill us before you can get us to town, you'll be sorry."

"Not very," Daggett said. "Dead men are easier to transport. You don't have to watch them as close."

Granger and Burns appeared increasingly nervous. Judging that Granger would be most likely to crack first, Andy sought to add to the weight on his shoulders. He asked Daggett, "Do you know if stealin' cattle is a capital offense in this county?"

Matter-of-factly Daggett said, "Depends on the judge. I would guess Zachary to be one who favors the rope."

Burns warned his partner, "They're tryin' to scare you. Don't pay them no mind." His voice was shaky.

Granger turned on him. "Why shouldn't we talk if it saves our lives? I doubt as any of them sons of bitches would be willin' to die for us."

Saddling his horse, Burns tugged violently at the girth, buckling it too tightly for his mount's comfort. He said, "There's some things a man just doesn't do, like peach on his friends."

Granger said, "There comes a time when friendship

ends and a man has to take care of himself." He turned to Andy. "Would you Rangers be willin' to make a deal?"

Andy glanced at Daggett. "What kind of a deal?"

"You just got a little rustlin' charge against us, and there's a good chance you might not make it stick. What if we was to tell you about all the regulators we know?"

"In return for what?"

"In return for lookin' north while we ride south. We'd leave this part of the country."

"And never come back?"

"We *couldn't* come back. Our lives wouldn't be worth a Mexican *centavo* around here."

Andy asked Daggett, "What do you think?"

Daggett said, "I always like to sample the goods before I buy. Give us some names."

Face darkening, Burns said in a loud voice, "Ed, don't you give him nothin'. If you do, I'll kill you myself unless the regulators get to you first." He put his foot in the stirrup and started to swing up into the seat.

A bullet sang past him and sent splinters flying from the side of the barn. Granger exclaimed, "Goddlemighty!" His frightened horse jerked loose and left Granger down on one knee, exposed to another shot. He flattened himself on his belly.

Stunned, Andy shouted, "Everybody down!" He was already in the saddle, but he swung to the ground, drawing his rifle from its scabbard. His horse danced excitedly. Andy tried to keep it between him and the source of the first shot.

A second bullet took Burns in the chest. He gave only a grunt and collapsed like an empty sack.

Daggett found a target and fired his rifle. Andy saw leaves fly from a cedar tree. A man darted from behind it and disappeared in the cover of another. Andy and Daggett both fired at the bush. A dark figure jumped up and ran. Shortly Andy caught a glimpse of a horseman galloping away. He took one shot but knew it was wasted.

Struggling for breath, Andy asked Daggett, "Did you recognize him?"

"Not for sure, but I smell Rodock. Him and that damned rifle."

Cautiously, aware that a second shooter could still be out there, Andy turned to examine Miley Burns. One glance told him the man was dead. He picked up Burns's hat and covered his face with it.

The clerk had kept his horse between himself and the ambushers. Now he walked over to help his brother to his feet. He asked, "Are you hit?"

Granger trembled. "No, but that bullet came so close that I could smell it." He fastened an accusing gaze on Andy. "Thought you-all were goin' to protect us. Look what they done to Miley."

Andy had no satisfactory answer. "If they want you bad enough, there's no ironclad guarantees."

Granger appeared almost ready to break down and cry. "I'm next. They'll never let you get me to town. They may get you Rangers, too."

Daggett walked out a little way, holding his rifle, search-ing for signs of a second man. Andy said, "We've got to try, anyway." He paused. "Unless . . ."

Granger was grasping at straws. "Unless what?"

"Unless you'd give us the names of all the regulators you know. Then maybe I could talk Daggett into lettin' you go."

"Wouldn't do any good. They'd trail me from here to the Pecos River."

"You'd need to go a lot farther than that, like maybe California. Stay put while I talk to Daggett."

Andy met Daggett just far enough out that Granger could not hear the conversation. He said, "It'll be risky, takin' him in. The regulators want him dead."

Daggett said, "It'd be a small loss."

"Gettin' those names is more important than jailin' one small-time cow thief."

"I see where you're headed, Pickard, and I don't like it."

"We can catch cow thieves any time. We were sent here to try and break up the regulators. If word got out that we have the names, I think you'd see a big cloud of dust as they left the country."

"I'd rather catch them and see them salted away in the Huntsville penitentiary. There's no punishment if you let them get away."

"They'd have to leave everything behind and start again someplace else. I'd call that punishment."

"Do it my way and they won't get to start again, not for maybe ten or twenty years. Damn it, Pickard, they're criminals. It's against my religion to let trash like this get away."

"What if you caught a little fish, then saw a chance to catch a big one? Wouldn't you take the little one off of your line?"

"But I wouldn't throw him back in the water. I'd eat him along with the big one."

Andy had sensed from the first time they met that he and Daggett would not agree on much except the weather, and perhaps not even that. He said, "Sergeant Ryker told me you have the final authority, but I'm askin' you to let me have my way about Granger. I believe it'd be a good trade."

Daggett's eyes threatened a fight. If it went that far, Andy suspected that Daggett would win. The older Ranger declared, "One of these days, Pickard, you'll turn some scoundrel loose, and he'll come back and empty a gun into your gizzard."

"That'd be my hard luck, not yours."

"And hard luck for your little wife, too." Daggett clenched a fist, then eased. "All right, tell him if he'll give us the names, we won't prosecute him."

Andy returned to the shaken Granger. He said, "I had a hard time talkin' him into it, and I don't know how long he'll stand hitched. You'd better give me the names before he changes his mind. Or before the shooter comes back."

The clerk urged, "Do it, Ed. Those regulators aren't your friends. They sent somebody to kill you."

Still trembling, Granger murmured, "There comes a time when a man has to watch out for his own skin."

Andy took the fugitive book from his pocket and turned to a blank page toward the back. Granger said, "One of them is Judge Zachary."

Andy almost dropped his pencil. "The judge? He's the last man I'd have thought of."

"He was a wheelhorse once. Now he's old and worn-out. They do what they want to and try to let him think he's still in charge. Mostly they take their orders from Scanlon, the wagon yard man."

Andy was not surprised. He had never seen Scanlon smile. He had noticed that the man was always careful in counting his change. Any mistakes made would be some-one else's.

Granger said, "Another one is the sheriff's deputy, Salty Willis. If he was left in charge of the jail while I was in it, he'd let them come in and get me."

Andy asked, "What about the sheriff himself? I always suspected he might've let them know I was takin' Bigelow to a safe place."

Granger said, "Old Pete? No, he's so honest he shines in the dark. The regulators would've killed him if they weren't afraid that'd bring you Rangers down in force. Anyway, Judge Zachary wouldn't have stood for it. They knew he'd try the whole bunch and hang them. Pete's his oldest friend."

"They could've killed the judge too."

"They need him on the bench, in case."

Andy wrote *Salty Willis* and asked, "Who else?"

Counting on his fingers, Granger began ticking off names until Andy had more than a dozen. Finally he said, "I can't think of any more. We never got to know them all. They guarded their secrets."

Andy asked, "Did they pay you to steal cattle?"

Burns said, "No, but they let us sell what we took and keep the money. They wanted each side to think the other one done it. Maybe the Teals and the McIntoshes would kill each other off. Even if they didn't, we'd eventually break both families. The regulators could pick up the pieces."

"Looks like you two were penny-ante players in a high-dollar game."

Granger said bitterly, "They'd throw us away like an old boot."

Andy had recognized a few of the names. Most were unfamiliar to him. At the bottom of the list he added a phrase: "I swear on the Bible that this testymony is true, so help me God." He said, "Sign it."

Granger asked, "Where's the Bible?"

"The thought is what counts."

Granger scrawled his name. Andy said, "Now you'd better catch your horse before Daggett changes his mind."

Granger was still dubious. "I hope you won't shoot me in the back and claim I tried to escape."

Andy said, "That's not the way Rangers do things," though he knew it had been done from time to time. The *ley de fuga* was an old custom imported from Mexico.

The clerk asked, "What about me?"

"We've got no hold on you. Go where you want to."

"I'd like to go back to town. I hope I've still got a job in the hotel."

"You don't want to go with your brother?"

"Him and me, we took different roads a long time ago."

"Fine. You can ride along with us if you want to."

The clerk shook his head. "Ridin' with you Rangers is liable to be dangerous now that you've got your list. I'd rather everybody thought I just took time off to go fishin'. That might get me fired, but it won't get me shot."

The two brothers shook hands, and the clerk rode away.

Ed Granger started to get on his horse. Daggett challenged him. "Where the hell do you think you're goin'?"

Confused and frightened, Granger said, "You-all said if I'd give you the names, you'd let me go free."

Coldly Daggett replied, "I said we wouldn't prosecute you. I didn't say we wouldn't keep you as a witness."

Andy protested, "But you made it sound like you'd turn him loose."

"It got us what we wanted from him, didn't it? He's just a miserable cow thief. All's fair in love and war, and this is war."

Feeling betrayed, Andy could see that Daggett had no intention of backing down. He said, "Are you ready to take the responsibility if somebody kills him?"

"I wouldn't have it any other way." Daggett turned toward Granger and asked, "Have you got a shovel around here someplace? You've got a man to bury."

# CHAPTER

## 12

Finding the ambusher's trail was no problem for Daggett. He said, "Looks like he's headed toward town. Once he gets there, we won't be able to sort out his tracks."

Andy asked, "You don't see anything special about them?"

"They look like a thousand others."

"Then they won't help us find out who he was."

"I figure it had to be Rodock, and I can figure who told him where we went. I'd like to have free use of that Deputy Willis for about ten minutes."

"Looks like he's the reason I never got Bigelow to the town limits."

"We'll get them, and everybody else on that list if they don't scatter like quail." Daggett frowned. "There's still the feud between the Teals and the McIntoshes. The job ain't done as long as that goes on."

"It's not our place to shoot two stubborn old men. That's what it may take."

All the way to town, Andy kept expecting someone to take a shot at the prisoner. Granger was slumped in his saddle, head down, as if he had already given himself up for dead. He was only slightly relieved when he saw the town ahead.

Andy said, "We've just about made it, and you're still alive."

Granger mumbled, "They'll get me all the same. That jailhouse won't stop them."

It was afternoon, and Andy was hungry. He said, "The hotel dinin' room is closed till supper, but maybe Kennison's chili joint is open."

Daggett said, "That old geezer talks till your ears hurt. He's not on the list, is he?"

"Granger didn't mention him."

"We'd better take Granger to jail first."

Andy shook his head. "And maybe leave him alone with that Deputy Willis? We'll take him with us to Kennison's. He's probably hungry, too." Andy made his voice firm enough to show that he meant to have his way. Daggett put up no argument. Andy was gratified at even a small victory over the strong-minded Ranger. There had been very few.

Noontime customers were long gone. The bewhiskered proprietor was asleep on a cot against the far wall of his small kitchen. Daggett shook him. "Wake up. You've got some hungry customers."

Kennison yawned and rubbed his eyes, trying to see clearly. "Why didn't you come and eat at noontime, like decent folks?"

"We were busy protectin' the public."

Kennison's eyes cleared enough that he recognized the visitors. "Rangers. Why didn't you say so? I can fix you anything you want as long as it's beef stew. I still got some settin' on the back of the stove. Won't take long to heat it."

Andy said, "Right now, even boiled cabbage would taste good."

Daggett said, "You don't like boiled cabbage? I always kind of favored it myself."

He would, Andy thought.

The cook noticed Granger for the first time and saw the handcuffs. "Are you feedin' him, too?"

Andy nodded. "It'll be a new experience for him, eatin' legal beef."

Kennison poked dry wood into the stove and stirred the dying embers back to life. He asked, "I know this man. What're you chargin' him with?"

Andy said, "We've got several things to choose from."

"He always had a partner when he came in here to eat."

"He won't be comin' in anymore. We buried him."

Kennison dropped a pot lid. It clattered on the stove top. "He's dead?"

Andy hesitated. He knew that whatever he told this man would be spread around town by nightfall.

Daggett declared dryly, "If he wasn't dead, we wouldn't have buried him."

Kennison moved the stew pot over onto the warmer part of the stove. "Shot tryin' to escape, I suppose?"

Daggett said, "That's as good a story as any."

Kennison ladled stew into three bowls and set it in front of the Rangers and their prisoner. He brought the blackened coffeepot and filled their cups. Instead of being critical, he seemed to take pleasure in what he believed Andy and Daggett had done. "It sure don't pay anybody to mess with the Rangers. Did he tell you anything before he died?"

Daggett said, "If he had, maybe he wouldn't be so dead."

Andy said, "We'd just as soon everybody didn't know what we've just told you. Or about us takin' Granger prisoner."

Kennison said, "The word'll get out. There's people in this town that can't keep a secret."

Andy sopped up the last of his stew with a cold biscuit. It was tasty and had the added virtue of being cheap. Daggett had already finished eating. He said, "We'd better take Granger to the sheriff."

He looked back as they left the café, Granger in tow. "Tellin' Kennison is like puttin' it on the telegraph. But maybe it'll make the right people more afraid of us."

Andy said, "Or make them shoot us from behind."

Sheriff Seymour sat in the jail office, working on the tax books. Deputy Willis was listlessly sweeping the floor, pushing the dirt just outside the door where visitors would track it right back in. Seymour stood up, looking expectantly at the prisoner. "There was supposed to be two of them."

Andy said, "We had to bury one."

"You killed him?"

"Not us. Somebody hid out in the brush and shot him."

"Too bad." Seymour took Granger by the arm and led him back to a cell. He removed the handcuffs, then locked the door. Granger looked sick at his stomach. Andy doubted that it was the fault of the beef stew.

Seymour asked, "Did you-all get anything out of him?"

Andy said, "After his partner was shot, Granger decided to give us all the names he knew."

"You got them?"

"In my pocket."

Seymour could not appear more surprised if a herd of buffalo had stampeded into the room. He glanced at Daggett for confirmation. Daggett solemnly nodded. Salty Willis looked as if Andy had kicked him in the stomach. He leaned on the broom and almost lost his balance.

Seymour asked, "Can I have a look at that list?"

Andy said, "You probably know them all." He turned to the page in the back of his fugitive list.

Seymour's mouth dropped open as he read. "Judge Zachary, for God's sake. One of the best friends I ever had." He ran his finger down the list and looked up quickly. "Salty!"

Salty Willis had slipped away.

Seymour exclaimed, "That damned whelp. And I've been tryin' to train him to take over my job when I get old."

"We'll get him," Andy promised.

Seymour said, "This list is like a wagonload of dynamite. What're you goin' to do with it?"

"Keep it safe," Andy said. "And notify company headquarters that I've got it."

"I'd as soon have a rattlesnake in my pocket. Mind if I make a copy?"

"Go ahead. It won't take long for the word to get out anyway."

Seymour copied the list onto the back of a WANTED poster. He said, "Andy, I'm worried about you carryin' this thing on you. It's like hangin' a big target around your neck."

"You've got a copy now. We can make more if we need them."

"But copies won't have Granger's signature on them. They won't carry the legal weight of the original. You could lock it in the county clerk's safe." He caught himself. "No, you can't. He's on the list."

Hearing heavy footsteps in the hall, Andy slipped the fugitive book into his pocket. He turned to see Judge Zachary stride through the office door, trailed by smoke from his black cigar. The judge said, "I didn't know you Rangers were back in town. Did you have any luck?"

Andy wondered if Willis had warned the judge. He tried to read the man's expression. "Some good, some bad. We took two prisoners, but a sharpshooter killed one of them."

"That's bad."

"The good is that we got the other one, and he gave us a list of regulators' names."

The judge's face flushed. He bit down heavily on the cigar. He asked, "Might I see that list?"

The sheriff handed him the copy he had just made. "You'll find a bunch of your friends on it. I regret to say that you'll find yourself there, too. On account of that, I'm placin' you under arrest."

The judge's face went a deeper red. "On what charge?"

"I'll have to consult the statutes. There's bound to be a law against a judge bein' part of an outfit like the regulators."

Shaken, Zachary demanded, "This so-called list, on whose word is it based?"

Andy answered, "A man named Ed Granger. He's in that cell yonder."

"Ed Granger? A common cow thief. His word would carry little weight in any fair court."

Andy asked, "How do you know he's a cow thief? According' to him, you were a party to orders for him and others to take cattle from the Teals and the McIntoshes."

"I never gave such orders. The fact is that the regulators have paid little attention to me the last few years. They act on their own volition."

"Be that as it may, we've got Granger's affidavit, witnessed by Logan Daggett and me."

"An affidavit signed by a known thief? You have no case."

Andy said, "Once we round up some of your vigilante friends and get them to testify, we'll see what kind of case we've got."

The judge asked, "Where is the original list?"

Andy patted his pocket. He said, "I'm keepin' it where it'll be safe."

"You are assuming that *you* will be safe. Considering what is at stake, that may be an empty wish."

The sheriff said, "In the meantime, Judge, I'd be obliged if you'd step back to one of the cells with me."

The judge looked genuinely hurt. "I thought you were my friend."

"I am, but I'd arrest my own mother if she broke the law."

"And if your case does not stick? What of your job?"

"I'm ready to retire anyhow. But first I want to see the regulators put out of business for once and for all. Me and the Rangers will see to it that you won't get lonesome. We'll bring you some company."

"I should be allowed to post bond."

Seymour nodded. "But we'd need a judge to sign the papers. We'll have to be send for one that's not under arrest."

Zachary began to wilt. "You know a prisoner was once shot in his cell here. What assurance have I that I will be safe?"

"They're more apt to try and free you than to try and kill you. It's the job of me and the Rangers to see that neither thing comes to pass."

The judge looked first at the sheriff, then at Andy and Daggett. Gravely he said, "You don't realize what you are dealing with. You could all three be dead before the sun rises." He paused, waiting for a response. Receiving none, he jerked his head at Seymour. "Very well, Pete, show me where you want me to go."

Andy heard the loud clang as the cell door slammed shut. He said to Daggett, "He's right about the list bein' shaky evidence in court."

Seymour returned, downcast. "I wish it'd been just

about anybody besides Judge Zachary. He's always meant law and order around here."

Andy said, "Maybe he couldn't get the kind of law and order he wanted in court, so he turned to the regulators."

Daggett said, "Rodock didn't come here just to play cards. It's my guess the regulators have been payin' him to keep things stirred up. He was probably part of that raid on the Teals. Like as not, he was in the brush and fired the shot that creased Ethan McIntosh."

Seymour said, "When Salty spreads the word that we've got Granger and the judge in here, the regulators are liable to come at us. And because you're carryin' the original affidavit, they'll be gunnin' for you special, Andy."

Andy had known at a subconscious level that everything was moving in this direction. Now the full cold weight of it sank in. Those men were deadly. His being a Ranger would not prevent them from killing him.

Seymour said, "I saw the county clerk in his office awhile ago. I'll go arrest him so the judge'll have somebody besides Granger to talk to."

The sheriff was back shortly, alone. He said, "His helper told me that Salty Willis stopped by and spoke to him for a minute. He left the office in a hurry."

Andy said, "Reckon he's quittin' the country, or is he roundin' up other regulators to make a fight of it?"

Seymour said, "I'd call it fifty-fifty either way."

Daggett said, "We'll lock ourselves in and stand guard here tonight in case the judge's friends try to break him out."

Andy agreed. "You'd better let Carrie know."

Daggett said, "I suppose, but I hate to make her fret."

Andy said, "She'll do that whether you tell her or not."

Seymour suggested, "You could send her away from town so she won't know what's goin' on. August Hawkins would put her up. He's got a good heart . . . for a sheep-man."

Andy shook his head. "She would see through that in a minute. I'd bet she wouldn't go."

Daggett declared, "It's a woman's duty to do what her husband tells her to."

Seymour gave Daggett a sympathetic look. "You've only been married for a few days, and to a redheaded woman. You've got some hard lessons ahead of you."

Andy saw no sign of excitement in the street. It was too early for news to have spread much. He and Daggett rode their horses to the front of the hotel and dismounted. To their surprise, Carrie sat on the veranda with her brothers Bud and Lanny. Daggett went up and self-consciously gave her a peck on the cheek.

She said, "I expected you-all to be back last night. I thought maybe you two went to Mexico."

Daggett said, "We would if we had to. Tell her, Pickard."

Andy explained while Carrie listened wide-eyed, without speaking. The clerk, Granger, stood in the doorway, listening. Evidently he had not lost his job for being absent without leave.

Daggett said, "Looks like we may be in for trouble."

He shifted his gaze to Bud Teal. "What brings you Teals to town?"

Bud said, "We came to see about our sister. I did, anyway. Lanny came to see Lucy Babcock."

Lanny did not have a happy face. Andy asked, "Didn't you see her?"

Lanny didn't answer. Bud said, "He saw her. She was with somebody else, and it wasn't Jake McIntosh. There's a new man workin' in the blacksmith shop. He's better lookin' than Lanny or Jake either one, and strong enough to whip them both."

Andy had been afraid the rivalry between Lanny and Jake might touch off a potentially fatal conflict between the families. Perhaps Lucy's fickle nature had reduced that threat.

Bud asked, "What's this trouble you mentioned?"

Andy explained about the list and the fact that Judge Zachary was in jail. Bud was shaken. He said, "I always knew he didn't care much for us Teals, or the McIntoshes, either, but I felt like he was fair to us when he was on the bench."

Andy repeated what Granger had said about the regulators taking their cattle and trying to promote violence between the two families.

Lanny took the news with a sour face. "We'll tell Pa. Maybe he'll be mad enough to fight somebody besides Old Man McIntosh."

Bud shook his head. "They've butted heads too long for him to get over it that easy." He swore under his breath.

"I'd've suspicioned just about anybody in town before I'd've thought of the judge. Mason Gaines, for instance. I never knew such a bellyacher, always wantin' to change things around."

Andy said, "Gaines isn't on the list. I wish he was there instead of the judge."

Bud asked, "What happens now?"

Andy said, "There's a good chance some of the regulators may try to deliver the judge. They'd like to get their hands on Granger and the original affidavit, too."

Bud said, "I'll help you-all stand guard tonight. What's more, I'll send Lanny out to the ranch to bring in the boys. Pa, too, if he'll come."

Andy said, "It's not your fight."

"That mob has been waitin' like buzzards to pick over the leavin's after us Teals and McIntoshes kill one another. Damn right it's our fight." He turned to Daggett. "Has she told you yet? She wrote the letter that brought you Rangers here."

Daggett was taken by surprise. He asked Carrie, "Why?'

She clutched his arm. "Because I was afraid some of our family would get killed if things went on like they were. I thought the Rangers could put a stop to the trouble. I didn't sign the letter because I knew Pa would raise hell."

Daggett said, "You were sure right about that."

Bud ordered Lanny, "Go fetch the boys, and don't stop to stay hello to Lucy."

Lanny shook his head. "I've got nothin' to say to her." He trotted to where his horse was tied.

Bud spotted a Bar F cowboy at the blacksmith shop. He said, "I'll go tell him what you told me. The McIntosh boys ought to be interested."

Carrie held tightly to Daggett's arm. She asked, "What makes you think they might try to free the judge tonight? If I were a regulator and thought my secret was out, I'd be busy getting away. I wouldn't have time to worry about what happens to the judge."

Daggett said, "Most of them have got cattle and other property they wouldn't want to leave."

Andy said, "Besides, they've held the whip hand around here too long to give up easy. The judge and his court have helped them hold on to that power."

Bud returned after his conversation with the Bar F cowboy. Carrie asked him, "Do you think Pa would really come, after all the hard things he's said?"

Bud said, "He wouldn't admit it, but he's been like a lost kid without you around the place."

She leaned against Daggett. "He has to get used to it. I'm a married woman now. I'll go where my husband goes."

Bud nodded. "That's the way it ought to be. If Pa can't see it, that's his hard luck. I think you picked a good man this—" He broke off short, though Andy knew he was about to say "this time." He sensed that Carrie realized it, too. Unlike before, it seemed not to upset her.

Daggett took her in his arms and said, "We'd better be gettin' back to the jailhouse. We don't want to leave the sheriff all by himself."

Carrie asked, "What do you want me to do?"

"If anything starts, keep away from the windows. Hunker down behind a stove or somethin' else solid. And don't worry."

"Don't worry? Logan Daggett, sometimes you say the dumbest damn things."

Daggett turned quickly and walked down the steps. Andy and Bud followed. Andy said, "We'd better turn our horses loose in the wagon yard."

Daggett said, "And arrest the owner. Remember, he's on the list."

They did not find their quarry. His helper was alone, forking hay into an overhead rack. He said, "Salty Willis came by here in a devil of a hurry. Boss saddled up and left with him. All he said to me was to take care of things till he gets back."

Andy said, "So he does intend to come back."

Daggett added, "And not by himself, I'd wager."

Sheriff Seymour sat in a chair away from his desk. He held a shotgun in his lap. He acknowledged Bud with a surprised nod, then said soberly, "The telegraph office has sent over a couple of wires. I'm afraid it's not good news." He handed one to Andy and one to Daggett.

Andy unfolded his and read. It said: STATE APPROPRIATIONS CUT. YOU ARE RELIEVED OF DUTY. REPORT BACK IMMEDIATELY FOR DISCHARGE.

He read it a second time before the full impact hit him. He was not sure whether to laugh or curse. He said, "I've been fired."

Daggett seemed in momentary shock. "Me too. All

those years, the outlaws kept tryin' to get me but never did. Now the money counters have brought me down."

Andy looked again at the wire. "It says report immediately. But we've got these prisoners. And what'll we do about the regulators? Are we supposed to turn our backs and walk away?"

The sheriff said, "To me, it says you've got no authority to do anything. You're supposed to dump it all in my lap and leave." Anxiety came into his eyes. "I ain't got that big a lap. I'd just as well open the cell doors and leave with you."

Daggett faced the wall and considered the problem, his fists clenched. When he turned, his look was fierce. "Like hell! They sent us to do a job, and be damned if we're quittin' with it half done. We've still got all the authority that really counts." He slapped his hand against the pistol on his hip. His gaze fastened on Andy.

Andy said, "We could get in trouble."

"I've been in trouble since I was eight years old."

Andy nodded. "Come to think of it, so have I."

The sheriff looked hopefully from one to the other. "Does this mean you're stayin'?"

Andy said, "It does."

Seymour reached into a desk drawer. "Since they've taken away your authority as Rangers, I'll swear you in as my deputies till this trouble is over with." He handed each of them a badge. Hesitantly he offered one to Bud, who accepted it.

Daggett asked, "What's the pay?"

"Salty was gettin' a dollar and a half a day."

"That won't hardly cover hotel expenses, but I'll take it."

Andy said, "So will I."

The sheriff said, "Now if you'll excuse me a few minutes, the judge has been after me to fetch him some cigars from his office. He's particular about the brand."

Dryly Daggett said, "Down at Huntsville, he'll smoke what they give him."

Seymour said, "I can't forget that he's been my friend."

Daggett shook his head. "Looks to me like *he* forgot it. I don't favor givin' him any slack."

"You haven't known him as long as I have." Seymour left.

Andy took another look at the wire, though by now he had it memorized. "I'd figured on leavin' the Rangers sooner or later, but this forces my hand. I reckon I'll start ranchin' a little smaller than I'd expected to. What about you, Daggett?"

"Everybody knows my name. I don't think I'll have much trouble findin' a job runnin' a cow outfit for somebody. I've got a wife to support."

Bud said, "I'll bet we can find you somethin' around here. That'd keep Carrie close to home."

Seymour returned with a box of cigars. Andy heard the judge tell him gratefully, "Much obliged, old friend. It is often the small pleasures in life that mean the most."

Seymour said, "I just don't understand why you let

yourself get into a fix like this, a man of your caliber mixed up with a band of ruffians like the regulators."

The judge bit off one end of a cigar. His voice was weary. "It was easy at first. Things here had gotten out of hand. Juries would not convict because they feared retaliation. The regulators could do what I could not, so I closed my eyes. In time, I was one of them. My court enforced the law in ways the law never intended. But the best intentions can go awry. I found myself with blood on my hands that would not wash clean. It was like being trapped on a runaway wagon and unable to jump off." He shrugged. "The truth is, they don't pay much attention to me anymore. They pat me on the head like an old dog and do what they want. They like me to be on the bench so I can rule their way when necessary."

Seymour said, "Looks to me like you could've gotten off that wagon if you really wanted to."

"I was not certain that I wanted to get off. Power can be more intoxicating than whiskey."

Andy stood in the open door for a time, watching the street. Passersby stopped for a moment and looked toward the jail. He sensed that the news was spreading around town. Though he saw nothing more tangible than that, he sensed a growing tension out there, or perhaps it was simply his own.

Daggett warned, "You better get out of that door and close it. You'd make a good target for a sharpshooter like Rodock."

Andy shut the door and barred it, then opened a small loophole at eye level so he could see out.

Seymour said, "People laughed about me puttin' up curtains in the jailhouse. None of them match. But at least nobody can climb up outside and shoot at us through the windows."

Bud seemed vaguely disturbed. He kept staring toward an empty cell. Andy made a guess. "Is that the one where Skeen was killed?"

"It is."

"From what I've heard, the regulators did your family a favor."

Bud grimaced. He looked around to see that no one was close enough to hear. In a quiet voice he said, "We never told a soul about this, not Carrie, not even Pa. It wasn't the regulators. Me and my brothers done it . . . for Carrie, and for us."

"The regulators got the blame."

"There wasn't many people blamed them. Most thought they did everybody a service. But you can see why we never wanted Carrie to know. In spite of him bein' a rattlesnake, she loved him, or thought she did. She's got a better man now."

"You'd better not ever tell Daggett. He might let it slip, or Carrie might read it in his eyes."

"I don't know why I even told *you*. Just wanted to get it off of my chest, I suppose."

Andy said, "It'll die with me. But not tonight, I hope."

Someone knocked on the door. Andy carefully approached the loophole and looked out. Editor Tolliver stood there. He said, "I bear a message."

Andy asked, "Are you heeled?"

"I never carry a gun. I do my fighting with a pen."

Andy opened the door slowly, making certain no one was waiting to rush in behind Tolliver.

Tolliver said, "The regulators out there chose me to be a go-between. They said it's because I'm neutral. I suppose that means I don't much give a damn one way or the other."

Andy said, "Do you?"

"Not enough to mention. Whichever way this all goes, I'll get a book out of it. Then I'll move to New Orleans and live the life of a rich author."

"You said you've got a message."

"Those men are in dead earnest. They say they'll lay siege to this jail until they either blast you out or starve you out."

Daggett angered. "The hell you say!"

"*They* say, not me. I'm just the messenger."

Andy asked, "Are they wearin' hoods?"

"No. I suppose they see no need inasmuch as their identities have been revealed anyway."

Andy said, "This jail has got stone walls, so they're not apt to blast us out. As for starvin' us out, tell them that if we go hungry, the judge goes hungry, too. He stays right where he's at." He paused. "And remind them that any bullets that find their way in here are as apt to hit the judge as any of us."

"I'll tell them."

Seymour asked, "Who all is out there?"

"Your deputy Willis for one. And Scanlon, who owns the wagon yard. Willis thinks he's giving the orders, but the rest appear to be looking to Scanlon for leadership. Willis is in past his depth."

Seymour said regretfully, "I'm afraid he always was. I don't know why I thought he might be the one to succeed me someday."

Tolliver said, "He has been seduced by the prospect of easy money. It is a delusion and a snare."

Andy thought Tolliver was probably deluding himself about the prospect of getting rich from writing a book. But, each man to his own dreams, and his own delusions.

The judge yelled from his cell, "How many did you say are out there?" On hearing there were eight or nine, he was disappointed. "I thought there'd be more."

Tolliver said, "I suspect some of the regulators are busy getting ready to leave the country. Fair-weather friends aren't of much help in a thunderstorm." He told Andy and Daggett, "I'll tell them the judge is hungry. Perhaps they will allow Kennison to bring something over from that greasy café of his."

Andy closed and barred the door as Tolliver left. The regulators gave the editor time to get clear, then opened up with a fusillade. Andy could hear bullets whine off of the stone walls. A few struck the heavy wooden door but did not penetrate it.

Granger howled in fear and flattened himself on the floor of his cell.

Andy said, "They're just lettin' us know they're serious."

Daggett said, "I never had no doubt about that."

Toward dusk, Kennison brought two steaming pots. He said, "Hope you-all like beans and beef stew because I've about run out of the makin's for anything else." He seemed eager to catch a glimpse of Judge Zachary in his cell. He said, "Remember me, Judge? You sentenced me to two days in here once. Said I was drunk and disorderly. I've never been drunk in my whole life, except for a few times." He turned back to the sheriff. "Who's payin' for this grub?"

Seymour said, "The county."

"With things so uncertain, I'd like to be paid now. You might not be in a shape to pay me later."

Seymour bristled. "You don't think we can handle it?"

"No offense meant, but there's more of them than there is of you. And I remember what happened to Skeen."

The sheriff said, "This jail is like a fort."

"So was the Alamo."

The sheriff dished out a bowl of beans and stew and passed them to Judge Zachary through a narrow slot in the cell door. Pain in the sheriff's voice indicated how much he regretted this turn of affairs. "I'm afraid he didn't bring any biscuits, but I'll fetch you some coffee directly."

Zachary sampled the stew. He said, "Whatever his hygienic shortcomings, the old rascal can cook."

Just before dark, Daggett said, "Pickard, lift the bar on the door. I'll go out and look around. Might get a better idea what we're up against."

Andy cautioned, "You may not get back."

"You be ready to let me in quick."

Daggett went out. Andy closed the door but did not re-place the bar. The big Ranger had been out only a few seconds when several bullets whined off the stone wall. Daggett shouted, "Open the door!"

He rushed back in, breathing hard. Andy barred the door behind him. Daggett said, "That damned Rodock and his rifle." He blinked hard. "I've got rock dust in my eyes."

Andy asked, "Did you see who-all's out there?"

"They didn't give me time for a tally."

Seymour said, "I'll stand watch a while. You'd all bet-ter try to get some sleep if you can. I have a notion they may worry us all night."

Andy stretched out on a cot in an unlocked cell, but his eyes were wide open. Sleep did not come on command. After a time he noticed a window curtain move. A hand appeared, lifting it. Andy drew his pistol, aimed above the hand, and fired. From outside he heard a startled curse. The curtain fell back into place.

As he had expected, shots were fired at irregular inter-vals during the night. They ricocheted off the stone walls or, a few times, thudded into the heavy door. In the wee hours, Daggett arose from his cot and walked to the door. He said, "They're tryin' to keep us from gettin' any sleep, but they're wastin' their time. I couldn't have slept noway."

He opened the loophole in the door, poked his pistol bar-rel though it and fired into the night. "In case any of *them* are tryin' to sleep," he said.

Time went by at a terrapin's pace. After a period that

seemed long enough for three nights, the promise of daylight began to show through the curtains. Andy walked to
a window and carefully lifted the curtain's corner. He saw
early orange streaks of sunrise. There was no movement
on the street. Usually much of the town was up and going
by daylight. No regulators were in sight, but he knew they
were there, biding their time.

Seymour rattled around the stove, rebuilding the fire,
putting the coffeepot on. He stood in front of the judge's
cell and said, "I'll have you some coffee directly, Judge.
Did you get any sleep?"

"Not much," Zachary replied. "Those men out there
mean well for me, but they don't seem to realize that old
men like us need our rest."

"They probably figure they've worn us down. I wouldn't
be surprised if they try to rush us this mornin'."

The judge said, "That would be a mistake on their part.
The war taught me that it is futile to charge an impregnable
position. One must find a different course of attack."

"Like what?"

"Even if I knew, I could not divulge it to you. My neck
is on the chopping block."

"I'm sorry to've had a hand in puttin' it there."

"You are doing your duty, Pete, as I have always tried
to do mine, by my own lights."

Seymour returned to the front of the jail, where Andy
peered beneath a window curtain. He said, "It's time I gave
up this job. There's some people I hate to have to put in jail."

Daggett grunted. "I doubt you ever jailed anybody for

singin' too loud in church. Most of them deserved what they got."

Seymour said, "I wish I could be like you. It's a lot simpler when you can't see but one side."

As the sun came up, a shower of bullets rattled against the walls. One penetrated the door, leaving a hole with splintered edges. Daggett said, "Rodock's rifle."

Andy said, "This thing between you and him must go back a long ways."

Daggett nodded. "We were boys together. Hunted, fished, rode over the country like two wild Indians. But as we started sproutin' whiskers, he went off in one direction and I went another. There came a time when I was sent to arrest him, and he tried to kill me. Almost did. It's hard to remember we was ever friends. I'll probably have to kill him sooner or later."

"You'll regret it like Seymour regrets havin' the judge in here as a prisoner."

"If your best dog gets the hydrophoby, you have to shoot it no matter how much you hate to. I'm afraid Rodock has turned into a hydrophoby dog."

Their conversation was interrupted by another short fusillade. One bullet came through a window and ricocheted across the room, prompting a curse from Daggett. "I'll make Rodock eat that damned rifle."

Presently Tolliver knocked on the door again. He shouted, "Is everybody all right in there?"

"Nobody's dead," Andy answered after peering through the small loophole. "You got another message?"

"I'm sorry to bring bad tidings, but the regulators have sent me to offer a trade. They want the judge. They also want Granger."

"They've got nothin' to trade that we'd want."

"I'm afraid they do. They have taken Daggett's lady hostage. Look at the hotel porch. You can see for yourself."

Andy caught a quick glimpse of Carrie standing in her nightgown, a man holding her. Daggett shoved him aside so he could see for himself. He exploded in anger, his voice wild. "Give up the judge? I'll kill him first! Him and the whole damned bunch." He brought up his rifle and tried to shove the barrel through the loophole.

Andy pushed it up so he could not take aim. He said, "It's too far, and your hands are shakin'."

"Turn aloose of me," Daggett cried.

"You're apt to hit Carrie. I don't think they'd really hurt a woman. It'd turn the whole town against them."

Tolliver said, "I wouldn't put too much stock in what they would or would not do. The hotel clerk tried to protect her. When I saw him he was lying on the floor. His head was bloody."

Daggett tore free of Andy's hold. "Stand aside. I'm goin' out. I'll hunt down and kill any son of a bitch that lays a hand on my wife."

Andy argued, "For God's sake, they'll cut you to pieces."

Daggett was a loaded cannon, on the point of firing. "If they do, I'll take a bunch of them with me." Daggett violently lifted the bar from the door and tossed it aside. Andy tried to wrestle with him, but it was like wrestling a bear. Daggett was in a frenzy. Andy swung a fist and caught him on the chin, but Daggett seemed not even to notice. He struck Andy a blow that sent him reeling backward. He lost his footing and went down on his back, hard. For a moment he could see nothing but lightning flashes playing against a stormy sky. Daggett opened the door and charged out, roaring like a wild man.

Bud took Andy's arms and brought him to his feet. He said, "Daggett's gone crazy."

"We'd better do what we can to help him. Sheriff, please let the judge out of his cell. Maybe the regulators will hold their fire if they see he's in the way."

Seymour said, "They might kill him by accident."

Andy found himself talking like Daggett. "Then it'll be their own fault. Let's do it."

His legs still unsteady, Andy went out, Bud Teal at his side. Daggett was already partway to the hotel, firing the rifle as he walked. He had surrendered himself to blind fury. The stable owner, Scanlon, fired at Daggett. Daggett fired back, and Scanlon went down on his face.

Andy saw that Deputy Salty Willis was the man holding Carrie's arm. Willis was distracted by Scanlon's fall. Carrie broke loose from him. She bent down and came up with a fist that struck Willis across the nose and sent him stumbling backward against the wall. Andy heard her shout something but could not make out the words. He suspected they were not for tender ears. She strode angrily back into the hotel and slammed the door.

Zachary said, "I want you to know that I do not condone the abuse of women. I shall see that Willis pays a price."

Andy admired Carrie's courage. "I think he already has. Wouldn't be surprised if she broke his nose."

The judge said, "I trust you are gentlemen enough not to shoot me in the back. I am taking my leave." He turned away from Andy and Bud and the sheriff and walked briskly toward the wagon yard.

Rodock had stepped onto the hotel porch to stand beside Willis. He cradled a rifle in his arms. He shouted, "Daggett, you'd better stop where you're at!"

Daggett never broke his stride. Rodock moved halfway down the steps. Daggett shouted, "Rodock, we've put this off a way too long!"

Rodock answered, "Then do your damndest." He swung the rifle to his shoulder.

Daggett dropped to one knee. The two rifles fired at the same time. It sounded as if but one shot echoed along the street. Rodock dropped to his knees, then sprawled forward across the bottom steps. Daggett pushed back to his feet. He seemed unhurt.

Carrie rushed out from the hotel, down the steps, and into Daggett's arms. Embracing her fiercely, he asked, "What did they do to you?"

She said, "Just dragged me out of bed. Nothing to kill a man about."

"They laid hands on you. That's enough. Thank God you're all right."

Andy saw a rip in Daggett's sleeve, and some blood. He said, "Looks like Rodock got you."

"It was Scanlon. Rodock ain't half as good a shot as he thinks he is." He turned Carrie back toward the hotel. "Come on, let's get you into some decent clothes. Can't have half the town starin' at you in your nightshirt."

Rodock was struggling to turn himself over onto his back. His right shoulder was a bloody mess. Trying to focus his gaze on Daggett, he wheezed, "Damn you, you ain't killed me yet."

Daggett picked up Rodock's rifle. "I intended to. Then I asked myself why I ought to give you an easy out. You crippled me once. I thought the fair thing was to return the favor."

"I'll come for you one day, Daggett."

"By the time you get out of the penitentiary you'll be too old to come after anybody."

Half a dozen horsemen galloped up the street. Andy squinted against the early morning sun. "Looks like your in-laws are here," he told Daggett.

Harper Teal led his sons Lanny and Cecil and two T Cross cowboys up to the hotel steps. The patriarch took in the scene with a sweeping glance. "Looks like we got here a little late."

Daggett did not reply. Andy said, "You're in time to help round up a few regulators." He pointed to Salty Willis, who held one hand to his face. "You can start with him. And yonder is Scanlon, if he's still alive."

Harper looked critically at Carrie. "What has my daughter to do with all this?"

"For one thing, she laid that bloody nose on Salty Willis."

Teal turned angrily on Daggett. "If you've done anything to put my daughter in danger . . ."

Daggett's only response was an angry stare.

Andy said, "Anybody who messes with her is in more danger than she is."

Tolliver looked down on Rodock with evident disappointment. He said, "It would have made a much more interesting story if you had killed him, Daggett."

Daggett said dryly, "You can kill him in your story. You'll make up most of it anyway." He looked down the street. "Ain't anybody sent for the doctor? Rodock could bleed to death layin' here."

Harper demanded, "Carrie, what're you doin' out here in your sleepin' clothes?"

Andy explained that the regulators had tried to use her as a hostage. He said, "She didn't take kindly to it."

Teal stood a moment, facing his daughter, then wrapped his arms around her. "Damn it, girl, we've missed you. I've missed you."

Carrie asked, "Am I back in the family now?"

Harper said, "You never was out of it. I was, for a while."

The Bar F riders appeared on the street, headed by Ethan McIntosh. Harper growled, "What're they doin' here?"

Bud said, "Same thing you are. They've come to help."

"We don't need no help from that old scoundrel."

Bud was disappointed. "I hoped when you realized what the regulators tried to do to us, you'd bury the hatchet with Old Man McIntosh."

"You boys can, if you want to. But damned if I ever will, not in a hundred years."

Andy suspected Ethan McIntosh would feel the same way. If there was to be peace between the families, it would have to come from the younger members.

Daggett said severely, "Pickard, the judge has gotten away. You turned him loose, so you go and find him."

The sheriff said, "I think I know where he went. There's no big hurry."

Daggett put his arm around Carrie and started up the hotel steps. He said, "I hate to tell you, but I'm out of a job."

She smiled. "I'm sure you'll find plenty to do."


Andy soon realized that the sheriff was guiding him toward the judge's ranch. Seymour said, "It's where he always goes for peace and quiet. He says it's his thinkin' place."

Andy asked, "Reckon he'll give us any resistance?"

"He's a gentle man at heart, in spite of what all he let the regulators do. He always said he did enough fightin' in the big war. He never wanted to do any more."

"It's too bad that so many didn't come back feelin' the same way."

The two men rode through a scattering of cattle bearing

an MC brand. Seymour said, "They're the judge's. He's always taken great pleasure in them."

"Does he own the land?"

"Just the cattle, and the section the house sits on. Like most others around here, he's a free range man. He claims the land by right of first possession, but legally the state still owns it."

"Somebody could take it from him and claim six-shooter possession."

"The regulators wouldn't have let them get away with it. They've had their good uses as well as their bad."

The judge's dog came to greet them, its tail wagging vigorously. It eagerly led them to the house, barking the news all the way. Judge Zachary stepped out onto his small porch. Andy looked for sign of a weapon but saw none. He reached down to his own pistol.

The sheriff shook his head. "You'll have no need for that. He has had shame enough without we add to it."

Zachary greeted the pair as genially as if they were on a purely social call. "Light and hitch, Pete. And you, Andy. Coffee ought to be comin' to a boil pretty soon."

Seymour dismounted and nodded in gratitude for the invitation. "Let's sit out here and talk on the porch. It'll be cooler than inside."

Zachary said, "We have a good deal to talk about." He seated himself in a rocking chair and gazed across the pasture. "I love to sit out here of an evening and just rock. I watch my cattle grazing and the calves playing yonder, and I don't feel alone. I doubt that heaven can offer much more."

Seymour said, "I envy you that."

Zachary mused. "You've always been a good friend, Pete. You don't have much to show for all those years of work and hardship, do you? You probably expect to keep working until they carry you away."

"I'm used to work."

The judge's eyes were sad. "I wouldn't mind so much going away if I didn't worry about my cattle. They're the nearest thing to family that this old bachelor ever had."

"You could sell them to somebody who'd pet them like you have."

"You deserve some pleasure out of life. I'd like to sell them to you, Pete."

"I ain't got the kind of money it'd take."

"You don't need to pay now. While I was waiting for you, I wrote out a bill of sale. Andy, I'll need you to witness my signature."

Surprised, Andy said, "I'll be glad to."

Seymour was stunned. Zachary went into the house and brought out a paper. He signed it, and Andy affixed his own signature. The judge folded the paper and handed it to the astonished Seymour. The sheriff summoned voice enough to say, "I don't know how to thank you."

"No need to say anything. This is my way of thanking you for being a good friend through the years." His eyes were sad, but he attempted a smile. "You could retire now if you want to. You could turn the sheriff's office over to someone else, perhaps Logan Daggett."

Seymour said, "I'll sure think on it."

Zachary arose from his chair. "Now, if you two will wait for me out here, I have a thing or two to do before we leave."

Seymour seemed to remain in shock. "I never expected such as this would ever happen to me."

Andy said, "I used to know an old preacher named Webb. He always said the Lord works in mysterious ways."

From inside the house, a shot rattled the windows. Andy and the sheriff glanced at each other, then rushed through the door.

It was turning dark when Andy rode up to the little house at the edge of Fort McKavett. He half feared that Bethel might already have gone to sleep, but he saw dim lamplight through the open door. Bethel's dog came out from behind the house and sniffed suspiciously, then recognized Andy's scent and welcomed him with a violent wagging that shook its whole body.

Andy stopped on the porch to wipe his boots on a sack Bethel kept there for the purpose. He called, "Anybody home?"

Bethel appeared in the door, holding the lamp high so she could see his face. For a moment her eyes betrayed her joy. Then her voice took on an exaggerated tone of severity. "How long this time?"

He said, "I've got some bad news. I've been dismissed from the Rangers."

"And you call that bad news?" She set the lamp aside and hugged him with all her strength. "It's the best news

I've heard. Well, almost the best." She pulled his head down and whispered in his ear.

Andy swallowed hard. "When?"

"It'll be a while, long enough for us to build that cabin and for you to put some livestock on the place."

He found himself trembling, momentarily overwhelmed. "It won't be easy. It's apt to be red beans and squirrel stew for a few years."

She kissed him and smiled. "I know seven different ways to cook squirrel stew."